Fan-Tan

Marlon Brando
and
Donald Cammell

Edited and with an Afterword by

David Thomson

THORNDIKE
WINDSOR
PARAGON

This Large Print edition is published by Thorndike Press®, Waterville, Maine USA and by BBC Audiobooks Ltd, Bath, England.

Published in 2006 in the U.S. by arrangement with Alfred A. Knopf, Inc.

Published in 2006 in the U.K. by arrangement with The Random House Group Limited.

U.S. Hardcover 0-7862-8217-7 (Americana)
U.K. Hardcover 1-4056-1318-1 (Windsor Large Print)
U.K. Softcover 1-4056-1319-X (Paragon Large Print)

Set in 16 pt. Plantin by Carleen Stearns.

Printed in the United States on permanent paper.

British Library Cataloguing-in-Publication Data available

Library of Congress Cataloging-in-Publication Data
Brando, Marlon.
    Fan-Tan / by Marlon Brando and Donald Cammell ;
edited and with an afterword by David Thomson.
        p. cm. — (Thorndike Press large print Americana)
    ISBN 0-7862-8217-7 (lg. print : hc : alk. paper)
    1. Pirates — Fiction. 2. Prisoners — Fiction. 3. Pacific
Area — Fiction. 4. Women pirates — Fiction. 5. Hong
Kong (China) — Fiction. 6. Illegal arms transfers —
Fiction. 7. Adventure fiction. gsafd 8. Large type
books. I. Cammell, Donald. II. Thomson, David,
1941– III. Title. IV. Thorndike Press large print
Americana series.
PS3602.R3596F36 2005b
813´.6—dc22   2005026548

Fan-Tan

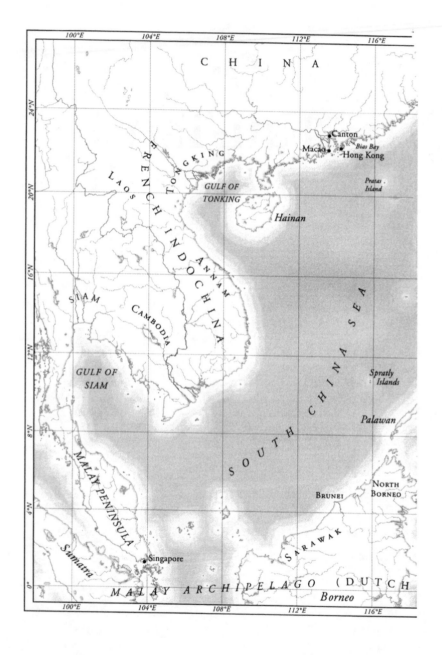

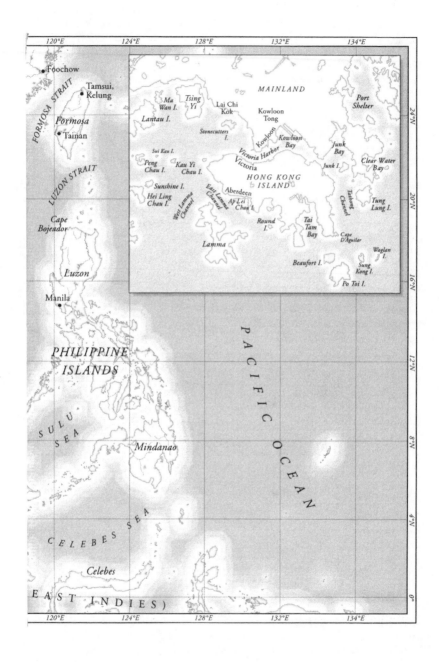

120°E 124°E 128°E 132°E 134°E

Foochow

Tamsui,
Kelung

FORMOSA STRAIT

Formosa

Tainan

LUZON STRAIT

Cape
Bojeador

Luzon

Manila

PHILIPPINE
ISLANDS

SULU
SEA

Mindanao

PACIFIC OCEAN

CELEBES SEA

Celebes

EAST INDIES)

24°N

20°N

16°N

12°N

8°N

4°N

0°

MAINLAND

Ma
Wan I.
Tsing
Yi
Lai Chi
Kok
Kowloon
Tong
Port
Shelter

Lantau I.

Stonecutters
I.
Kowloon
Kowloon
Bay
Junk
Bay

Sui Kau I.
Victoria Harbor
Junk I.
Clear Water
Bay

Peng
Chau I.
Kau Yi
Chau I.
Victoria

HONG KONG
ISLAND

Sunshine I.
East Lamma Channel
Aberdeen
Taulong
Channel
Tung
Lung I.

Hei Ling
Chau I.
West Lamma Channel
Ap Lei
Chau I.

Round
I.
Tai
Tam
Bay
Cape
D'Aguilar

Lamma
Beaufort I.
Waglan
I.

Sung
Kong I.

Po Toi I.

chapter 1
The Prison

Under a black cloud, the prison. And within the prison, a bright rebel. The walls were extremely high, and although this was not possible, they appeared to lean inward yet also to bulge outward, and they were topped with a luminous frosting of broken glass. Seen from the heights of the modest hill named Victoria Peak — from the summer residence of the governor of the Crown Colony of Hong Kong — the prison must have looked very fine. "If the sun were ever to shine," said Annie to the Portuguee, "the glass would probably glitter. It would look like a necklace of diamonds, Lorenzo. Or a big margarita, in a square cup."

The sun had not shone since November. This was March 2nd, "In the year of Their Lord" (Annie's words again) 1927. The vast cloud, several hundreds of miles in diameter and near as thick, squatted upon the unprepossessing island and pissed upon its prison. Annie Doultry (named

9

Anatole for Monsieur France, the novelist) was negotiating the one hundred and eightieth day of a six-month stretch. Born in Edinburgh in the year 1876, he looked his age, every passing minute of it.

His father had been a typesetter, a romantically inclined Scotsman whose hands played with words, a man who loved puns and tragedy, *King Lear* and Edward Lear. His mother was an unusual woman, lovely and liked, but not quite respectable. She was a MacPherson, but she had a flighty side. She had had lovers, the way some families have pets. Though raised in logic, common sense, and strict economy, once in a while she took absurd gambles — for one, her husband. Later the Doultrys emigrated to Seattle, the boy and the paternal grandmother in tow like many a Midlothian family in those days (when at least there was somewhere to emigrate to). The whole story was vague, though, and Annie was not much given to reflection upon his childhood. His memory was a mess, as full of giant holes as an old sock. Scotland was an accent he loved.

On the other hand, he thought a lot about the future. "That is one of my characteristics, Lorenzo," he said firmly to the bum of a Portuguee who occupied the bunk above, all aswamp in his own noisome reflections. Annie spoke out like that as a matter of principle, as a way of resisting the danger of thinking silently about one's own thoughts. That could lead to more thinking and so forth in a potentially hazardous spiral of regressions, the sort of thing one had to be careful of in Victoria Gaol. Men went mad there.

"If you think like a prisoner," said Lorenzo, "you are a prisoner for life."

"Not me," said Annie Doultry.

"But you are here," said the Portuguee — and it was undeniable. The loose Annie, liberty-loving, unpredictable, spontaneous, was as confined as anyone else in the prison.

"Soon you be old, man," mocked Lorenzo. "People grow old fast here."

That warning sank in. It helped explain Annie's thoughtful look. Once in prison was once too often. Annie Doultry had had little time to ask himself, "Where are you in life? Are you going to be a jailbird or are you going to be your own man?" He had taken that latter hope for granted, but he was too old to be lingering. You could say that it was prison that turned him into a full-blooded fatalist — and made him dangerous.

The grown man himself had a nose bent a little to the left. This is what he had written in pencil under March 1, his yesterday: "They say follow your nose. If I followed mine I guess I would be a Bolshie. But mine is a nose that knows who is boss." There, his own words hint at it: at a level above mere punnery the nose stood upon its battered cartilage as a sort of memorial to the mockery of the name that might have graced a fair highland woman. "Annie Doultry, rhymes with 'poultry,' " he repeated a number of times, testing his earplugs of candle wax as he screwed them in. Nothing wrong with the ears, their lobes pendulous in the style that indicated wisdom according to the Chinese, but the main organs compactly fitted beneath the hinges of a lantern jaw notorious for its insensitivity. "A face to sink a thousand ships," said Annie sonorously, as a final trial, and with the satisfaction of one who could no longer hear himself except as cello notes in his own bones.

To turn from the inner life of the man to his three-dimensional situation: the lower bunk of a cell in D block, seven feet by five with the usual grim appurtenances, shit pail and ignoble window, glassless but thickly barred, its sill over five feet from the concrete floor, making it fiendishly difficult for a Chinese to see out. Not so hard for Annie Doultry, however, for he was a large man and terribly thick of thew. Thick-chested, thick thumbs and eyebrows, thick tendons of the wrist and below the kneecap and at the insertion of the hamstring, a valuable asset for a violent man a little past the years of youthful resilience when being thrown out of bars and down companion ladders were just laughable excursions. Thick-bearded he was, too. They had tried to make him shave it off, but he had fought a moral battle with them, from barber to chief warder to the governor himself — and won it. So they had taken his hair but left him his beard to play with. Subsequently each hair had grown prouder, though admittedly grayer. It was an unusual gray, with the cuprite tinge that bronze develops when it takes what the imperial metal workers called the water patina.

Annie had often looked at himself in his mirror — before he lost it. It was a metal mirror, not of great antiquity. It was stainless steel, with a hole to hang it from, four inches square and probably Pittsburgh-made, for trading with Polynesian natives. The mirror was both kind and perceptive, like a rare friend. It stressed equally the deceptive youth and petulance of Doultry's mouth and the inexpressible, faltering beauty of his eyes. Faltering, because they never quite looked back at themselves, in that or any other mirror. The eyes were guarded because he did not wish them to expose him in any way. Beautiful, by way of his mother presumably, for his father was an ugly fellow; or perhaps just by way of contrast with the rustic ruin of the nose.

His hair was not so thick, of course, and it was cropped repulsively short back and sides. This style was all the rage in the prison, for it denied living space to the poor overcrowded lice.

The next thing was to get his socks in his hands in the correct manner. The heels should fit one in t'other, hand heel in sock heel; but the latter were giant vacuities, and the light was poor. The task had to be done. Nothing else guarded against the roaches.

The Portuguee was moaning, which meant that he was asleep. No earplug was proof against that sound. "He is in the fearful presence of a Jesuitical dream," said Annie softly. He wished he could write this down in his schoolbook, but the socks made it impossible. "Or perhaps he is praying." Damnation was what the man wished to avoid at all costs; he had told Annie so. But what made his moans all the more impressive was their coincidental harmonic precision with a Chinese type of moan, straight from the throat in E-flat and out through a mouth agape and then the open window of the hospital ward. This pit of suffering was on the ground floor of A block, just across the alley. The one who moaned had been flogged two or three days ago; his wounds were ulcerating and so on. But it must be made clear that the problem for Annie was not emotional or spiritual: it was a sleeping problem, for the buildings were all crammed together and the acoustics were excellent.

Annie lay back with the socks on his hands. On the great hairy pampas of his chest stood a ravaged tea mug, its blue enamel all mottled with dark perfusions like aging internal bruises promising worse to come. Yet Annie treasured it, for it was his one remaining possession inside this tomb of a prison. The other things — the lighter without a flint, the metal mirror, the brass buckle with the camel's head — he had gambled away at the roach races. Besides, Annie liked his tea, and Corporal Strachan (Ret.), chief warder of D block, would slip him an extra in this mug, Annie's own. Now, however, it was empty as an unrewarded sin. On either side of it lay his big bunched mitts, gray as stone, *manos de piedra* indeed, whose knuckles were protuberant but the fingers astonishingly delicate considering what they had been through — no pun intended.

He remained still. Around his tea mug, his chest was decorated with dried pellets of sorghum (a sort of mealy stuff) flavored with ginger. This was a taste much favored by cockroaches. His broad belly carried a trail of these pellets past his navel via the folds of his filthy canvas pants down to his bare feet. The big toes rested with a look of weary dignity on the rusted bedstead. Along it was laid an enticing line of roach bait, like the fuse to a keg of TNT.

Annie Doultry was lying in wait for his prey with all the punctilious preparation of a hunter of tigers, or of leopards, using his own person in lieu of the tethered goat. For this was the essential feature of his plan: his personal attractiveness to the animals in question. If there is one dish a Chinese roach prefers to sorghum and ginger, it is the dried skin of a whitee's feet. They would not dream of devouring the living epidermis, they were not looking for trou-

16

ble, but they favored calluses as an epicurean rabbi does smoked herring. To hold it against them — the roaches, that is — would be rank prejudice; but the fact was that a vulnerable foot was denuded of its natural protection. Feet became little engines of sensitivity. In Annie's case it was worse, for the roaches nibbled his fingers too throughout the torpid watches of the night — oh, how delicately they chomped away at the husks of his fingertips! Never did they wake him, and circumspection was their motto. No doubt the fearful size of the man gave them pause. "Do not wake him," they whispered one to another as they satisfied their desire. Hence the socks on his hands.

In a mood of stillness, Annie Doultry waited. The light became dimmer, the black cloud thickening with the approaching night. Under the black cloud, the prison.

Doultry's cell was no different in shape or size from the other three hundred and twelve. But in status it was one of a select few, like an ancient and appalling Russian railway carriage with First Class all in gold letters on its side. The top-floor view included the top strata of Victoria Peak and the governor's summer residence, its

Union Jack weighted in the moist atmosphere like a proud dishcloth. The grub was better too — pork twice a week, which was twice as much pork as the others got, the others being Chinese, a smaller race and less needful of meat, according to colonial doctrine. (And who will say they were wrong? Too much pork rots the colon's underwear and the upholstery of the beating heart.)

The top floor of D block was called the E section, which need not confuse the student if he remembers that the E stood for Europe, or European. The exalted E loomed on brooding signs and likewise on Annie Doultry's institutional garments, stenciled on the canvas in blood-clot red above the broad arrow. The arrow pointed at the letter with pride or with accusation, depending on how you looked at it. In Annie's case it was also with indignation, for he was an American, a true-blue American since the age of five or thereabouts (though in his heart's heart he knew he was ever a Celt from the land of mists, and a wanderer).

Doultry was not the first Yank to wear the big E. As the superintendent had patiently explained to him, the E referred not to geography but to race, and in the view of the prison service a white or whitish American was indisputably an E. There were five-hundred-odd A's and fourteen E's in residence in March of '27, including remand prisoners awaiting trial. This proportional representation was surprisingly close to that of the colony as a whole. This again could be regarded as praiseworthy, pointing at the proud blindness of British justice, or as shameful, for obvious reasons.

But enough moral speculation; back to the facts, blinder than justice. Annie, prostrate in his bunk, his socks on his hands and all strewn with cockroach bait, his leathery face menaced by the sagging paraboloid of the Portuguee's mattress, protruding like an appalling fungus through its fret of rusty wire, an instrument that sang tunes of despair with each twist of the poor wee bugger's bum. A great stain resembling Australia pressed on Annie's eyeballs with the whole weight of that meaty continent, which he had seen more than enough of in the course of his erratic voyages. And to think this was but the mattress's underside! What must she be like topsides — in proximity to the wooly back, the shriveled buttocks, the leaky sphincter of the Portuguee?

Perish the very thought.

Although it might be pretended by a certain superintendent that Victoria Gaol was named for the sovereign on whom the sun never set, this was not so. The naming was at second hand, like a wife's, bequeathed to the prison by the city of Victoria, erected all higgledy-piggledy on Hong Kong Island. There was very little old-fashioned imperial pride about the project; a place to make a few bob was all that was behind it. Noting the pussyfooting of the English, the Scots moved in and cannily organized things. The colony was run by them, they made the bureaucracy tick, they owned the richest merchant houses. They ran the docks and the engines of the ships on the China Seas.

However, though he was once a Scot, it was not the future of the city that bore on Annie Doultry's brain, nor the world's, either; his own future it was, or would be. The reality to be expected, the facts of it. But was there such a thing as a future fact? There was one for Mr. Wittgenstein, indeed. Common sense answered "Yes!"; logic hollered "No!" To hell with philosophy, thought Annie. It was too much reflection had got him there in the first place, too much thinking and too little action. "If I had only shot the bastard," he thundered at the Portuguee's vile mattress, "instead of standin' there weighin' the pros and cons of it! God blind me for my compassion — Lord, do you hear me now? Act, damn your guts! ACT!" The tin mug on his chest danced to the tune of his recriminations, the great sob that he would not allow to emerge gonging its enamel bottom. Annie overcame the sob and filtered it out as a sort of sigh, or wheeze. "Ah, now there was a good firearm. That Luger. Nine-millimeter Parabellum, disastrous to the flesh as any .45 and a helluva sight straighter-shootin'." Pause. "But all said and done, nobody makes metal like Smith & Wesson." He caressed the dull enamel of his mug. "The color o' the pit of the night. There are pearls that color, Lorenzo." (Manuel was his name, but no matter.) "Like ink on a leather apron."

The Portuguee slept on, moaning in the swamps of his own dreams.

This one was big, too: a good three and a half inches long. He stood upon the rusted iron bedstead at the foot of Annie's bunk. He eyed Annie and then stepped with circumspection onto a toe. The toe, the whole foot, Annie had attempted to wash a little to make it as appetizing as possible. But this creature ignored the riches spread before it. Him, her — how in Christ's name do you tell the sex of a cockroach? (Well, Hai Sheng could — and later did, pronouncing it to be a he.)

To the eye of the roach, Annie's size 11 must have had the appearance of that Buddha's foot forty feet long, carved from the pale gray throat of a Singhalese mountain. Its calluses and corns were already well pruned by previous visitors; the terrain was smooth and sweet as an adolescent girl's. The cockroach pressed on, up the pants to Kneecap Knoll and then downhill to Groin Canyon, where certain morsels of sorghum roach bait, moistened to make them stick, lay in a crevice. But the beast ignored this feast. With a cautious but unhesitating step he descended ledges of dirt-caked hemp to the very lip of Fly Gap itself — that fault in the world's crust to which (Annie thought, with respect) your average roach would give a wide berth. The pit itself yawned there, with boredom no doubt, spooky bronze-gray tendrils curling forth, shameless and buttonless (for Annie had gambled away the buttons). The splendid creature's antennae felt the moist ether and his carapace glittered like Beelzebub's armor, the perfect color of fresh tar. He looked downward, into the shadows; and the view must have dizzied him, for he did not seem to hear Annie's whisper: "You are not a gentleman, sir." Annie said it so that it could not be said of him later that he said nothing, that it was a betrayal of confidence. Then the gloomy cauldron of that tea mug descended like a shroud upon that proud cock of the roach walk, making him prisoner too.

The roach races were held in a gutter about twenty-five feet long that traversed the exercise yard. By convention this gutter demarcated Europe from Asia. It was concrete, eight inches wide by four deep, and rimmed with a vile greenish tinge that Doultry liked to call "this Emerald Sward" or sometimes "the turf of grand old Epsom." Understand, please: he was trying to be British.

As the clang of the starting gong did the trick (it was a tin plate), the roaches were released with a lot of noise and exhortations up at the north end. Most often they chose to keep to the straight-and-narrow, encouraged by the stamping feet on either side. With a following breeze the best entries reached (or roached) fifteen miles an hour, the speed of a man with the devil at his heels. It was imperative to catch the critters before they disappeared down the drain a yard beyond the finishing line, except in the case where a runner's sloth made liquidation by the sole of the disappointed foot a more likely fate, and the drain became life's sanctuary. "They're a fatalistic lot," said Annie to Hai Sheng, an owner like himself. "They prefer dishonor to death any day of the week."

Hai Sheng spat with a rich sound, signifying his approval of these words. He spoke pidgin, but understood considerable English. His wiry thoroughbred, Wondrous Bird of Hope, had yet to lose. His winnings were well over ten dollars in cash alone this season, though he was only a few weeks old. The rains didn't set in properly until June, so you can see the profit to be made from a good roach in Victoria Gaol.

Beyond the gutter, the greater part of the yard was devoted to the hard labor of the Chinese inmates, on a shift basis. They unraveled old rope, many miles of it. The shredded hemp, called oakum, was nominally destined to caulk sprung seams in the oaken hulls of His Majesty's ships. However, this was 1927 already, and the navy had built its ships of steel for over fifty years. So the oakum was stored against the day when the wooden walls might arise again from the deep of Trafalgar, and the Bay of Tientsin too, where a frigate had gone down in 1857 under the ancient guns of the Dragon Emperor's fortresses.

The rope picking was pointless, but it pretended to a point. It was officially called Hard Labor No. 2. The east end of the yard was where the cream of the condemned worked at Hard Labor No. 1, or Shot Drill. Their labor transcended purpose; it was labor consecrated to itself alone.

The "shot men," as they were called in the prison, walked all day in circles. At four points on the perimeter of the circle there stood small pyramids of twenty-four-pound shot, or cannonballs, so that no more than five paces separated them. The shot were of cast iron, black and featureless as the back of Death's hand. For over three centuries they had fed the secondary armament of His Majesty's ships and the army's all-purpose cannon. Then, overnight, about the middle of Victoria's reign, the belated adoption of the rifled cannon had made the twenty-four-pound shot quite obsolete. The whine of the spinning shell became their dirge.

So the shot accumulated in their millions. Like a vast and despicable population confronting genocide, they brooded in their pyramids great and small in dark corners of the empire, schoolboys pissing on them. It was left to this ageless penitentiary in Hong Kong to find a proper use for them. Here, the shade of that irrefutable old lady, Queen Victoria, lifted her petticoats for the last time to reveal to the forgetful that those iron balls of hers were not yet impotent; that they could still break men's hearts.

The labor consisted of each man picking up a shot from a pyramid as he reached it, carrying it those few paces, and placing it carefully on the next pile. Then five paces, light-footed, to the next one, and once more the stooping, the lifting of the shot, the carrying, the setting down, and so forth, and so forth, in two-hour shifts, eight hours a day.

The shot could not be dropped upon its pile, of course. The equilibrium of the pyramids was important; it required precision from each man and an overall rhythm, a disciplined momentum to the wheel of guilty Chinamen (for Europeans were never condemned, in Annie Doultry's day, to Hard Labor No. 1). Their overseers were Indian warders, burly men (a number of them Sikhs with immense beards fastened up behind their ears) who paced the rim of the circle with their rattan canes (three feet six inches long and one inch thick), smartly uniformed and marvelously impartial. They would poke and pat, encouraging the Shot Drill, for it was a drill, and they were mostly professional soldiers who had been lucky enough (old wounds or sickness would do it) to get this cushy job. They were by no means sadists. Still, when a man fumbled his shot, they beat him, for that was part of the drill.

Between races Annie sometimes watched the shot men. The Chinese convicts all wore straw coolie hats of uniform size — it was regulation. The effect was symmetrical and easy on the eye: the pale pointy hats dipping at the circle's four corners, the chinking of the twenty-four-pound shot, the forming and dissolution of the pyramids, the bending of backs, the bending of brains. Once he said out loud: "You're a lucky sonofabitch, Annie."

Annie's six months was a mere slap of the wrist according to the barrister who defended him, Mr. Andrew O'Gormer. It was not even so much as hard labor, but mere imprisonment. Apart from cockroach racing, Annie's hardest labor was an hour's walking up and down each morning after breakfast. No talking, of course, but Annie had formed a friendship with Corporal Strachan, and they would often walk together, chatting circumspectly. In short, Annie knew how to do his time. He handled the situation.

O'Gormer had taken Annie for every last cent, naturally. On the other hand, the prisoner could have got ten years under the Arms and Ammunition Ordinance of 1900. There's no knowing what goes on in the judge's chambers over a gin and tonic. Annie had shipped in to Hong Kong, all fair and aboveboard and properly entered on his ship's manifest in his own neat handwriting, "for transshipment, bona fide cargo to Tientsin, Province of Shantung, Republic of China," a modest quantity of firearms procured in Manila from sources close to Uncle Sam's fine army in those regions. Specifically — it was all down in black-and-white — nineteen hundred and twelve U.S. Army Garand rifles, in good shape with regulation bayonets; eighteen Maxim .50-caliber machine guns (well used) plus nine excellent Hotchkiss heavies; two

28

hundred thousand rounds of .300-cal (for the rifles); twenty crates times twenty-four Mills grenades; and an assortment of side-arms: several hundred Army Colt .45 automatics (the classic 1910 model) and revolvers (mostly .38's) and some interesting old mortars, heavy with grease and dents.

According to the quite liberal colonial law, no licenses or red tape need be bothered with provided these goods were ultimately destined for elsewhere. With arms, Hong Kong liked being a marketplace, but not a customer. The problem arose when a certain Polish gentleman approached Annie in Torrance's bar and offered a ridiculous sum of money for half-a-dozen Colt autos plus a few cartons of .45 ammo to make them go pop. "I was deeply offended, sir," Annie told the judge. "I told him to keep his damned money, for I was well aware it was an offense, Your Honor, to sell a gun to a Hong Kong feller without a permit from the captain superintendent, Hong Kong police. I was well aware of that. There's Communists about, Your Honor, and we don't want 'em getting their dirty hands on good American guns, I'm with you on that right down the line." Annie figured this would go down well with his audience. This was at the supreme court, before a jury.

"Please address me as Your Worship, Mr. Doultry," said the judge.

"Your Worship," said Annie.

But one thing had led to another. Though Annie maintained that the guilty weapons had been stolen from off his boat while Bernardo Patrick Hudson (his first mate) was suffering a bad attack of malaria brought on by drinking Chinese beer, the jury, though sympathetic, had declined to believe him. The thieves (or buyers) had not been apprehended; the guns were gone: the maritime police counted every last one remaining on board. The emissary of Annie's legitimate customer, Marshal Sun Chuan-fang, warlord of Nanchang and the plains south of the Yangtze at the time, was no help at all. In fact he was extremely annoyed, since delivery of his lawful shipment of arms was canceled at short notice, the entire shipment being confiscated by the Hong Kong police according to the letter of their law. The marshal's rapacious army was then engaged on several fronts in desultory warfare with Chiang Kai-shek. The details are fatiguing, but it was quite natural that British Hong Kong rather disliked stories in the *South*

China Weekly News about the colony's role as a bazaar for arms open to both sides — or to all sides, more accurately, since there were at least a dozen independent armies fighting each other up and down China. There was even a theoretical international arms embargo in force, dating from May 5, 1919. It had been sponsored by the American minister in Shanghai and signed by Britain, France, Russia, Japan — everybody but the Germans, whose arms business in China was huge. Then the Russians broke the embargo in a big way when they started supplying armaments to the Nationalist-Communist alliance, and soon the embargo was just another bit of paper. America supplied new machinery for the Nationalists' main armory at Canton, to build British Vickers machine guns and ammunition for Russian rifles (seven hundred thousand cartridges a month). In Hong Kong, deals for anything could be made, including gas masks and airplanes. It was only indiscreet publicity that was taboo.

Annie knew and understood all this — the situation he was getting into, the niceties of it. It was depressing to have to keep up with this ongoing Chinese catastrophe,

31

but he was doing business with them; and though he was not keen on the food, Chinese women were exceedingly attractive — along with the steady rumination on why he was so drawn to them. No, Annie was not naive. To rub salt in the wound, Barney (Bernardo Patrick) Hudson had had the wind up all along about peddling the Colt sidearms to the Polack, and when the shit hit the fan he persisted in repeating, "I told you so, I told you so," and laughing in a hysterical fashion. He was lucky not to be in the dock himself.

Annie felt he was getting soft. He knew perfectly well he had been framed. Nonetheless, the philosophical way to look at it was like it was just a bad bet, a bet with the odds rigged, the dice loaded, and the dealer's drinks paid for by the opposite party. But it was in prison that Annie became a real gambler.

Something profound had happened to Annie since September 4th, the day he first donned his E and his red arrow. He had never been in the slammer before, for one, and his age was too old for a first time. He was also plunged into forced proximity with the Chinese for the first time in his life, the Chinese of the narrow alleys and great effluvious slums, the coolies who were as another species to the white men on the outside. Willy-nilly, a sympathy was seeded in him. It might have been disgust, but no, it seems it was sympathy.

Let it be clear, Annie had always got on with most Britishers — a getting-on that got to the point where nostalgia for the Scotland he could barely remember and his pernicious talent for mimicry had led him to pretend to be a limey just for the hell of it. (He could impersonate a cockney near as well as he could a Scot.) But this tolerance for the British, an odd race who (as the Chinese pretended to) lived in the certainty of their superiority to all others, may have made the temptation to cock a snoot at the limeys irresistible. Annie had no chip on his shoulder on account of his conviction and punishment. He had been caught bang to rights, as Detective Inspector Kenneth Andrews put it; his was a gamble taken and a gamble lost. But the loser incarcerated is an animal destined to six months of the paid principal, of emphatically aversive conditioning toward the powers that put him there. Thus, if the British Empire rubs a man's face in his own dung for six months, he cannot be expected to feel the same way about that empire or the dung. Add to the stew Annie's aversion to authority in any shape or form. To prove the origins of this antipathy would require a pilgrimage into a childhood forgotten by everyone, particularly by Annie. But it was there in the way so large a man insisted on a girl's name. The long and the short of the matter is that what had been merely a rebellious pimple on his psyche must have swollen up in Victoria Gaol into a boil: a boiling boil on the soul's posterior, coming to a fiery head, almost ready to pop.

"Him too much big," said Hai Sheng, the well-known Chinese owner, eyeing Annie Doultry's entry for the 3:15 race. "Wondrous Bird fly fast by velly, velly small foot." Hai's Wondrous Bird of Hope, the richest prizewinner of his day, was still only a colt, according to Sheng, who knew his roaches. Sheng had a collection of small change in many currencies, also safety-pins, aspirin tablets, buttons, toothbrushes, opium scrapings, bandages, and Annie's belt buckle with the camel's head, as proof of this knowledge.

"What callee you fat animal?" asked Hai Sheng, with skepticism.

"Dempsey." On the glossy back of his enormous animal Annie had engraved his mark, a great D, white lime rubbed into it to show it up.

"Ha. Dim-see no more champ."

A longish pause. Doultry wondered if the man was insane. "What?"

"Jackee Dim-see he beat-up by young fella."

Annie rubbed his face. Its surface felt like an old automobile tire. "Come again?" he said.

"Jackee Dim-see he beat-up by Chin Tun-hi."*

Annie realized where the confusion must lie. Gene Tunney, that fellow from the Marine Corps, had found fame being whipped by Harry Greb in his dotage — Tunney, a smartass, a real fancy dan. It couldn't be true. Tunney was a light-heavy; he had challenged Jack last summer, but the champ had laughed at him. "Shengy, old buddy," said Annie lightly to the short Chinaman, "whoever told you this yarn was having a spot of fun at your expense."

Hai Sheng's lips were pursed in his pudgy

*In fact, Jack Dempsey had lost the heavyweight title to Gene Tunney in Philadelphia on September 23, 1926. He would also lose the return fight, in Chicago, on September 22, 1927.

face; it was not a smile but a politeness. The two men were seated side by side in the latrine at the back of the washhouse, a three-holer where business could be transacted and conversation flowered. "Whoever told you this tall tale was taking the piss out of you, my son," said Annie.

Hai Sheng said it was a decision. Chin Tun-hi had walked all over the champ; Dim-see had seemed like an old man. It was outdoors, the rain had come down from the clouds, the young fella's blows were thunderbolts. Hai Sheng had heard this tale because there had been considerable betting in Hong Kong, where men bet on everything under heaven and on earth. Hai Sheng's ear was close to the ground.

At last Annie accepted that fate had caught up with Manassa Jack. Annie had never contested that the Chinese were well up on matters of fate; it was a thing they specialized in. "So goes the way of all flesh," he said, nodding his acceptance, somber with violent memories. "He was unusual, Jack. A terror to the body he was, and a sworn enemy of the liver and ribs." Hai Sheng nodded, lips pursed. "On the other hand, you had to call the man a right-hand artist, out and out. While your run-o'-the-mill everyday body puncher normally favors a left hook. Like myself."

Universal justice decreed that Dempsey the roach should win the 3:15 race by four lengths going away from Wondrous Bird of Hope. He did better than win: he escaped. The great speeding beast swerved out of the gutter four inches past the finishing line, scorning the sanctuary of the finishing sack. Nobody tried to stomp on him. Stomping losers was one thing; escapees were different. Dempsey spun sweetly around the sack man, a lovely maneuver, and disappeared down the drain. "He was a virtuoso and an exhibitionist," said Annie. He felt a deep sense of loss, but he did not hold it against anyone, least of all that noble creature. It was typical that a roach should bring out all that was best in a man. Hai Sheng paid up with the others. Doultry collected nearly a dollar, plus two safety pins, a small opium tablet, and his old belt buckle with the camel's head. Hai Sheng nevertheless shook his jowls sympathetically over the loss that clouded the win. "That's life," said Annie. "That's typical of life." He clapped the Chinaman on the shoulder. He tended to clap their shoulders and deliver genial little punches under their shoulder blades to emphasize his points. The Chinese detested that sort of thing but never protested, which amused Annie and provoked him to do more of the same.

The only place the E's ever spoke to the A's, unless you include the can, was over the gutter in the yard. It was against regulations, talking between Chinese and whites, god knows why. Was some sort of clandestine passing of information feared? Revolutionary small-talk? Contamination of hearts or of minds? Only at race time were the regulations waived; it was the British way: sport was sport. The warders liked a bet; everyone needed a bet. So the gutter separated, but it also joined: E's, A's, and Sikh guards with their great hooked-up beards. Human frailty breathed sweetly among the roaches, with their images blazed on the back, Demon of the Left River and Apple Blossom and Wondrous Bird of Hope and, before he blew the coop, Dempsey, the Manassa Mauler.

"Sheng," said Doultry the next day, "you and I are men of the world. We share an interest in the sporting life, am I right?"

"Lightee."

"All right. So I want to do you a favor, pal. I'm prepared to make you an offer for Wondrous Bird."

38

"Wondlous Birdee no for sale."

A lie, a barefaced lie. The negotiations took only three days. Something drove Annie to it, he knew not what. He might have tried to find another world beater, but his brain told him he had been lucky and his luck was now changed. The other possibility is that Hai Sheng had decided to sell and conned Annie into it. "So now you want to sell the bastard, eh?" sneered Annie. " 'Cause he lost? Just once? Fuckin' typical."

He paid for the cockroach in gold. It was half the filling in an extracted molar, a nest egg hoarded against a rainy day or an investment opportunity such as this. The filling, split by Corporal Strachan's bayonet, was weighed for the parties by the dentist himself, a pleasant Bengali. Four grains of gold, worth close to five U.S. dollars, which was ten dollars Hong Kong at that time: a tremendous, unheard-of price. "I bling him you tomollow, Mistah Annie. In he boxee of Jonkau wood." Hai Sheng made his mark on Annie's receipt, a most elegant mark.

The shot men circled amidst their metal pyramids, like the faithful in fog-bound Purgatorio.

It was the night after the sale of Wondrous Bird. The night before his delivery, in his box of Jonkau wood. Hai Sheng said this box had once held a great pearl set in a sign of emeralds, stolen from the dowry of Tzu Hsi, the Dragon Empress, by one of his illustrious forefathers in Tientsin. Annie lay on his bunk in the dark; it was almost eight.

He sucked on his opium pill. It was like a peppermint in size and duration, but black and not meant to be swallowed. It tasted disgusting, like a tablet of rat shit, which made the pleasure that ensued the sweeter. There was already the pleasure of solitude, for the Portuguee had been carried to the hospital. The doc was of the opinion he was suffering from advanced phthisis — tuberculosis, he was talking about. In those days, there were qualified docs who reckoned flogging led to tuberculosis — perhaps this danger helped them miss the ruin of the body!

In any case, whatever it was, he could look forward to meeting his ancestors shortly. He was called the Portuguee, but he was Chinese three parts in four. In Macao, where he hailed from, that was considered Portuguese; it was a matter of snobbery. Although most of them had come to Christ and the pope by parental tutelage, a few of the more realistic ones worshipped their ancestors. The Portuguese who lived above Annie was one of those. His E must have been a courtesy to the governor of Macao.

From the heart, Annie thanked Dempsey, the Big D, for his pill. Not only was his heart a little heavy on account of their parting of the ways, but he also missed the Portuguee. And in addition, there was a bad flogging on. It was damned insensitive of the boys in the band to have one so late, but they were a thoughtless bunch. Just when you had achieved a level of tolerance and compassion for them, they would pull some ugly stunt like this, a bedtime flogging — to put the frighteners on, as the limeys put it.

The frequent floggings were the one aspect of prison life that Doultry felt was a threat to his sanity. The rites of punishment were staged in a small yard reserved for the purpose, but it was a small prison, and the screams were not to be missed. The rattan cane (a new one for each beating) was applied to the buttocks of the Chinese with great force and damaged the skin to the extent that scars for life were inevitable. This aspect of the punishment was the one the Chinese abhorred the most. Their general theory was that the louder a man screamed, the more likely the doctor was to tell the discipline warder to ease up a bit. Of course, this was not true. And there were some who did not make a sound.

Annie, lying there, tried to put himself in a Chinese way of thinking about all this, because they were the ones being flogged. They had also done most of the flogging in this world. The Chinese had always flogged each other mercilessly; thus there was no logic to guilt on the subject on either Annie's part or that of the discipline warders who beat malfeasant prisoners in Victoria Gaol. One of them was Welsh and the other a cockney from Stepney, a personal acquaintance and the darts champion of Hong Kong. Any way you looked at it, it was disgusting to a sensitive person, and to the naked eye. But it was worse to the naked ear. There was no strictly appointed hour to perform the rites — it could be dawn or it could be after tea — but it was always a street called Pain for Annie. God help us all in our hour of need.

Annie Doultry to Corporal Strachan: "Give me a topping, Stew, over a flogging, any day of the week."

Corporal Strachan: "I never minded a toppin', meself."

Strachan — he was from Carlisle, on the border — had been discharged from the 52nd Battalion of the line, the Argyll and Sutherland Highlanders, still a private after twenty-six years. A sergeant twice over, twice reduced to the ranks, he was called corporal, even by the superintendent, Major Bellingham, out of a sort of respectful compromise with history. He had an Afghan bullet in his hip, which gave him trouble, and medals from a number of places with names that brought tears to a Scotsman's eyes, including the bloody Somme, where two-thirds of the great regiment laid down their battered lives. Drink was the problem with Strachan.

Hanging was all in a day's work to Strachan; he had been at it for years, appreciating the job for the extra pay, which was one pound fifteen a throw. He enjoyed gallows humor, too. In this jail there was a literal example. Every damn day, the European prisoners mounted their proud gallows in a body, twice over — going and coming. This because as a measure of economy it had been incorporated into the short concrete bridge that connected D block with C block. This bridge had to be traversed to reach the exercise yard beyond. There was a square trap in the middle of it with a fifteen-foot drop to the alley below.

"Stewart, it's not a good thing," said Annie once. "There should be a wee bit of respect. Not for the buggers as hang, but the buggers as hang 'em." He always spoke a sort of bastard Scots tongue to Strachan. Annie was unable to control his tongue; it spoke for him. "For what is left of my heart, this tongue speaks," he said to Strachan, and he showed him the guilty member. It was tuberous in form, a dusty gray on top but a lovely rose beneath, and the fat tip of the thing was a delicate instrument, cute as a young girl's. "The ultimate sanction is what they call it, man. They should've built you a proper gallows. That blasted hole is like a privy. What it calls to mind is turds dropping through it." Strachan had a good chuckle at that one.

An easy fifty percent of those who took the long drop in 1927 were pirates by trade. The penalty for piracy was death, with no mitigation as to circumstances. A pirate, caught in the act or the planning thereof, or in association therewith in any form or manner, was hanged, and no beating about the bush. They deserved it, for they were a barbarous breed of men, and too numerous upon the China Seas.

At a quarter past five, when the sun must have been rising in Singapore, Annie awoke from a disintegrating dream that we will not go into. In Hong Kong there was only a desultory pale-yellowish rinsing of the shameful heap of cloud above the prison — it was not enough to call it the light before the light. Annie awoke by way of having decided to do so before he retired. This was a trick, a knack, another of the facilities of this talented but unsuccessful man. He would bang his head on the wall, quite hard, once for every hour o' the mornin' and a wee little tap for the quarter past. It was finely judged. The hanging would have woke him up anyway, but by then the fun would have been over.

Although this ceremony was routine as the floggings, it was less frequent, and a number of the more energetic E's roused themselves to witness it. This opportunity offered because the Bridge of Sighs stood right beneath the windows of the E section, affording a grandstand view if one's shit pail was dragged into service. The tramp of booted feet was the opening effect, a hollow doomy sound on the concrete vaulting like the sound of death's drums in a sewer. The soft croak of Mr. Hugh Llewellyn's orders — he was the head warder — floated up from the gloom, followed by Strachan's appraisal of the Chinaman's person as it enjoyed its last moments of life's breath. "Aboot nine stone an' a half, sir. I'll gi' him eight inches over wi' that neck on him."

Annie shifted the shit pail to the necessary spot beneath the window. It was an act of faith to consign his weight to the lid of it. He must have still pushed two hundred and twenty pounds even after considerable losses to the vile and insufficient jail food. Many a dawn vigil had that rusty lid borne for the sins of others. Between the bars above, Annie's eye peered at the fuming sky. The putrid phosphorescence of the great cloud revealed that it was palpably moldering, the victim of its own excessive humidity. Beneath, the governor's posh house was plain to see, its great flag so low-hung with the vapors that it was next best to half-mast. Half-mast, for the soul of Li Weng-chi.

His face was asymmetrical. It had received some great blow at an early age. That rage in the face made it memorable. Rage was not characteristic of the condemned in this prison, though there is no truth in the notion that a Chinaman can accept death with greater calm than a whitee. Quite the reverse; Annie Doultry himself had reason to believe that they had a horror of death and a fascination with its panoply greater than any papist's or Mussulman's.

Li Weng-chi had been brought in from Lantau Island after his capture by a party from the gunboat HMS *Thames Ditton*, and spent no more than a week in solitary before his trial. Doultry had never seen him before. He was shackled between two Punjabi warders, their turbans tight-wound for the dawn detail, their pants pressed, their minds on their breakfasts. Strachan had in his hands a dusty black sack, fit for Irish potatoes, pretending to be a hood. Li Weng-chi scorned it with a great gob of luminous spit, slap onto the gallows trap. He began to speak, or to chant an invocation in his language, whatever it was. (It was not Cantonese; it was a variety of the Chung Chia language from some wild region of the south.) The chaplain, the Reverend Edwin Trevor (Church of England), ignored this heathen prayer and commended Li Weng-chi's soul to the God of the Jews.

Annie kept his eyes off Trevor, offended

by his unworthiness, his grubby collar devoid of faith, shamed by the impeccable Indian warders, lowly men though they were. Annie studied the rage in Li Wengchi's eyes. In many Chinese faces there was a frightening cast to the skull. To Annie, the fashion in which the eyeballs nestled in their slots, protected by bone, suggested the priorities of survival and the inevitability of violence. Boxers got themselves eyes like that after fifty fights, but this Chinese was born with them. As he watched him, this thought, along with others equally pessimistic, stroked the lining of Annie's stomach, causing it to creep up on itself in minuscule ridges. (He had not had breakfast, either.) And the bright black movement of those optical instruments in their little bunkers was unsettling. It was Doultry's opinion that the Chinese could see in the blinding sun like no white man. This opinion may have been erroneous; science might well deny it. But then the superiority of Chinese eyes at sea or of Scots determinism in the engine room was not something that respectable scientists wished to quantify, either then or now. Well, was this not a reason to have one's doubts about scientists? Annie respected science, and he was hurt when it let him down with its pusillanimous moralizing, worse than religion's.

And now he observed, from behind his bars, from upon his shit pail, that Li Weng-chi was no longer praying; he was accusing, and he was doing so in intelligible Cantonese.

Li Weng-chi was already standing on the trap, the noose around his neck, Strachan adjusting it with choosy fingers. He addressed himself to Dr. Cathcart, the colonial medical officer. Cathcart had lived twenty years in the colony and was fairly fluent in Cantonese. He listened attentively. Head Warder Llewellyn was heard to inquire irritably what all the chitchat was about. "Let us proceed, Doctor. Unless the prisoner is unwell." A man has to be theoretically healthy to be hanged.

"He wishes to make a statement, Mr. Llewellyn. To have it written down."

"Let's get on with it, Doctor. He cannot make a statement now."

"I gather it's a denunciation."

"The bugger's just stallin', sir," said Corporal Strachan. "Let's get on with it."

"Whatever you say, Mr. Llewellyn," said Dr. Cathcart. "But the chappie here says there's some influential pirate or other is at present sojourning in this prison. Our man

49

has decided to denounce him, I gather."

Annie watched like it was a picture show. He sucked his teeth, a salivary sound, a sign that he was impressed. On the Bridge of Sighs, Mr. Llewellyn took out his watch and studied it. "I assume the prisoner has asked for a postponement of his execution?"

"No, Hugh, he has not."

Thereupon Llewellyn agreed to the taking down of the statement. Dr. Cathcart did it with his propelling pencil on the back of his mess bill. In the growing gloom of the frustrated day, the doctor's ear tilted toward Li Weng-chi's deliberate sentences. Once the doctor asked for clarification. The pirate explained, the doctor nodded, absorbed in the linguistic challenge. He then turned to the head warder, who was blowing his nose with every sign of impatience. "All right. This is how it goes." He coughed and proceeded to read aloud, with some pride and a fine feeling for the intent of the original.

" 'If wolves of the sea must die' — no, 'be destroyed' is better, I beg your pardon, yes — 'be destroyed by the hand of syphilitic foreign dogs, dogs of the street, then the one who calls himself Hai Sheng must die the death of ten thousand cuts. For he is a leader of sixty' — a lieutenant, I presume — 'under the banner of the Mountain of Wealth, who betrayed the men of the West River.' I assume that simply means the West River Gang, wouldn't you say? 'May his gonads rot. May red worms make their home in the bowels of his sons.' That's rather well phrased, I think, don't you?" The doctor's pencil adjusted an adjective.

"Corporal Strachan," said the head warder. "You will append your signature as witness."

This Strachan did.

The pirate Li Weng-chi was smiling, a thing he did rarely; his physiognomy had no provision or talent for it, no flexing points in the skin, so it adjusted with difficulty. But there was enough light now for Annie to see this grim smile, while Strachan readjusted the knot behind the left ear. Then the drunken old Scots warrior kicked the wedge out of the trap and gravity claimed another wicked man.

Five minutes later, standing on a stepladder steadied by Strachan, Dr. Cathcart checked the pulse of the prisoner as he swung gently in the alley. Li Weng-chi's neck was absurdly extended and his naked feet dripped with excreta, but his expression had not changed. Worse, a pulse was still there. This was not all that uncommon. Within a few minutes more he was irrefutably a goner.

The sun rose above the horizon, clear as a brass gong. For the first time since November its light penetrated the prison. A brazen ray pierced the alley (which was aligned east to west) and embalmed Li Weng-chi's smile within the memories of those privileged to witness the moment. Then the light withdrew into the black cloud; and with it went the stoic endurance of Annie's shit-pail lid, which gave out a groan as it buckled along its diameter, lowering his naked foot into a couple of quarts of mild pee, which was all the vessel contained at this early hour.

And with one humbled foot and an empty stomach, Annie guessed that this was his chance to intervene, to make a play. Why? Why does a man trained over fifty years to mere survival, why does he volunteer? Was it for truth's sake, or did Annie Doultry see opportunity?

"Your Honor," said Annie to the superintendent. "Hai Sheng is not a pirate. Shudder the thought." He shuddered his ample frame. This interview was being conducted in the superintendent's office, which had less of a view than Annie's cell. Major Anthony Bellingham (Ret.) was seated behind his desk, the fans thunking away, moisture on the walls. Prisoner No. 43141/E, Anatole Doultry, was at attention before him, Dr. Cathcart sat in the other chair with an abstract look. There was an orderly at the door, and the rain was dripping down outside.

"Doultry, kindly refrain from calling me Your Honor. Sir will do."

"Sir, Hai Sheng was my cook aboard my vessel *The Sea Change*, a schooner, sir, a trading schooner of ninety-six tons. She's a fine vessel, I know you'd appreciate her refinement. This man was my cook May through January last. He was uninstructed on the fine points o' his craft, sir, but he was skinty wi' the provisions, he didn't put up wi' any answerin' back from the crew, and he was a fair seaman. I instructed him meself in the art o' porridge oats, sir."

Annie not only sounded sort of Scots, one of those very slow-talking Clydesiders who got pleasure from boring people to death, but he had done something with his facial hair to help the illusion: more than a touch of candle wax in the mustache so that it stuck out like two spears with yellowish points. He had an upright bearing, the weight on one leg and the other forward-planted, the feet splayed like a regimental piper's, and the hands cupped gently together, at ease below the belt as if a sporran were there to support them.

"Your cook, eh? A damned violent cook, by all accounts," said Major Bellingham.

"Violent? Well, I'd no say he was particularly violent, sir. He had a temper, mind. You criticize his noodles, for example, you try to tell him they was like old torn-up underwear wi' sodding glue sauce, and Shengy would take after you wi' his cleaver every time. Any wee criticism and you took your life in yer hands, I tell you, sir, you could ha' had him up for attempted murder any time you liked."

Here Annie chuckled heavily, a sound to match the weight of his boringness. "If he couldna get you wi' his cleaver, he'd get you wi' his sea-snake stew. But let us be serious, Major." Annie looked around his audience. "Does bein' a murderous cook make a feller a pirate? As I recollect, it was end o' January Shengy got waylaid in Mrs. Trentham-Smith's by that rating from HMS *Suffolk* — his name escapes me now. He was a stoker's mate. That was the first trouble my Hai — I call him 'my Hai' — first trouble he was ever in. I've got no particular use for Chinks, Your Honor, as everybody knows, but a man can't stand by and see justice perverted by wild accusations o' some cocksucker on the gallows."

"No swearing, Doultry."

"I apologize, sir. My feelings are a bit overwrought, sir. Shengy is a good cook."

"Doultry, I understood you were American. You don't sound American to my ear."

Annie sighed deeply and shook his head, as if hard put to find the words for so emotional a subject. "Sir, I'm British born. Born in Edinburgh, Royal Navy at age fifteen, served in the North Atlantic in the war, sir. HMS *Derry Castle*, minesweeper, sir, she was torpedoed under me, twenty-six survivors. I could go on, sir. I have me discharge papers and me medals, sir."

There was a pause. Major Bellingham had a way of raising his straw-colored eyebrows to the very top of his mottled forehead. His head tilted far back to add to the impression of extended skepticism, the brow furrowed by compression from beneath, the nostrils narrowed, the jowl stretched above starched khaki. From a low angle (Bellingham was over six feet four) those eyebrows looked like an unnaturally low growth of head hair. The man was bald as a bean, let it be added. He eyed Doultry slyly, his eyebrows up there — such elevation would be an impossible strain on your average face, thought Annie, whose next lie lay ready on his tongue, freeing the mind to wander a little.

"Your passport is American, is it not?"

"The family settled in Seattle, sir. I have many memories of that fair city. I apologize for my language earlier on, sir — I'm just bloody stunned that the ravin's of a condemned man, obviously a matter o' personal grievance, should be given credence over agin my cook. Now, as my Hai gave me to understand it, this bugger Li thingamibob got all out of order in this little dim-sum joint, teahouse type o' place, drunk and disorderly, got himself flung out on his earhole. My Hai was workin' part-time there, in the back, see, while my vessel was laid up in Whampoa, number 11 dock, gettin' her bottom scraped. Anyway, he was obliged to go after this thug Li with his trusty meat cleaver." There was a pause. "Shengy is a very solid laddie, sir. You know how he landed up in here, don't you? Sheer ill luck, sir. He got into a spot o' bother in a house of ill fame, it could have happened to anyone. Fact is, he missed me. It was an impulse of the un-

56

conscious, sir, he abruptly flew off the handle and —"

Major Bellingham interrupted the flow of it. "What absolute drivel, Doultry!" He pointed to Hai Sheng's admission sheet. " 'Grievous bodily harm'! 'Assault with a deadly weapon,' old boy! He excised the man's eye — with the lid of a sardine can! I remember the case perfectly."

"Well, like I said, sir, he's a solid lad. But he's no bloody pirate. That's a load of old bollocks, sir."

Dr. Cathcart raised his hand, as a schoolboy does, or did, in the old days. The major said, "Yes, David?"

"I personally feel the condemned man was telling the truth, Tony."

This dildo must feel like he's the author of that statement, Annie thought, what with his pride in the translation of it.

"Who or what is this 'Mountain of Wealth,' David?"

"I really don't know. I would guess the commander of some gang or other. *Tao-shou* was the word he used — that's a very archaic word. I think that's what it means, a chieftain or commander."

"David, you should have asked the man. 'Mountain of Wealth' is really too melo-dramatic for words."

Dr. Cathcart lit an inexpensive cigar in a way that signaled irritation. "Llewellyn was in a hurry, old boy. He wanted to get on with it. I simply offered my services. He kept saying get on with it, get on with it. My heavens!" The doctor exhaled fumes with a loud sigh. Doultry sighed too, in harmony with the doctor, and with great resonance.

There was a tramping outside — another orderly at the door. "No. 294991/A is here, sir." Hai Sheng himself was ushered in and stood before the major.

"My good man, it has been alleged that you are a pirate."

"Me no pilate. Me cook."

Annie had got the word to him. It was not hard to pass messages around Victoria Gaol if you knew the ropes — and the strings attached to the ropes. More difficult to explain was why: what reason did Annie have for this amazing attempt to save the skin of a Chinaman he knew only from the tenuous world of roach racing? Did he have some perverse sympathy for Chinese pirates, a kindly disposition toward these bloodthirsty wolves of the sea, as they liked to call themselves? The answer is no, not at all, by no means. Annie Doultry was a man of the sea himself, and pirates were his natural enemies. Annie Doultry was acting on a hunch or out of some profound boredom — the very man who would claim he never gambled!

In the last year alone — between December 18, 1925, when the *Tung Chou* was taken, and January 27 of '27, when the Ho Hong Steamship Company's SS *Seang Bee* (3,784 tons) was hijacked en route from Singapore to Hong Kong, fourteen steamships had been pirated on the South China Sea (not counting innumerable local junks). Every year since the end of the Great War, the toll of ships had mounted. What started as a nuisance had become a consuming pillage. Casualties were numerous. By 1924, all coastal steamships were equipped with special defenses and armed guards, either privately recruited or supplied by the Hong Kong police under provision of the Piracy Prevention Ordinance. The following year, largely as a result of the attack on the Singapore-registered SS *Hong Wha*, these precautions were extended to ocean-going vessels serving Indo China, Malaya, and the Philippines.

The *Sunning* was an interesting affair. She was carrying only a hundred passengers, two of them Europeans in first class.

She left Shanghai on November 12th, 1926, called at Amoy, embarked more passengers and cargo on the 15th, and seven hours later was overrun by twenty-five men, one with a Thompson submachine gun. The assault was made as the guards were changing duty at four p.m. Their radio, the first target, was destroyed. There was a lot of gunfire, but only one guard was wounded. The pirates thought the *Sunning* was carrying half a million in silver, but the specie was on another ship. However, there was a rich cargo of silk aboard and plenty of loot from the passengers and the ship's safe.

The unique part of the story was that the second engineer, William Orr, and the third engineer, Andrew Duncan, refused to take the situation lying down. Orr got hold of a deep-sea sounding lead, of all things, knocked out an armed pirate, got his gun, and with Duncan got hold of two revolvers hidden in his cabin.

They shot two other pirates and retook the bridge, freeing Chief Officer Beatty and Second Officer Hurst. For hours they fought off repeated attacks from about twenty experienced pirates, who in the process tried to advance using Chief Engineer George Cormach and a pair of Chinese cabin boys as a screen. Cormach was shot in both arms; five Chinese passengers were killed or wounded.

Then, at three o'clock in the morning, the raiders set fire to the ship, under the bridge, to smoke out its defenders. The pirates still held the engine room, but of course they could not steer the vessel. A storm got up, the wind spread the fire, it got out of control, and the pirates decided to abandon the ship. They killed an English telegraph engineer who had been interpreting for them, and left in two lifeboats, leaving four dead and five wounded.

The *Sunning* was a raging inferno, her engines immobilized, but her officers managed to launch a half-burned lifeboat under Second Officer Hurst's command, which, after weathering nine hours of evil seas, was picked up by a Norwegian freighter, who radioed Hong Kong. Several warships set forth. One of them, HMS *Bluebell*, sighted one of the fleeing pirates' boats and captured seven of them. Several drowned themselves — they knew what their fate would be.

The *Sunning* was reached by the SS *Ka Yid* and taken in tow. She was burned out, but got back to Hong Kong. The total death toll was thirteen; five Chinese from the purser's staff were missing, presumed to have been working with the pirates. A great testimonial dinner was given for the heroes, and Second Officer Bill Hurst and Chief Engineer George Cormach were awarded Orders of the British Empire.

Li Weng-chi was not one of the seven captured pirates, all of whom were tried and hanged before Christmas. But he was fingered by one of those doomed men, for some old revenge. Li Weng-chi was a well-known desperado, and they picked him up on Lantau Island on the Christian New Year's Day.

Annie had been in jail when this happened, of course. But he had been sailing in these parts since the spring of '25, mostly to and from the Philippines, in the arms business. That was where he had his connections, and where a small operator with a small boat could make a little money below the line, and if necessary, beyond the pale. Making money was Annie's pretext for being here, such a long, long way from the San Juan Islands in Washington State, which he had called home for close to sixteen years now. Obviously, he knew all about the plague of piracy. He even had an old acquaintance, First Officer Hans Eriksen, who had got himself shot up when the SS *Sandviken* was raided last summer, only a month before Annie's own downfall. Eriksen nearly lost his arm, and Annie had cursed the filthy bastards, as did all decent seafaring men, whatever their own sins.

So is it not a matter of bewilderment that Annie should stick his thick neck out to save the skin of a suspect sea wolf like Hai Sheng? To invent a saga of imaginary cookery and a career of Royal Navy minesweeping for such a perverse purpose? His behavior boggles the mind.

He may have had a soft spot for the man. Annie may have simply liked Hai Sheng. But he would never in a thousand years have admitted as much. If you had pinned his knees against a wall with a steam caterpillar tractor, the most he would have offered was that the whole thing was just a fucking lark. So why not take him at his word?

Annie had no shame for his perversity. It was immense, and pointless. The Spartan rewards to be had from a minor art, or vice — to wit, lying for the pleasure of it — were riches enough for Annie, who was poor in near all else. Untruth was a violin on which he played like a Paganini of bunkum. He lied for the dear loveliness of it and with as much devotion as others purport to give to the church of fact.

Enough of aimless speculations: who can say what springs turn the cogs of a mind like Annie's, now forward, now backward, now sideways? Sideways let us slide, then, to the superintendent's office, the rain becoming vengeful, the window steaming up with the writhing fug of Dr. Cathcart's cigar.

Cathcart was well aware that the superintendent was not weighing issues of truth and falsity, of the maybe and the maybe not. The major saw no earthly point in condemning himself to hard labor; there were better places to spend one's morning than in this blasted office, in the toils of this gaunt prison — the Kowloon Bowling Green Club, for one. In front of the major's nose was the big E on Doultry's sagging tunic and his face, salt-weathered but of a resilient pinkish hue, or rather a nonhue, for white was its name. Although Annie was a sinner and a felon, Li Wengchi, the pirate of Bias Bay, was a creature of an altogether lower order, whose cadaver the color of lard was already on its way to the university medical school to endure a destiny that inspired far greater horror in a Chinese mind than the mere hanging of it — a wholly pragmatic horror, for a dismembered and eviscerated body has a hard time ahead of it in the reincarnation stakes. As for Hai Sheng, the current object of scrutiny, the head warder reported that he seemed to be a respectful little bloke and a hard worker in the bookbinding shop. He stood there now with dewdrops on his smooth round forehead and his dimpled upper lip and pained bewilderment in his eyes. He did not have a piratical air.

"We'll forget the charges," sighed the superintendent.

chapter 2
Annie at Liberty

The superintendent's private opinion of Anatole Doultry was that the man might be unhinged. After dismissing what he referred to as "this whole nonsensical imbroglio" from his office, he discussed Doultry somewhat facetiously with David Cathcart for several minutes, while his boy gave his boots a touch-up to fit them for the bar of the Kowloon Bowling Green Club.

It is undeniable that Doultry was a preposterous figure, even by Victoria Gaol standards. Contained and restrained therein, his whole large being absorbed in the effort of enduring the vileness of it (for it was vile, make no mistake about it), he was easily mocked. Yet he seemed not to notice. Major Bellingham himself used to indulge in this Doultry mocking — the superintendent was a genial but undoubtedly twisted man, and that is all one need to say of him. But Dr. Cathcart, equipped with a more searching intellect, did not trust Annie an eighth of an inch. He had no confidence whatever in the man's brawny, bumbling good nature and fake Scots vernacular; he saw no whimsy in the phantasmagorically different versions of Doultry's personal history you got depending on which day of the week you made an inquiry. Doultry left David Cathcart feeling profoundly uneasy. In Doultry's presence, intimations of the fuming rage in the man prickled the nape of the doctor's neck, a rage hibernating like a demented bear within some hollow of that thick tree trunk of a body, which stepped so lightly, but so slothfully, down the alley from administration to his den in D block. The biggest of all the prison's warders, a retired mule-skinner from Peshawar, followed him. But Doultry made the man look insubstantial. By chance they passed the dentist, the Bengali, on his way to work, and Cathcart (watching from the office window) saw Doultry clap the little chap on the shoulder with a wink and a crack — something about the decline of the British Empire, like as not.

In the armory, a small severe room, stout ranks of Lee-Enfield Mk II rifles stood against the walls and guarded the pair of them. "Time for a wee dram o' the good stuff," said Strachan. He took from his pocket a blue bottle, Phillips Milk of Magnesia, and poured the dram into Annie's tea mug. "Where will you be goin', then?"

"I shall be goin' back to my vessel," said Annie.

He sipped the Johnnie Walker and scrutinized the *Hong Kong Weekly Press and China Overland Trade Report.* It was a newspaper nearly as weighty as its name. The news of the war in China was as incoherent as always, but the National Army of the Revolution, the Kuomintang Army, commanded by Generalissimo Chiang Kai-shek, appeared to be winning for sure. The Generalissimo's home base had been right next door, in Canton, the immense City of the South (famed for the multiplicity of its merchants, for its cuisine, and for its corruption) of which Hong Kong had once been but a parasite. But in recent months the illustrious Commander of the South had advanced northward, winning many battles, both real and imaginary.

Changsha fell. Marshal Wu Pei-fu retreated. The Generalissimo took Wuhan, the City of Three Cities, which sat astride the crossroads of the immense nation, where the Yangtze River traversed the main railroad northward. Here, much to the annoyance of the Nationalists, their allies the Communist Party of China set up their own government. Chiang Kai-shek would not forgive them this effrontery, although at the time he could only smile and (seething behind his hand) congratulate them. (To assuage his anger, he shelled a British destroyer on the Yangtze.)

What Annie wanted to know, politically speaking, was just two things:

Were the Reds in or out? (This from the point of view of a sensible man of business, circumspect about his contacts and with a nose open to the winds of the future.)

And what was up with Marshal Sun Chuan-fang, his number-one customer?

The Northern Armies, under their disparate and idiosyncratic marshals, of whom the chief was nominally Marshal Chang Tso-lin, got the worst of things in 1927. Marshal Chang called his army of armies the Ankouchun, a lovely name that means roughly "the Great Army for the Tranquilization of the Country." His headquarters were in Peking, the nominal capital of the fragmented republic. Tradition, which was all that was left of most things, still held that whoever sat in Peking was the government of China.

At the perimeter of every city, as the trenches were dug and redug and the artillery slugged away, deals were made by the ubiquitous marshals at the back doors of their private railway cars. There was wheeling and dealing, the betraying of old allies, the bargaining for first rights of pillage to an unpillaged town somewhere, the buying and selling of shabby battalions of men become savage with endless war. It was a cartoon; it was a caricature of perfidious China: a stink pit of corruption and venality, the bodies of demented infantry and despairing peasantry heaped together on the windswept plains and awash in the sad canals, with gangrene running amok in the field hospitals. For years, it had been like this. It had taken the Dragon Empire two centuries to fall to bits. Here were the bits, then, all pulverized to an exhausted sameness but serving still, like a nauseating congee, to thicken the plot on each page of the *Hong Kong Weekly*, thick and inky on Annie Doultry's knees as he attempted to see into the future.

"So the Generalissimo has taken the fatal step."

Strachan was cleaning the feed block of the early-model Maxim gun that was the prison armory's pride — a gun built to

70

mow down hordes. "What has the Generalissimo gone and done now, Annie?"

"He has announced that all the Reds are traitors, Stewart. They are traitors to the new nation of China. He has fired his pal Chou En-lai; he has said 'Up yours, Comrade' to Joe Stalin."

Annie did not share Strachan's loathing of the Reds. He had not made up his mind about them. He was seldom sure of labels, anyway. But what was, was. "The Communists have reached the end of the road, Stew. Their emissary, Mr. Borodin, has fucked off, back to Russia. What treachery! Those Russkies must be eating their boots."

Strachan's ripe nose glowed with satisfaction. He was not good at reading, so the news was fresh to his ears. "There never was a Chink army wore boots before the Generalissimo's. But did boots buy those Bolshies loyalty, Annie? Never on your life! From the Chinks, boots will only buy you treachery, sir. Treachery is sown across this land like the dandelions in auld Dumfriesshire, d'ye remember 'em, Annie?" Strachan was near to the bottom of his milk of magnesia bottle.

"I think the Reds are done for, Stew. There's no future for 'em in China."

★ ★ ★

And then of course there was Marshal Sun Chuan-fang, Annie's favorite customer.

If ever there was a warlord owing no fealty but to war itself, it was Marshal Sun. He had a flexible army of between fifty thousand and two hundred thousand, depending on the winds and tides of conflict. He had occupied Shanghai in '25 and looted it systematically. From within their concessions, the foreigners had watched him, stunned by his tortuous iniquity. Nominally he was allied with Marshal Chang Tso-lin and the Army for Tranquilization, but Marshal Sun traveled with a private trainload of concubines, and his transcendent loyalty was to gold. His were two hundred thousand guns for hire. He was a masterly tactician, too, the best general in Asia. Consortiums of Shanghai bankers and Hong Kong merchant princes had paid Marshal Sun great heaps of gold to protect what they felt to be their interests — in other words, to fight the Reds. Marshal Sun had grown fat on his reputation as a Red hater. His mistresses had multiplied; he had started a private air force. The planes broke down (they were fine French Cauldrons), but not the women.

Marshal Sun's troops were fairly frequently paid — he could afford it — and his army had fought Chiang Kai-shek to a standstill in '26. Then abruptly, in '27, the marshal had retreated. There was a great battle for Nanchang, with slaughter on both sides, but the rumor was rife that Generalissimo Chiang Kai-shek was making a deal with the swaggering marshal and the battle was only for show. Sun Chuan-fang, devious manipulator of war and gold, had retreated in good order. Many of his women (who were mostly French, White Russian, and American girls) were wearing the latest Paris hats. The next thing, the Nationalists had marched unopposed into the city of Shanghai, and Marshal Sun's soldiers were helping Chiang Kai-shek's stout men, newly booted at Russian expense, to slaughter the Communists who infested the metropolis and called themselves a proletariat. It almost made a bloke feel sorry for them.

"It must be said, those fuckin' Reds have got guts," said Annie, nose in the newspaper. "They have a belief. The rest of 'em would sell their own mothers. They have no religion, the Chinese, their religion is a fake, and no faith in human nature whatever. They are a desperate people."

"Better to sell yer mother than be a Bolshie," said Strachan.

The next day, Annie Doultry was released and went back to his boat. To Strachan he bequeathed Wondrous Bird of Hope, in his box of Jonkau wood, as the gift of a jailhouse friend.

Annie did not see Hai Sheng again. Having sold his famous animal, Shengy did not appear again on the turf of grand old Epsom. This taciturn individual was apparently keeping himself to himself now, since the tasteless denunciation business. Annie received no message of gratitude, but a little knot of newspaper with three of his fly buttons accompanied the delivery of Wondrous Bird to his cell. He forgot about his imaginary cook, for his mind was on his future again.

Upon leaving Victoria Gaol, Annie shook Mr. Llewellyn by the hand, or rather the tips of the fingers, and said in his normal American voice: "Hugh, this is fare-thee-well. It's sad, isn't it? Boy, I shall miss you, scout's honor. But I just want you to know how tremendously I enjoyed my stay at this lovely place. I want to particularly congratulate you on the cuisine. I wanted to leave a little something for the chef, but unhappily I seem to have forgotten my checkbook. I have something for you, though."

Annie was wearing his brown suit with the Prince of Wales check. It was rumpled from six months' inactivity, and Llewellyn's office was perfumed by mothballs, but Doultry looked a fine figure of a man. He had given his blue polka-dot necktie to the dentist as a gift for his tact and gentleness (one never knew if one might not be back) and fabricated a substitute from a small flag, a Stars and Stripes pennant of yacht-club quality bunting that he kept in his suitcase for emergencies. Under his arm he had his gift for Llewellyn, rolled up. He gave it to him.

Llewellyn was at a loss for words. He had no ready reply. But he accepted it.

It was a very nice pencil drawing of the exercise yard. Annie had put in a picture of Corporal Strachan, outside the door of the latrine. On the right you could just see down the alley; the bridge was beautifully done. From it hung a body. The body might have been Li Weng-chi's; it was too far off to tell. But the chap leaning with his arms on the parapet and smiling at the viewer was obviously Llewellyn; the broad rectangle of his face was unmistakable, with its small red mustache. Annie had colored it red with a pin's drop of his own blood. There was a great deal of the artist within him.

Llewellyn took the drawing and said, "Thank you very much, Doultry." It was signed "Anatole Doultry, with best regards to Hugh." Llewellyn was still studying it expressionlessly when Annie made his exit with a big smile for the guards and others on duty, carrying his lightweight imitation-leather suitcase and his umbrella. His imitation Rolex shone. As he stepped through the postern gate, he gave a little wave with his hat before donning it. This fedora from San Francisco was in excellent shape considering its age. It had one small bullet hole in the brim, on the left, which was less of an imperfection than a decoration, a conversation opener.

It had stopped raining for a while, but the weather was still cooler than usual for March. Annie's suit was appropriate, the forty bucks he had had in his sock in September had been returned from the prison safe (with the sock) and was worth as much as ever in Hong Kong (about twenty U.S. dollars) though inflation was rampant in China. As he strolled down Chancery Lane and grabbed a rickshaw on Hollywood Road, he noticed there were more

76

beggars about. There was a feeling in the air. There was a pressure on.

The way was all downhill, the rickshaw riding the brake, the coolie in a good mood as Annie directed him in a loud voice, practicing his Cantonese and his air of authority, which he had naturally not been able to do too much of recently. At his instructions they paused in front of the windows of Borsalino's, the hat shop. Annie began to feel like himself again: a captain. Turning the corner into Ice House Street, he saw the four words written on the stone wall that had once aroused his curiosity. A Chinese fellow had told him: I DARE TO DEFY, it said. The message was addressed to any demons who might be flying down Queens Road, looking for a victim. According to the Chinese vision of things, the demon would recognize that whoever lived in this house was no pushover. The demon would turn right or left, and keep moving, and pick on somebody else.

Annie told the coolie to take the long way round Statue Square. The coolie stopped, and they discussed supplementary payment for a few minutes. The coolie pointed out how large and heavy Annie was, and Annie kept agreeing, and asking if the rickshaw man had ever offered a rebate to a small person — a dwarf, say, of which there have always been many in China. Or maybe a lissome young thing, a real dilly little dolly? Annie described her with his hands and the rickshaw man laughed, he was most amused, but he would not give a straight answer. "Yes," he said. "Always me give small people fast ride."

Annie put a lot of mental energy into the discussion. He explained that he wished to look at the statue of the Duke of Connaught. They reached an agreement and continued.

In the square Annie descended from the rickshaw and stretched his legs. There were nannies and children around, everything looked normal, but when Annie studied the duke's bronze face he saw that the great man's expression had changed. He was a nephew of Queen Victoria and a well-informed man in his lifetime. Annie was by now himself well enough informed about the Chinese vision of things to know that the duke's statue was considered by the most perceptive among them, men who were philosophers and intellectuals, to contain a demon. The nature of this demon was arguable; the subject was never discussed with foreigners. It is one up to Annie that he should have found out about it; it reveals an enquiring side to his nature.

The demon intrigued him. Obviously, it must in some way partake of the duke. Did it, for example, share his memories? Or some other aspect of the man's reputedly urbane and observant character? Captain Doultry looked into the Duke of Connaught's eye. "What's goin' on, Duke?" he asked him. A couple of small English children were playing at his great bronze feet with a metal battleship ten inches long as the duke's eyes answered Annie's. The rickshaw coolie eyed the duke too, stroking his upper lip but keeping his distance. He had gained a new respect for his passenger — greater than he deserved, one would think.

The great cloud, or palace of clouds, had become brighter at its western edge. Annie studied the meteorological indicators as they proceeded at a gentle clip down Hennessy Road, into the district called Wan Chai, and turned left at the tram stop into Lun Fat Street. The bars were lighting up, the girls were hitting the streets, the many food shops were stoking up their bright stoves made from old kerosene cans, the workingmen were taking it easy as Annie went to work.

★ ★ ★

Stoffer's Bar and Grill was less distinguished than its name. But Annie was more interested in its food than in the social standing of the establishment. The cook was German; the grub was excellent. Annie Doultry only ate Chinese food when he had to; he did not go for the taste combos involved. For six months he had thought about Stoffer's. But this preoccupation was not solely motivated by food.

They kept up the brauhaus atmosphere with the verisimilitudinous faith characteristic of expatriates. There was Tsingtao beer on tap, brewed in the city of that name far to the north in the strictest German way. Two seamen, a Norwegian and a Swiss, were full of it, arguing about a horse. The language of their discourse was English. Doultry knew the Swiss; he was an expert sailing man despite the jokes. Oh, the simple pleasure of shaking hands with old acquaintances! It cannot be overrated.

The barman was a new face to Doultry, a half-caste fellow, very well-spoken. "Tell me, Pete," said Doultry, after his second Tsingtao, "do you happen to know a feller called Fred Olson? 'Philly' Fred?"

The barman smiled; his cheeks were like

ripe pomegranates, his teeth big in the middle and rippling away to a tiny size at the sides like a necklace. "Mr. Fled?" His eyes were all lit up. Annie nodded. "No, sir. No Mister Fled come here, sir, no sir."

Annie sat himself at the back, and ordered himself the dinner he had been thinking of for six months, and ate it.

The place filled up a bit, but business was obviously slow. Stoffer appeared about midway through the roast beef, solemn and preoccupied as usual, and welcomed Annie back from his voyage. How was Java? he asked. He knew where Annie had been, of course, but Bernardo Patrick Hudson had put the word about that Annie was in Java, having a look at some pearling business. Annie told Stoffer that the weather had been terrible and Stoffer said there had never been such a terrible winter in Hong Kong, rain and gloom. They patted each other's hands. Later, Stoffer sent a bottle of Stummelpfennig's schnapps to Annie's table with his compliments. By the time the Muenster cheese arrived Annie was in a position to think about China.

Did flogging the Chinese help? Annie was a man who liked to hear a question out loud inside his mind, and then follow it up. The past was already assumed; there was no reason to go over past events ad nauseam. This was the only way to handle problems like the flogging question — or else, as Annie knew by long experience, they got stuck in your craw, and thence proceeded to the back of the brain box, where dreams were fabricated and stored. If you got it early on, it was no more than a problem of reason, of further inquiry at the worst — a question of the future. The dreaming had been outwitted.

It was while he was immersed in the flogging question that Philadelphia Fred came in. He didn't see Annie for a while. He remained at the bar in the company of a man who looked Italian. Fred's own person had taken on an Italian look; he was wearing flashy clothes with a stripe to them. He looked healthy and prosperous — one is tempted to say "until he saw Annie Doultry." But his look of prosperity didn't change, although the smile became perhaps overbroad, like that of a stoic greeting an old friend in a hospital. Annie was smiling too as he slapped the table next to his apple strudel in a gesture of invitation that could not be denied.

Fred Olson must have thought of making a quick exit. This idea would have occurred to any man in his position. But while thinking of it, he was irresistibly propelled by convention toward Annie, with that smile broadening behind which his fear blossomed all in a fragrant bunch, and he leaned over Annie's table and stuck out his hand. Annie took it by the fingertips with big gentle fingers (the way he had done with Hugh Llewellyn). At the same time he was thinking: I've learned this from the Chinese. The Annie Doultry of yesteryear would not have shaken Fred Olson's hand like this, even with the cold touch conveyed by these fingers. To Fred himself he said, "Sit down, ol' pal. You know I was just saying to myself, 'Boy, I sure hope Philly stops by tonight, I'd sure love to see him.' " He felt Fred's fingers begin to withdraw, and tightened his own into a vise. "Have a drop of the good stuff, laddie," and pushed the Stummelpfennig over with his left hand. "Hey, where you been hiding?"

"Annie, I would if I could," Philly Fred replied. "But I gotta handle this guy, he's a customer. It's good to see you, buddy. Hey, long time no see, hunh?" Here, because he could not detach his fingers from his host's, he sat down. "Let's get together tomorrow, whaddyasay?"

"Fred," said Annie. "The Chinese live in a world of appearances. They're brought up to believe that all the world's a stage, ahh!"

Fred nodded warmly. "Shakespeare," he affirmed. Annie nodded back at him. "Fred, I'm trying to come to some conclusions about these people. For example . . ." He paused to fill a glass for Fred. "For example, in the can here they beat 'em when they get uppity. Some of 'em refuse to work, see. Insubordinate bastards. They decline to carry these cannonballs around in this circle."

Annie's forefinger defined the circle. Fred's eyes followed it, wondering where the catch was.

"So they beat them, Fred — they are flogged. Now, I discussed this with the people in there. It's gotta be morally repugnant to the British Empire. They're supposed to be the civilized ones." He filled his mouth with the last of the apple strudel. "I can prove that. Thirty years back you could get a hundred and fifty lashes with the cat-o'-nine-tails in there. Then it went down to sixty tops, then no more cat, just the rattan, now it's thirty-six, and anything over twelve it's got to be okayed by the visiting magistrate, that's

84

what they call a low-class judge around here. You see the trend. It stands to reason they would like to drop it. The Brits by and large are not sadists, in my experience. Except with their own families, of course. Also, they have lots of old ladies back there complaining about it, you know what I mean?"

Philly Fred nodded, paying the closest attention.

"But despite it all, they go on steadily flogging those goddamn Chinese. Why is that, Fred?"

A short pause. "I guess it's to put the fear of God in 'em, Annie," Fred said, with conviction, though he was just hazarding a guess.

Annie was already shaking his big head with its bent nose and its terrible haircut, his forefinger shaking, too, like a metronome. "No, Fred. No. It's for the humiliation. They looked at the Chinese. They asked themselves, 'Why have the Chinese always flogged each other?' They've never bothered with prisons themselves, the Chinks — it's always been flogging, branding, amputations, and so forth."

He leaned forward, lowering his voice. "For the humiliation, Fred. The Chinese always flogged the guy in front of a crowd.

You strip him bare-ass naked, then you beat that ass, you flog it. There's no point goin' into the pain of it, the suffering, et cetera — you know why?"

"No," said Fred.

"Because to a Chink it don't matter. It's irrelevant. It's the scars is what he's all cut up about, no pun intended, which marks of humiliation he will carry with him to the grave. And beyond, to where it's decided what his next life will be. They're gonna ask the feller, up there in heaven or whatever they call it, 'Hey, buddy, how come you got flogged? What did you do, boy? What did you *do?*' " Annie paused here, moved by his own words. He stared into Fred's eyes. "That way you can get to be born again — as a cockroach. Did you know that, Fred?"

"No," said Fred.

"When you lose your ass that way, you lose a lotta face with it," said Annie. "People talk about 'face,' they don't understand what it means. In your average Chinese, it means the whole works. Face is life. Life is the front you put up. It is pride gone bananas, Fred. Okay, so you're gonna say to me, 'Is that any fuckin' excuse for the British, who call themselves a civilized nation, to go on floggin' the Chinese here in 1927? Is it? That is uncivilized. They gave it up in the navy years ago.' "

Fred shook his head slowly. "I wasn't going to say that, Annie. It's common knowledge you've gotta have a firm hand with the Chinks, everybody knows that."

Annie looked around Stoffer's, without registering what he saw. He rubbed his face and swallowed all the schnapps in his glass. "I guess that's it, Fred. You were right. It adds up to the fear of God." Fred was encouraged by this; he did some more nodding. Annie filled the Philadelphian's glass to the brim, looking introspective. "Fred, you've helped to give me insight, you know that? Into the British Empire. They're scared to stop flogging 'em, is what it is. They know the Chinese would say, 'The red-hair barbarians are getting soft, they're a buncha softies, let's cut 'em to pieces.' " He had himself a solemn little chuckle, which Fred joined half an octave up the scale.

Annie pushed back his chair, wiping his mouth with his napkin, and his nose too. "Fred, I got to be off. I'll be in tomorrow night, in here I mean — let's get together tomorrow, okay, pal? I want to tell you about Java."

Fred gave him a big sappy smile, nodding away and saying "Sure, buddy, sure," as Annie rose and laid his hand gently on the man's shoulder and wandered off, through the bar and out. He did not ask for his check, for he knew Fred would take care of it.

Outside, Annie put on his hat. A gentle drizzle was softening the gaslight's ginger glow, which matched the blowsy light to the west where the sun was unobtrusively making its exit.

Annie turned down the alley next to Stoffer's. He was familiar with it. A well-known food stall lived there, it did a bigger business than Stoffer's to the locals, it was big on eels and the strangest kind of fish. Little old gentlemen in their baggy blue pajamas sat under the awning stuffing themselves and discussing business, the eel pots steaming, the cook chopping some-thing fishy with his great cleaver. A family of cats lived beneath his portable kitchen; cats and fish guts flew everywhere, and the aroma was reassuring, if you were fond of Hong Kong.

Annie stood eyeing some Chinese puff cookies. He had never tried one. They were less fearsome than the eel fare; they looked tasty — a kid could see they were just a bobble of pastry with plum jam inside. He raised his umbrella and glanced at his watch. Then, by pointing, he attracted the cook's attention and purchased six of the pastries. He still felt amazingly hungry, starved almost. The puff cookies were extraordinarily delicious. On the spot, he took another six. Danger gave him an appetite.

Nobody paid any attention to Annie. He stood under his hat and his umbrella and experienced bliss. He asked the cook what these Chinese pastries were called. The cook was unclear about his question and kept shaking his head, saying, "No today. Tomollow." But a boy who worked at Stoffer's stuck his head out the kitchen door and grinned at Annie and supplied him with the riddle's answer.

Philly Fred Olson paid Captain Doultry's bill with never a murmur. Now he felt perfectly calm, and headed for the gentlemen's toilet. He was physically unprepossessing, but his short body under his vulgar striped Italian-style suit was resolute and quick-moving. He unbuttoned his fly as he went in, anxious to relieve the pressure. The place was well known for its green tiles, imported from Delft or somewhere, and the urinals were very large and fine, with thick architecture of creamy china, oozing with water and browned by mankind in a comforting way.

Freddie attended to his affairs with a long sigh. This passing was emotional; it breathed feeling into the pungent air. A very old Chinaman sat on a stool beside a table of marble with colored bottles and brushes on it and various other instruments. He was at his ease, reading a newspaper, close to a basin with a square mirror above it, brass-fixtured and adequately lit. The old man's purpose, as soon as he saw you, was to force you to look into that mirror, because when you did, you owed him money: five cents, ten, a dollar if you were exceptionally pleased with the sight of yourself after you pissed.

The door of one of the two stalls opened and Annie came out. He was eating the last puff cookie from a paper bag.

"Hey, Freddie," he said in a high, piping voice. "How the hell are you, still?"

Freddie, peeing at full throttle, said: "Who's that?"

"Your pal," said Annie, in the piping voice, very high in register.

"I ain't got no pals," said Freddie, still not bothering to look around. Annie crumpled the paper bag and dropped it in the waste basket beside the attendant.

"You got one," says Annie, quietly, giving the old man, who wore a long green jacket with brass buttons, a five-dollar bill. The Chinese gentleman nodded his gratitude without overdoing it, as Fred turned, doing up his fly, and saw who it was he'd been talking to.

"I thought you'd be in," said Annie. He had pink jam on his pinkie; he licked it off. In a confidential way, he said to Fred: "I have yet to meet the feller who didn't need to take a piss after getting a bad fright."

Freddie made his move, but it was too late. Annie knew that his old pal's right hand was going to reach for that pistol under his arm. He was so sure of it that both their moves coincided. Annie's was the old left hook, and catching Fred in that vulnerable position, it got the Philadelphia finagler deep in the side at liver level. That punch ended it right there, to all intents.

Annie's one overlooking, if you could call it that, was of the odd fact that Fred Olson carried a pistol under each arm. Annie's fist impacted the spare one, a .32 in a suede holster, and felt a bad pain in the middle knuckle. In the process it drove the gun into Fred's ribs, cracking a couple of them, so that Fred was robbed of all breath and willful motion for several moments. So Annie was obliged to finish him off almost exclusively with the right hand, and it was a longer and more troubling business than he had hoped for. Fred kept his head down (it was not the first time he'd been beaten up), Annie clubbing him underneath and then using both his knees, heavy as logs of wood. When Fred started to collapse, Annie held him up with his damaged hand and got in one clean right uppercut that Manassa Jack would have approved of. It was sweet dreams for Fred, then.

Among those dreams may have been one about Annie dragging him over to the urinal and sticking his swollen head in the puddle there. If it was a dream for Fred, it was a real pleasure for Annie. A pleasure, too, to lean on the flushing handle and watch a surge of soggy cigarette butts play havoc with Fred's vocalization as he tried to breathe and plead for mercy in his dream. "Wake up, Freddie," said Annie, breathing a bit hard and looking at his knuckle. "Wake up, I want to talk to you."

Gurgle, gurgle from Philadelphia Fred Olson. Annie put a foot on the side of his neck to keep his old friend's head in the urinal. On the foot he applied pressure.

That was one thing Annie had plenty of to apply.

"Can you hear me, Fred? Oh, Freddie, can you hear me?"

"It was you or me, Annie." That is what he said, but you could hardly make out the words.

"Where's the dough you got for turning me in?"

"I lost it," said Fred. "At Happy Valley." What an original excuse. Annie applied about another forty pounds to the side of Fred's neck. "Oh, Annie. Oh, Annie. You're hurting me. Gimme a break."

"The only break from me you'll get is one in your neck. Undo that money belt. Get that money belt off right now." Annie sounded strict and pitiless, and Fred managed to get his trembling fingers working at the belt problem even though his head was in the pisser. It was a thick, heavy belt, and soon as it was unbuckled Annie bent down and whipped it out like an ivy root. He undid the snappers on the inside and removed some folded-up bills. "You just lie still, Fred. 'Cause if you move I'm going to break every bone in your dumpy little body. I really am." There was twelve dollars in the money belt and two lottery tickets. How disappointing.

Annie undid his fly buttons and dragged out his cock. He wanted very badly to piss on Freddie's face. He wanted to drown him like a sick dog. But somehow the mechanisms of his body, full of beer and schnapps and indignation, were reluctant to respond to the demands of the brain, which had by now suspended its enormous penis over Fred's scrunched-up face, the foot keeping an ineluctable pressure on his neck. The rest of Olson's person had begun to writhe about on the dreary way back to the light of the mind. The old attendant read his newspaper, paying no attention. Somebody came in, presumably to take a leak, but left immediately. Annie did not look round; all his concentration was on his purpose, the pump primed, the vengeance in his gaze, but the circuits and valves refusing for some reason to function. He tried to relax. He thought of great tankards of beer as he aimed for Fred's quivering eye.

That worked.

He sprayed Fred's various facial orifices, which their owner was trying to keep closed. But he had to breathe, so he breathed Annie's piss. He made the best of a bad job, in short. Annie was naturally filled with a deep sense of gratification quite separate from his initial and, let us admit it, rather petty lust for the humiliation of his enemy. This was the gratification of the conquest of body by mind. One's own body, one's own mind. It was a sort of meditative feeling, outside of the self, which was engaged in aiming and keeping weight on the squirming prisoner. So, meditatively, Annie said, "There's nothing worse than a tattletale, Freddie. There's nothing worse. If there's a next time, boy, I won't just piss on you."

As Annie left the men's room, the old Chinaman looked up at him, then at Freddie still lying there in that unusual position. "What matter with him?" he asked. "He's just having a drink," said Annie. "One they don't sell at the bar." He readjusted his hat. He checked his appearance carefully in the mirror; for five bucks he figured he could take all the time he wanted.

By the time Annie boarded the steam ferry to cross over to the Kowloon side (the mainland, that is), night had fallen again with all the weight of those regions and with it a gentle drizzle as a reminder that the great black cloud was still there. Still, it was pleasant to ride the Star ferry, for a boat was a boat, and to feel the sea under his feet was a pleasure. He rode top deck, first class (ten cents), to imbibe the perfume of the harbor, one of the greatest on earth and tremendously populated with vessels of all descriptions. The sight of Victoria Harbor could never pall and at night it was exquisite, for even the smallest sampan had by law to carry a light. The maritime police were strict about this. They themselves rode about in natty steam launches; you never knew where they would pop up.

The ferry was bowed at both ends so she did not have to turn around to come back. Leaning on the starboard gunwale, Annie positioned himself to inspect the wonderful apparition that loomed alongside the naval station (which was called HMS *Athena* in the navy's quaint fashion). The large and bizarre vessel moored there was the first built-from-the-keel-up aircraft carrier that Doultry and the rest of the world had seen. The shadowed silhouette of HMS *Hermes* in the sparkling night, blurred by mist and rain, was ineffably powerful and mysterious. The lights of junks and sampans clustered abaft of her where the boat people were conducting business with certain of the ship's crew, a practice officially frowned on but sanctioned by custom on the first night in port since the men could not go ashore till the morrow. However, their British loins were aching (though that is not to deny that quite a few were queer as all get-out), and the smuggling of Chinese females aboard His Majesty's ships, especially one as big as the *Hermes*, was not much of a problem if the petty officers were in on it — which they were, for they had first pick. The girls did tremendous business that first night, to be sure. These were Tanka girls, the aforesaid boat people who were in principle despised by their nation as a caste of primitives, but feared by them too, because they manned the pirate fleets and were a people apart. Until the time of the third Manchu emperor the Tankas were not permitted to live on dry land or to send their children to school. On the other hand, much of the daily business of China was in their hands, for it went by the waters, the seas, the rivers, and the canals. So they were a people to be reckoned with.

There were few first-class ferry riders at this hour, for the Chinese in general preferred the nickel ride on the lower deck. But a number of those with Annie observed the great floating mountain that was the *Hermes* with interest, and perhaps they were impressed by the omens she portended. For she had sailed half across the world to join the China Squadron and to do battle with the pirates, whose spies were even now aboard her, fucking her crew.

There was a bar in Mongkok that Annie used to frequent. He sidled into the place. There were few places on God's earth in which one could find sleazier bars than those of Mongkok, the red-light district of Kowloon. The establishment was dark as sin and a hell of a lot scarier, the gloom relieved only by the luminescence of the faces that turned to look at Annie as his largeness loomed among them. Scared faces, one-eyed men, scroungy-looking individuals uniformly engaged in the business of blurring the tedium of their fear, their apprehension of the terror of life. The reek of opium oozed inexorably from the room beyond the curtain at the back and hung there among the other odors like a pall of evaporated dung.

"Where is the fat man?" Annie inquired of the bartender, who was slowly wiping a glass with a rag. He returned Annie's gaze with eyes like weevil holes in a drum of Dutch cheese. He was not Chinese; it was a face from some archipelago among the waste waters of the great nameless ocean that the Chinese despised and loathed, and which some Western explorer imbued with religious sentiments had called Pacifica. With a clear enunciation Annie repeated his question. The bartender made an immensely lugubrious movement of his head, indicating the back room.

The fat man was seated on a stool smoking a cigar and getting his head massaged by a small Filipino woman. She was a barber; you could tell from the sticks she wore stuck in the bun of her oiled hair. The fat man was all wrapped up in some kind of cloth, his obscure figure thickened by the exhalations of his vile cigar, which oozed through the opium fog like axle grease through crankcase oil. He smiled at Annie. It was an unmistakable smile, as the captain laboriously asked him a question in his rudimentary Cantonese. Around the four walls of the narrow and windowless room lay the forms of those smoking opium. Two or three little boys scurried about underfoot, rodentlike, ministering to the necessities of the customers.

She's upstairs, the fat man told Annie; he spoke with his shining, cheerful little eyes, rolling them upward on their axes.

Annie made his way to the stairs at the back, stepping light and dainty as some great furred creature to avoid disturbing the realms of dreams that nestled between these walls. The stairs were narrow. At the top was a door upon which many layers of paper prayers, signals and signs to the protective gods, were stuck; red, black, and pink. Upon this door Annie knocked.

A woman opened it. She stood there in a cheongsam that was a caricature, tight as the folds of her dimpled flesh, the garment split up the side to where the hipbone nestled in its voluptuous padding. She arranged her weight on the leg in question so that its shiny skin popped out like butter from a sweet potato to dominate Annie's peripheral vision as his face smiled into hers.

"Hullo, Princess. How are you?"

She belted him across the chops with her right hand. Tiny and soft though the hand was, this young lady's stance must have been geared to delivering the blow as well as advertising her charms, for it rocked Annie's famous jaw upon its moorings, and involuntarily he raised his own hand to the abused place with a gesture as delicate as hers was crude. His eyebrows rose up above his handsome eyes, which had a look of decorous pain in them.

As she stood in her door Yummee's polished little face was a hostile sight indeed: wide as a flattop Filipino fishing canoe across the chiseled cheeks, tapering dramatically above and below to suggest the lozenge shape of a paiachi fruit, her nostrils flared and her chubby lips so far asnarl that they stained her bright teeth with their greasy Hong Kong lipstick. Her breathing was short and sharpened with the surge of sweet adrenaline. She positively spat venom with each word, which she spoke in a fashion that expressed her hatred of this language that the circumstances of her profession forced her to employ.

"You are late," she said.

"Baby, I'm sorry. My boat broke down."

"One half of a year late. Stinking prick!" She looked like she would hit him again, but she was satisfied with Annie's flinch and redirected her violence into words. They came squirting out of that angelic mouth, their brakes shot to shit and screeching protest, flecks of pearly saliva speckling his face like a sulphurous dew.

"You say, 'Oh, I come ova tomollow night'! Oh, I going to cut your face off, mister! Maybe soon you have bad times, you gonna see! Where my fuckin' money? Where, where, where, where?" That little hand perfumed with sandalwood oil stuck out under his nose. "Where my fuckin' money? You fuckin' fat stinky prick?"

"I've got it in my bra," he said with that lovely leer with which he had battled women for forty years. (More or less, Annie allowed, it had been a battle — he was too old to be a child, too filthy to be a saint.)

"Don't try to fool on me! You try to fool on me alla time, now is me who is gonna do foolin'! I make joke, oh yes, maybe one day you gonna wake up with yo' fat prick all cut off, oh yes, Annie, oh yes, oh YES!"

She took such pleasure in this notion that involuntarily she smiled too, a smile of delight and delightful to any eye, even Annie's. He took the opportunity now to ooze past her — his belly caressing her bounteous breasts — into the room, the familiar room.

"That sounds nice," he murmured to the silk drapes that hung everywhere to obscure the decrepitude of the walls. "That sounds nice, that sounds delightful." A tiny green lamp bathed his grin in a mysterious glow as he sat down on the sagging bed and lay back with a sigh of deep content.

"When does the fun start?"

"Fun already started." Yummee's mind was quick as a skinning knife. She knew he would next announce that he was hungry. Whether stuffed to the brim or an aching pit of nothingness, this man's stomach was the mother of most of his behavior, and his genitalia the father of the rest, in Yummee's opinion. Remember that this was a behavior that almost everyone exposed to it considered entirely unpredictable, and you may appreciate how shrewd she was.

"Listen, babe, I'm hungry," he said.

"Only ting I got for you is poison."

"Okay then. Gimme one order of poison and a bottle of schnapps, darlin'. Chop-chop, okay?" The grin on him was shining in the recesses of her bed, shadowed by its chaotic drapes. "Yummee, you don't give me some grub, I'm gonna take a big bite right outta that big ass o' yours, sweetheart." The saliva dripped through the sighs between each word. In Filipino, she thought: This bum is incorrigible. He is the one my mother warned me about, and the goddess Tsai-ah-Mieu also. Thus thinking, she closed the door and wiggled ominously across the little room to the bed. Standing there looking down at him (an angle that she preferred in her relations

103

vis-à-vis all males, blackguardly or benign), she reached for the cord of a bell and yanked it.

A large and languorous finger landed like a butterfly on the peachy thigh in the cleft of her cheongsam.

"Keep yo' dirty hands off me," she whispered.

"Princess, I can explain everything."

"Keep yo' big stinky, dirty hands off me."

"My little Princess." The fingers, scrupulously scrubbed for the occasion, each nail honed and polished, did their dirty work.

"My little Yummee. I missed you. I missed you a lot. I missed the way you smell. Y'know, I never met a girl that smelled as nice as you. When I was down there in Java, I looked all over for that perfume. I couldn't find it. I realized it wasn't perfume, it was just you. Yummee, tell me something nice. I just sailed two thousand miles to hear it, and I'm a tired man."

(Pause here; the heavy butterflies grown heavier but still softer, the plump little woman standing motionless with his hand invisible, buried to the elbow's crotch in the cheongsam's cleft, expressly invented in Hong Kong for these purposes.)

"A tired man. Then I saw you, babe. And now I am not tired at all."

The bed creaked and its old springs twanged as he levered into action with his hungry stomach and his big slippery mouth. Annie was at work again. With a practiced flick of the wrist designed for heavier work, he eased the cheongsam's slit wider to expose the entire butterball thigh. Without perceptible movement, her legs were now definitely farther apart, and their musculature was unresistant and frothy, as if they were no longer bearing her weight. In a sense, she seemed to float upon the musty air like an arrangement of balloons. Evidently the dexterous licking of the inside of her left knee was contributing to her support, as it would soon to her downfall.

When it came, it was a float rather than a fall. Annie's left hand was completely occupied, each finger playing a separate tune upon the delicate complexities of her pussy, so it must have been the right one that slid under her ass and elevated her and floated her onto the bed — or more precisely, onto Annie, onto his broad stomach, the sturdy muscles beneath expressly relaxed to provide the comfort of a mattress of familiar Celtic flesh. An unintelligible muttering sound came from Yummee as she subsided on top of him. It could have been a prayer to one of her goddesses, or a threat.

A boy entered the room. He was wearing quite elaborate makeup, dressed in green silk pajamas, his hair inordinately long and done in the sleek style that was intended to identify him as a homosexual. Yummee was naked by this time, seated astride Annie's amorphous form, which had not moved though she had undone all his buttons, both shirt and pants. He lay opened now to the warm air and her cool hands, like a large, amorous fish symbolically slit up its ventral seam by the fingers of an Oriental mermaid. Huskily, he requested the attentive boy to bring him a plate of chop suey and a couple of bottles of Tsingtao.

She was unarguably a fat little woman. But her polished quality, her moistness, her devotion to her art of the flesh — and to what we must call the spiritual aspects of it, also — made her exceptionally appealing to Annie Doultry. This was a woman who had made so much love, from tender childhood onwards unremittingly through a life devoted to this practice alone, that she was completely at home in the universe of lust, like a fisherman upon the sea or a farmer among his fields. On the other hand, if she was prevented by circumstances from making love for eight or ten hours a day, she became quickly irritable. No doubt it was because Annie had kept her waiting since seven o'clock, when he had promised to come, that she was in such a disgusting frame of mind when he showed up at ten. These three hours of impatient inactivity when she could have been fucking were more to blame for her evil mood than the six months of supposed "waiting" to which she attributed it.

Annie did all he could to make it up to her. He was successful. She said those bad words were all a sham, because her feelings were hurt. She did not say she loved him, but she said other things that were intended to make it clear that this was the case. She also gave him a bath.

Lying in the bath at Yummee's, Annie looked for Australia among the stupendous discolorations of the ceiling. Relieved not to find it, his gaze wandered among familiar sights: the pink light playing on the fearsome tangle of pipes, the thundering water heater, its dragon's glare of flaming gas plainly visible if one dared to peer into its mouth. Yummee had installed this novelty to impress the clientele. It had been Annie's suggestion when first they became friendly. It cost a great deal of money, but he was right: business had boomed. This was when he began getting free fucks, and a lovely feeling of having deserved them. Yummee had three or four girls working for her at the house in Lun Fat Street; she was expanding, in a business as well as in a physical sense. She must have been nearly thirty, after all, and deserved success after so much devotion to a profession into which she had been sold by her father, who was a farmer in Luzon when the famine of 1906 had struck. The fact that she had managed to escape from (or possibly buy herself out of) a brothel in Manila was a sign that her goddesses were well disposed toward her.

Another was the Norwegian seaman who had treated her honorably and had given her insight into the heart of the alien race. She had learned that unlike Chinese or Malay or Filipino customers, the whitees desired a touch of the heart, or the pretense of this touch. It was a tradition with them, apparently, which may have been connected with their Christian religion and all its exhortations about love, or may have been something to do with their mothers. Or else white women in general may have been responsible for this need in their men for a special kind of lie. Whatever it was, Yummee investigated it, and learned to perform the rites these men secretly desired. She gave them a touch of the heart, clothed in the flesh of Asia.

Annie had worked all this out in his own head, of course. Yummee was not given to introspection. But when Annie lay in her bath, an old enamel tub of a greenish hue seamed with veins of rust and rime like it was ancient flesh, he sometimes thought about women in a grand, landscape-artist sort of way. At other times he lay there beneath the dragon's glare and reflected, with a greater particularity, on those special and memorable women who had helped, or hindered, to make of him what he was.

Yummee's sensitive hands were in the bath too, deep in the murky waters, as if to help Annie in these quests of memory. At this moment, the hands were gently stroking Annie's enormous but still relatively flaccid sexual appendage. The soap was pungent in his nose, the steaming scum; the dragon's roar, the hot gush from the brass tap all green in its joins like a seaman's bones. Yummee's little fish of a forefinger crept under his scrotum, lending thereby a curious flotation to the whole engine — an engine that had a specific gravity slightly heavier than unity, thank God. Annie had from time to time observed the sexual parts of other men unashamedly floating in their bathwater, and he felt a deep gratitude that his own were made of weightier stuff. Once in a Japanese bathhouse he had gazed on a whole legion of rather small cocks bobbing like fishing floats in the communal waters. What a joke! — a joke he had shared with Barney, only to spot a few days later, in this very same bath of Yummee's, the pointy black tip of Barney's foreskin floating flagrantly on the water's surface.

The waters of forgiveness lavishing their favors upon Annie. The ovoid bar of Wright's coal tar soap in Yummee's hands an instrument of unmentionable pleasures. The steam. The piano of desire. Annie's engine ticking over nicely.

She climbed into the bath. By and by she sat upon the pillar of his wisdom. "You bitch," he breathed in her moist ear. The water sloshed onto the tiles. Above Hong Kong Island, the great black cloud parted along its ventral seam also, and admitted the light of the stars.

In her bed, he told her: "I could never really be without you. I thought about you, Yummee. I had a dream about you." He reached for his beer on the floor. "I dreamed you were a mango. With the shimmering wings of a moth." He lay back. He absorbed his beer, his comfort, her head on his shoulder. He sighed. "It makes me sad to think that I must be off again so soon. I shall miss your laughter. I shall miss watching your ass jiggle when you get out of bed in the morning and run to the can."

"My ass is no too big?"

"Of course not." He had half of it in his right hand. "Yummee, I owe you, what, nearly six hundred dollars?"

"You no gonna ask me for some more?"

Annie was silent for a while. He finished off the bottle, he dropped it on the floor, it rolled across the boards. Below, in the opium den, the stupefied eyes of a bank clerk turned up to the ceiling; he imagined that he heard distant thunder.

Annie said: "How's about maybe two hundred? To fix my engine? The one in my boat, I mean."

"What a prick you are!" said Yummee. But a little later she gathered up a handful of old bills for him. One day! she told herself.

chapter 3
The Sea Change

The next morning, with Yummee sleeping on him like a sprawled puppy, the still-stalwart Annie slipped out from beneath her delectable body. He did not wake her, no matter the temptation. He had his duty to do, and two hundred dollars to do it with. For Annie had taken it for granted that his loyal but unreliable first mate, Barney Hudson, would have neglected the ship while Annie was languishing in prison. But a seaman like Annie is not himself without his ship, and now in the bones so lately rattled by Yummee he had a hunch that a boat would be necessary.

Lord, said Annie to himself, a hundred yards away — for he had picked out the trim lines of his own vessel in the harbor, and it stirred him as much as any memory of Yummee. *The Sea Change* had been built in Gloucester, Massachusetts, in 1892, a two-masted schooner, ninety-two feet long, twenty-four feet in the beam.

There were faster ships, and many more handsome, perhaps; but none of them belonged to Annie Doultry. He had acquired *The Sea Change* in Portland, Oregon (it was a gambling coup; but that's another story), after the ship had been sailed around the Horn for the Klondike gold adventure in 1897.

But then the nearer Annie got to *The Sea Change*, the more his heart sank. He guessed that the ship hadn't been to sea more than ten days in six months, and a ship has memories. *The Sea Change* was draped in sadness, just as if there were mourning clothes hung in its limp rigging. The paint on the hull was cracking. Not a dab of polish had been applied to the decks. The sailcloth seemed to be in tatters. And what of the engine? groaned Annie, for that was the heart of the ship.

"There ain't a goddamn thing wrong with dat engine, Annie," said Barney. Bernardo Patrick Hudson was a tall black fellow from Tupelo, Mississippi, who had been raised on the river. Later, in New Orleans, he got into trouble and took off. Annie had picked him up in the Solomon Islands, where Barney had gotten pretty sick and was in bad shape. Maybe he was only forty like he said, but he looked a lot older.

Annie took him on as a deck hand. Being the kind of sonofabitch he was, Annie tried to make out that it was charity that made him do it. But it was really because Barney could tune a piano, and play it too.

They were aboard *The Sea Change*, moored to the north jetty of the Yaumatei typhoon shelter. The shelter was a new construction, a sort of artificial harbor with strong, high breakwaters of Hong Kong granite enclosing it all around. It was already jammed with junks of all description, each one supporting an entire family — sometimes two or three families, a whole clan — in the physical as well as the economic sense. The typhoon shelter had already metamorphosed into a crammed little village of junks, plus a few old lorcas — Portuguese-style traders that carried Chinese rigs, mat sails, and so forth — and a few, a very few, Western sailing vessels. Steam launches didn't like to berth at Yaumatei. It was a place for junks, for the fishing people — and for a few guys like Annie Doultry, who couldn't afford to berth at Wan Chai.

The sky was wide open to the brassy sun. The black cloud had gone. The air was warm and as usual excessively humid; there was a whiteness about it — it was a vast translucent fog loaded with the moisture that the black cloud had left as a reminder. Barney was shirtless, his own tremendous blackness glistening reptiliously. He was thin, the way a lattice of black wire is thin.

Annie Doultry sat on the taffrail and contemplated the vessel that was his father and his mother. She was in seedy shape. He could smell her, too. He looked grim as hell.

"You mudderfucker," he breathed at Barney. "You might at least have tried to keep her fuckin' brass clean."

Barney laughed. He had a hammer in his hand. With it he beat a tin can into an approximate flatness. He was on his twentieth can this morning, but he did not let up. His banging emphasized the rhythms of his laugh, which had a clanging sound to it anyway. "Hey, Annie!" he croaked. "Hey, my man, my captain. Lawd have mercy! You didn't even send me a fuckin' postal card, Cap." He bopped the tin can, holding it down with a pair of pliers. Next door, at the rail of a junk strung end to end with drying fish, a number of Tanka children watched the proceedings aboard the whitee boat with fascination.

"You sonofabitch," said Annie. "You

115

could've come and paid me a visit. That's the least you could've done."

Barney went on cackling and beating his tin cans. He had a sack full of them. The sweat trickled down from his head, filtering through his faded sideburns and collecting in pools in the rocky concavities of his collarbones. His whole body seemed worn away as if by some tremendous, ubiquitous ocean.

Annie rubbed the compass binnacle with his forefinger and looked at it like an old maid checking her sideboard for dust. He moved over to the door to the saloon, went down the steps, and stared in. He sniffed. He entered. His home. The chart table, his special chair, his sextant in its rack, his bunk, the picture postcards, the pictures of his children. His piano.

"You been carrying opium, right, Barney?"

The banging continued. Annie sniffed a couple times more. To a layman the mingle of smells — the reek of the galley a few feet forward, of tar, of diesel oil, of paint, of paraffin, of old wood — might have been capable of masking any particular odor.

Annie exited the saloon. He walked forward to the galley skylight and eyed Barney. Barney had stopped laughing; he was concentrating on the job in hand.

"We had a long discussion, Barney. We agreed, no fuckin' opium. Not on my fuckin' boat, Barney. I got enough problems, Barney." Annie's cheerful state of mind, stemming from the bliss of freedom, was beginning to return to normal. He was grumpy. Men of the sea incline to be grumpy, for it is a hard life.

Barney stood up. At six feet three he was taller than Annie. With the hammer in his hand, his glistening sinews, and his scarred Ashanti face, not to speak of the expression of indignation on it, he had an appearance of ferocity. If any white genes polluted his chromosomes, it was kept a big secret by his physiognomy. He said: "Yo' boat? Yo' fuckin' boat? What you talkin' about? This here boat is *my* fuckin' boat, man. What you talkin' about?"

Annie just looked at him. Barney was tapping his chest. "*My* fuckin' boat, man."

"Barney, are you havin' one of your spells?"

"No, I ain't havin' one o' my spells. You bet me this fuckin' boat, Annie. You tellin' me you didn't bet me this boat?"

Annie gave the man the benefit of his blankest stare. The stare said, "Barney, you are crazy, you are ready for the nuthouse."

Barney shook his head vigorously at the stare and at the implied allegation. "No, suh. No, suh. You tryin' to welsh on me, I ain't havin' it, mudderfucker. You bet me this heah boat, Annie. I tol' you you was gonna git yourself fucked over, I tol' you those mudderfuckers was gonna sell you to de fuckin' cops, I could smell it. Shit. I tol' you."

"I tol' you, I tol' you," Annie mimicked him, grinning. He was beginning to enjoy this.

With his hammer Barney pointed at the white sky and made supplication to its owner. "The Lord is my witness, de man bet de fuckin' boat. Hey, dis feller tryin' to git out of a bet, Lord. What am I gonna do wid him?" His blazing eyes demanded an answer. Maybe he got one, for he became calm. Then he took off his hat, drew down the stained hatband, and took out a scrap of folded paper. It was torn from a page of Annie's schoolbook and bore writing in pencil. Barney held it a long way from his nose and struggled to read it. In a voice like a preacher's that rang across the typhoon shelter, he read: " 'I promise to pay one boat to Bernardo Patrick Hudson if he don't git his one thousand Hong Kong dollar an' no cents on de deal with Marshal Sun' — whatever dat mudderfucker's name is." Pause. "Den it say, 'A. Doultry.'"

"That is not my signature. You forged my signature."

"Dis ain't yo' signature?" Barney thrust the crumpled scrap under Annie's nose. With an amazingly swift swipe of the left hand Annie snatched it; it disappeared into his fist. "Nope. That ain't my signature. That looked to me like the moniker of a blind drunk man, and it's a well-known fact that I don't ever get drunk, now isn't that right?"

"Gimme that IOU," breathed Barney, raising the hammer with a grotesque gesture.

"Sure," said Annie, and flipped the tiny white ball over the side.

Barney remained frozen in his violent pose like a statue of some hero of darkest Africa wearing a homburg. The neighbors on the junks on both sides of them were crowding the gunwales to watch the fun.

"Barney, Barney," murmured his captain. "You wouldn't take my boat, would you? Shit, I don't believe this. Givin' my boat to a goddamn nigger." He shook his head too, now, his eyes wet with tears. (How did he do it? Was it a trick? Or true distress?) "Shit. Seven years. Look what I did for you. I saved your ass a score of times. You didn't have a pot to piss in."

Barney lowered the hammer and sat down on the skylight.

Annie said: "What have you ever done for *me?*" The reproachful look on his face was not lost on the audience. A murmur of sympathy was audible in the Tanka language (for of course the sea gypsies had their own language, like all the peoples of China). "You never gave me a damn thing."

Barney looked up at him. "Why should I give you sumpin'? You a white man, Annie. I never gave a white man nothin' in my whole life. An' no white man never gave me nothin'."

Annie hauled out a pack of Woodbines and lit up.

"You know sumpin'?" continued Barney, warming to his theme. "I wouldn't loan you the teeth in my head if you was starvin'. What did you ever give me? A fuckin' bunk? Full o' cockroaches? And me tunin' your fuckin' piano? For seven years? And smilin'? An' tellin' you jokes?" There was a catch in his voice now. "Cookin' your fuckin' food? An' how often didn't I never git paid? You want to gimme a dime

120

on the dollar?" His chin thrust forward; it was trembling. "You owe me money, mudderfucker. Here, I wrote it down."

Annie leaned against the main mast and sighed. From here on the proceedings were predictable, they always went the same: Barney taking off his hat again — it was fossilized and preserved in salt — and extracting from the crown of it, from under the sweat pad, which was purposely loose, a little paper notebook small as you could buy, blue in color, all crinkled and the pages yellow. Annie's patience was wearing thin, and as Barney opened his mouth to recite the bad news, his captain waved largely at Hong Kong and all its works and said, "Barney, you gonna get paid soon. You gonna get paid soon as we get a little cash in hand."

"Forgit de pay. Dis here boat is mine, man, you standin' on my deck. I gonna ask you nice, now, to sign over dem fuckin' papers, de ship's papers, 'cause dis mudderfucker is mine, man, it *mine.* Dat dere was a legal bet, man. It was legal."

"Barney, you ain't lookin' the real world in the eye, my friend. There ain't nothin' legal about a nigger in Hong Kong. I could shoot you right here an' now and dump your goddamn black carcass in this here harbor bang in front of the maritime police station, an' those ol' boys would just smile and look the other way. What's to stop me?"

"Nothin' — 'cept my razor."

"I could shoot you while you were sleepin'."

"You ain't got the nuts to shoot me."

The sun rose higher beyond the white vapors, turning them into translucent steam. The sweat dripped off Annie's nose as he stood there, his thick arms folded. Barney's mesh of sinew seemed to have collapsed into a black bag of bones as he sat staring eastward (above the roofs of Kowloon) into the glare where the ocean began. "I'm gonna go on over to Los Angeles now," Barney said, "and sell her. Or San Diego — I know a feller there. I'm gonna sell her, stick an' canvas an' all found. An' I'm gonna go home. An' I'm gonna buy myself a little place down there on this bayou. Dead Dog Bayou is what it's called."

Annie just looked at him. Barney had spells like this, when he acted crazy. "I ain't gonna hang around here," he was whispering to the faces of the kids at the rail of the portside junk, the one with the display of fish. "Or I gonna end up in one of those opium dens. I gonna go home."

"You asshole," said Annie. "I told you to lay off that opium."

"Where we git money den?"

"I could have made a big haul with those guns," said Annie.

"You mudderfucker. You stole 'em. You stole 'em off of the American Army," said Barney. "An' de chicken come home to roost."

Barney did know how to tune the piano. And he knew how to play it, too. He would take the bass and Annie would take the top end and sometimes when the sea was becalmed they would play stride piano all afternoon. But the heat and the moisture could fuck her up really bad. It was a Brinkerhoff, made in Jackson, Michigan, and it had a lovely clanging tone that suited the acoustics of the saloon. And here was a funny thing: Barney had played pianos on steamboats up and down the big river all his youthful life, until he got into trouble, and he was the one with the ear, with the perfect pitch. But he didn't care if she was a bit out of tune; it was Annie who cared.

"Barney, you play that stride piano better'n any sonofabitch west of San Francisco, never mind the color," said Annie.

"You ain't gonna sweet-talk me outta this boat, man. You be talkin' about *my* piano now, an' don't you forget it, mudderfucker."

From a long way away, Annie noticed the small and apparently blind woman who seemed to be coming directly toward him. Why? For a start, because she was as pale and bright as the moon after rain, but also because her lack of sight seemed to have so little to do with the way she came toward him, just as surely as if she were being steered between rocks and shoals.

"Captain Dowtry," she said, as she bumped against him. There was no question mark on what she said, just the bare fact of meeting.

"What is it?" said Annie. Close up, he saw she was much older than she had seemed.

From within her jacket, she slid an old matchbox — it was a vesta box, for pipe smokers. "For you," she whispered.

"I don't smoke, mother," said Annie.

"Not smoke," said the old woman.

Nor was it. As Annie took hold of the box, the woman slipped away so swiftly he wondered if she expected an explosion. Still, Annie eased the box open and found an old friend: it was the dead body of his cockroach, Dempsey, bronze-colored and a relic. And beside the perfect corpse was a roll of paper.

Annie's thick fingers opened the paper out and he was able to read, in black ink handwriting, in English, yet not quite, this instruction: "Captain, sir, your entrance is called for at the House of Strange Dreams, Soarez Street, Macao. I am waiting."

Determined to feel no alarm, Annie boarded the afternoon ferry to Macao, chuckling to himself at the way every dark design made its way through that fearsome city — the most unrestrained city in the Orient, the one where anything might happen. Macao was a place where gambling seemed implicit in the curve of every street and the impassivity of every face. Only forty miles west of Hong Kong, it was its antithesis. For whereas Hong Kong pretended to observe English order, Macao was as casual and hedonistic as the Portuguese who owned it. It was the oldest European settlement in Asia, and the most wicked. There was not a man or a woman who had adventured in the East who did not have scars, treasures, and black jokes that ended with the single word of explanation "Macao."

Like a ball on a roulette wheel, Annie hardly needed to make his own way. A boy of nine or ten, but without ears (some ordinary cruelty, no doubt), came up to him as he stepped ashore, took hold of his arm, and led him through the crowded streets. After five minutes, they were outside the House of Strange Dreams. Annie marveled at all the crowds of Macao refusing to notice his staged entrance.

He stood there in the doorway, where the money changer's booth was. That man would give you a price on your watch too, sale or pawn, or on jewelry, cameras, anything like that. Two girls in garish cheongsams (practically a uniform for fancy ladies) were raising cash on a pair of earrings. There were numerous girls of all shapes and sizes. Bobbed hair seemed the fashion. Annie looked around the room, filled with smoke, opium fumes from upstairs, and the passionate mutter of the gamblers.

Many of the players were very poor; quite a few were coolies and dock workers with bodies remarkable for their sinewy spareness. They left their straw hats in careless piles along the wall as they gambled with pennies, standing next to farmers who had come into town for a monthly spree, soldiers on the lam, and old people in old silk clothes who couldn't be bothered to make for the second floor. The second floor was first class; you paid a two-dollar tip just to go up there. The earless boy was standing on the stairs, his gaunt face shining, beckoning to Annie in an anxious, impatient way.

Annie ignored the boy. He listened to the impenetrable muttering, the clack of cash, and the hiss of paper. He moved over to the table. There was only one, but it was thirty feet long. Eight assistant croupiers — *loki,* they were called — were ranged on one side, each with a cashier beside him. The chief cashier and the croupier himself, both very old, were seated in an almost mythological state up the far end.

Shoving his way through the crowd, Annie observed a bunch of European sailors leaning on the table with their bodies in exaggeratedly aggressive poses, like in a musical show, all in those tight pants, a uniform that knit them together though they were from many different countries and different ships. Two were French navy boys with the red pom-poms on their caps. There was a Dutchman, a couple of Boches, Portuguese, Scotsmen, who knows what? They were merchant seamen wading through their pay, drunk as coots, a ring of lovely little women in cheongsams and bobbed hair pawing at them, touching their asses in their tight pants.

Seamen. The word made Annie smile.

He liked to watch the fan-tan. He had never played. Annie never gambled. That was his story. He never played cards; he never bet the horses. He bet on cock-roaches, true enough, but that was in prison; it was a special case, a case of des-peration. And he had once bet on a dog, on a greyhound. That was another story al-together, a long story.

Nonetheless, fan-tan sometimes tempted him, because it was a beautiful game. Part of its charm lay in its limpid simplicity, part in its rigorous dealings with the laws of chance, part in the rites of its justice.

The hole in the ceiling from which the rich people looked down upon the poor was also part of it. Annie looked up. He could see their faces, leaning over the rail. The hole was rectangular and long, exactly the same size as the table. The attendants up there let down the bets of the upper-crust gamblers above in small baskets on long strings. Amidst all the chaos, or seeming chaos — until the clang of the bell

128

brought aching silence and the croupier raised the silver cup and began his fateful count — the baskets fell like felled birds, smack in front of the croupier's assistants, each in his place before a copper plate whose sides were numbered 1, 2, 3, 4, the copper stained by the ink on the banknotes that had licked it all these years. The baskets fell in this way because they were thrown, not lowered, a special throw arrested just so by the string, like savages in New Guinea who jumped off two-hundred-foot cliff-tops attached to 190-foot vines and were occasionally killed before visiting royalty. And as the basket fell, the attendant holding its string — who was always old, sometimes very old — sang out in his special voice how the bet was to be placed: "Fan!" or "Ching!" or "Kwok!" plus some extra singing details. What lovely words, thought Annie.

The face of the woman looking down at him was not strikingly beautiful, for a Chinese; after all, beautiful Chinese women are undoubtedly the most beautiful in the world, so that is a tall order. But she was, said Annie's eye as it saw her, beautifully striking. She was ten feet above him in the gloom of the upper room, standing beside one of the oldest croupiers in Macao, who was on his night off. He was plump, but she was lean. A lean little woman, watching Annie Doultry.

He was admitted to a room. It was in the house adjoining the Yung Chung fan-tan house, reached by a little bridge that reminded him of the gallows in Victoria Gaol. It was a small, anonymous room with black wooden paneling. An abacus lay on a table. After a while a servant in a traditional black outfit came for him and conducted him to another room. It was long and narrow, and on the walls hung paintings upon silk. Porcelain was displayed in the proper way: Kuang Hsi, Chen Lung, and Ming. There were other objects of value — an elephant of jade with emeralds in its imperial panoply and in its eyes — but the room was not overburdened or ostentatious in its wealth, save for the screen that divided its western end. It was a screen fabricated for the viceroy of some Ming emperor of the early years — the Viceroy of Fukien, possibly. Upon it was depicted the sea, with a dragon upon that sea.

The woman came into the room alone. Annie was waiting with his hands behind his back, solemnly eyeing the elephant. His cap lay on the table. She said, "Sit down, Mr. Dowtly."

"The name is Doultry, ma'am. Rhymes with 'poultry.' "

She did not attempt to repeat it. Later on she may have tried, but it always remained Dowtly on her tongue, though she spoke the English language remarkably well when she wanted to impress idiots. "Do you know who I am?" she asked him.

"Miss Butterfly?" His expression was earnest, his eyebrows raised like Major Bellingham's. Miss Butterfly — Hu Tieh in Mandarin — was China's most famous movie star, under contract to the Star Motion Picture Company in Shanghai; she was from Canton and a real pinup. The lean little woman almost smiled. Annie thought: where is there a woman immune to flattery?

"I am Madame Lai Choi San," she said. And Annie knew he had met a mate, a match, a woman who might kill him one day.

He sat down on a chair. His hat remained on the low blackthorn table, black and plain and pricey like the other furniture. He noted how soft and flattering the lights were; they were oil lamps, not gas. There was gas piped all over Macao, he knew; she was cunning, she must have been about thirty-five, thirty-six. She watched him silently, seated opposite, moving her hand in a curious way on the table, as if she were counting imaginary money. She wore a white silk dress of traditional Kwantung cut, with green dragons on her sleeves and green jade at her throat and ears and on the pins in her hair. Her skin was dark, very sun-tanned for such a woman. It shone like bronze in the light reflected from her robe, and Annie guessed at once that she was a woman of the sea.

"Is that a relative of yours, Mrs. Lai?" He indicated the dragon on the screen, breathing blue fire, engulfing a ship with tall sails, a Portuguese or British merchantman. Such a question was a compliment, and she smiled and nodded graciously like a Chinese widow woman, which is what she was. On her left hand she wore gold rings, some with emeralds, but the other was naked. He noted the shortness of her nails; he noted her narrow feet in green slippers, unbound feet like a peasant's or one of the sea people's.

"Yes, I am Tanka person," she replied. "My father, my father's father, back and back." The hand with the rings waved. Her movements were imperious and elegant as an arrogant boy's. "We are Tanka. We own many ships. Now for me to ask you, Captain Dowtly: what will you please drink?"

He asked for schnapps. She had never heard of it, but she ordered a servant girl (a very dinky little piece, thought Annie, eyeing her as she scurried out) to deal with the problem. "Mistah Dowtly," she said. "You are a very kind person. You have make gift to my servant. My servant name of Hai Sheng, master of sailing on one of my vessels." She smiled, a positive smile, though momentary. "My master of sailing, not Captain Dowtly's cook — oh, no, no, no, no!" She wagged her finger at Annie. He shook with laughter. She said, "Why you make this gift? Gift of life to Hai Sheng?"

"He owed me a cockroach," said Annie.

The servant girl came back. She brought a tray with a porcelain bottle and three tiny cups, exquisite as eggshells, and was followed by a small Chinese man of about Annie's age, wearing an amazingly well-cut suit of dark gray worsted with a discreet stripe and a blue polka-dot tie the twin of Annie's own that he had given to the dentist in Victoria Gaol. Annie now regretted the gift.

Madame Lai introduced him. Chung

Hou was his name. "My accountant," said Madame Lai. "We say, 'my writing master.'" She waved her elegant hand; his bow tie was equally gracious, he shook his own hand most warmly. He had eyeglasses with curiously large pearl-colored bridge pieces to compensate for the absence of a bridge to his nose; it was unlikely he was a boxer, thought Annie, he must have been born like this. The other thing Annie noticed at once was the telltale bulge low on Mr. Chung's left breast. His jacket was too well cut for such excesses.

"Please give the captain what he has earned," she said in English to Mr. Chung, with a wave at Annie.

Mr. Chung reached for what Annie was sure must be his gun. Annie's hand dived under his seersucker jacket and yanked his nine-millimeter Walther from his waistband and beat him to the draw. Mr. Chung did not flinch; he kept moving even as Annie's thumb flicked off the safety with a clank. The mad Chinese widow cackled with laughter like an insane bitch. She clapped, shrieking with delight, covering her mouth in the gesture of a Chinese maiden to hide her wide teeth and pink gums as Mr. Chung suavely pulled a bag of gold from his inside pocket and laid it on the blackthorn table without batting an eyelash (like many Manchurians, he had no eyelashes worth speaking of anyway).

"I'm sorry, ol' feller," said Annie, faintly embarrassed. He shoved his sidearm back into his waistband under his limp seersucker. "You know how it is."

Mr. Chung waved a little hand that mimicked his mistress's, not bothering to say, "Okay, don't worry about it." His English, Annie was about to learn, was not as good as Madame Lai's.

The girl poured a liqueur into the cups. Mr. Chung said, "Patience, please, Captain, soon you get number-one schnapps. Tly this drink, velly fine Chinese vino." There was something ludicrous about the writing master, but you had to admire his sangfroid; he had come within a fifth of a second of a bullet in the brain.

The bag of gold was not mentioned until after Annie had accepted the vino in the porcelain cup. Madame Lai explained that there were about a hundred English sovereigns in it. She tipped out a few, a rather vulgar gesture in Annie's opinion.

"One thousand dollar. My gift, Captain Dowtly. For your gift of life to Hai Sheng. I have many sailing masters" — a big wave here, like the one the dragon on the screen was riding — "many, many. But I take care of my people."

He sipped the liqueur. It was disgusting. He tried to conceal his distaste by redirecting it, as it were, toward the bag of gold. He put down the cup, picked up a sovereign, his upper lip puckering. "Mrs. Lai," he said, mastering all emotion. "Thanks a million, but I couldn't accept this."

"Oh, you must accept. I say yes."

"Mrs. Lai, I never been paid yet for saving a man's ass. For bumpin' 'em off, sure. But not the other way round. I wanted that cockroach. It would be against my principles to get paid for being human." Even as the words came out of his mouth, he could hear an inner voice squealing: "Principles? What is this hokum? Annie, is this some kinda bet? Are you betting a cool grand on another dumb hunch, or what?"

"Have some more wine, please." Madame Lai raided the little bottle, a gleam in her eye. Annie raised a negative palm, a polite negative. He read her thoughts: "Hell!" — or whatever it was in Chinese — "This fella want no British gold, no Chinese wine! What the hell he want?"

Silence; a silence like the lingering echo of a gong. Then: "You no like this welly fine vino?" Mr. Chung's bridgeless nose

136

wrinkled with the embarrassing question. Annie suddenly felt exasperated with the whole scene. "Mr. Writin' Master," he breathed, "I love it. It's the best hummin'-bird weewee I ever tasted."

As if on cue (for another silence was imminent) the tall servant in his smart black outfit entered carrying a quart bottle of Stummelpfennig's schnapps. Annie felt a hell of a lot better.

Mr. Chung, Madame's writing master, bowed deeply. He made his exit silently. He took the bag of gold with him before Annie could change his mind.

She said to Annie: "Yes, I watch. I watch to see you play fan-tan."

"You musta been grievously disappointed, ma'am." He refilled the eggshell of porcelain with schnapps for the fourth time; it didn't hold much.

"Yes. I am disappointed." Her face gave no hint of anything but alertness.

He shook his head. His eyes wandered round the room. He did not care particularly for Chinese porcelain or screens or flowers of dark jade embedded in metal mirrors. He had owned a metal mirror, a bit rusty in back but more functional than the one on Madame Lai's rosewood table in front of the great screen. It was a thousand years old and its surface, though highly reflective, was peculiar. "I never gamble, Mrs. Lai," he said. "Except on cockroaches."

"Never play cards?"

"No."

"Never bet on horses?"

"No." Annie could lie for days on end.

"Never bet on nothing? Ooh la la!" Wherever she had got this expression, it wasn't Paris. With each "la" her pointed tongue clacked effortfully against the back of her tigerish teeth; still, her "la la" sounded more like "ga ga," in Annie's opinion. She saw him smile as his eyes wandered sleepily and hers drilled into the bones of his face with an effort at perception that positively fatigued him. It was like the death rays in H. G. Wells. Her expression did not change.

"I did once bet on a dog," he remembered.

"Please tell me story."

A pause. "I knew I was betting on a dog," he explained patiently. "But I didn't know it was in a race, okay? I thought I was betting on its life." Another pause. "It was a trick."

"Ah!" she said. "Ah, yes!" Her eyes were

shining like nickel-jacketed bullets. "I have heard of this dog's life, yes!" She nodded energetically; she would have gone on, but his palm was rising, his broad pink palm, an imperative to stop, to desist, to give him a break, that even this bullet-eyed woman, one of the most notorious gangsters in Asia, could not withstand. She shut up.

"It was a trick," he repeated. "A pal of mine played a dumb trick on me." (Bernardo Patrick Hudson, it was, that damn creepy nigger.) "This pal o' mine led me to believe that I was layin' a few bucks on whether this dog would live or die. A sick dog. He said there was this bozo with a sick dog."

She stared at him. She understood the gist of it. He would bet on a sick dog willingly, any day of the week. Annie nodded several times to confirm her thoughts. Madame was getting the point. "Well, there's no damn need going into the details, is there?" he said reassuringly. "It turned out it wasn't a question of rabies; it was the dog was in this race, is what it was. It was a trick."

She nodded. "A tlick. Ha!" She clucked her tongue. He nodded some more. He felt like nodding off, but it had to be gone through with, he had to follow through.

Miraculously, she lent a hand. "I see. Except cockroaches. You do not like to make gambles on running animals — except cockroaches. No cards, no fan-tan. Hong Kong Stock Exchange, maybe?"

"No stock exchange." He changed the nod to a shake. His head was heavy, it moved in its own rhythms; but with an effort of the will he could alter their direction and wavelength. "No poker. No backgammon."

"But the death of dogs, yes?"

"Matters of life and death, yes."

"A dog's life. Ha!" She saw the symmetries, now that she knew what it meant. She was a student of the language, a wonderful learner. But she had been born knowing men.

"You got it, honey," said Annie.

Behind the screen with its great dragon devouring the ships of the barbarians, Mr. Chung, the accountant, the writing master, was seated silent as a sphinx. He played an incomprehensible game with himself with a pack of old and fragile gold-backed cards (they looked French; but what was the game? Did he invent it?). For a table he used a Rand McNally *Atlas of the World*, the latest edition, laid across his lean knees. He listened attentively to his mistress's conversation with Captain Doultry and from time to time observed the latter through one of the slim gaps where the screen was hinged.

"You are a true gambler, Mistah Dowtly."

"Well, I dunno." What the hell was all this about? The schnapps was building up in his limbic system; it was definitely time for a nap. "Let us put it this way. I don't bet on organized things, sweetheart. I bet on disorganized things. For or against, it don't make much difference to me. I take a stab at it. I like to have a little fun."

She averted her eyes from him. This movement was enough to imply that she had seen enough of him. "Captain Dowtly, you are a very interesting man. I thank you for coming to see me. But now I have some business." She rose from her chair with elastic decisiveness, like a white cat stretching before going out on the prowl.

Annie gazed up at her. He liked gazing up at women as much as women liked gazing down at him. He fixed upon her his sumptuous, needy eyes, sucking hers back into them, sideways, against her will. He held fast her nickel bullets in the sockets of his head. His brain said, with a drawl of fatigue: "What the fuck does she want?" His mouth said: "I think everyone should maintain a little mystery. That is my opinion."

She stood there. She was hooked again. Two can play this game, Madame. You are an archthief, I can tell it from every move you make. But I, Madame, am an archliar. "Perhaps women should remain a little more mysterious than men; I don't know." Annie put on his lovely act of searching out an answer. "But there has to be something about everybody that makes you want to find out more, don't you agree? If I told you everything about myself, you might become bored very quickly."

"Or very slowly," she said.

"It's a matter of curiosity. It is human nature to be curious. When the curiosity is satisfied, we've got to find something new to be curious about. Right?"

"I must go to my business." She was nervous now.

"There's something about you, Mrs. Lai, that intrigues me and interests me a great deal. May I ask you about it?"

"Maybe I will not answer." Now it was fear.

He arranged a smile on his face, an it's-up-to-you-baby smile. "Well, we're alone now, okay? So anything you say, you know, anything of a personal nature, is just between us. I mean, no one else is around to hear, it's just you and me, isn't that true?"

She stared at him. "Yes. That is true."

"So what is Mr. Chung doing sitting behind that screen? Behind me and to my right?"

She didn't miss a beat. She didn't even reply too quickly, she didn't even bother to smile. "Oh, he is just a servant. With my servants I am alone. We are alone." A brave response. Doultry nodded his satisfaction, but pressed his point. "I never saw a Chinese servant who wore a three-hundred-dollar suit made by an English tailor."

"He is waiting to have business talk with me. Now, I must go."

"Now, I must smile," said Annie.

"A smile makes face more pretty," said she.

"Not if you got real bad teeth."

"Your teeth pretty good. Now I give you something small, which you will keep, please." She went to another table and took a box of ivory and removed from it a mah-jongg tile, ivory also, with a red sign and on its back an inlay of jade. This she gave to Annie. "Maybe I like to see you one more time, Captain. My servant will have this tile, this same one."

Annie took a look at the tile. It bore the sign of three balls (a shrewd choice, he thought), and the jade inlay on the back portrayed a vibrant tiger of meticulous ferocity. Annie dropped it in his pocket. "If I don't come," he said, "I'll send it back."

"You keep. I have plenty more mahjongg."

"Maybe we'll catch a movie together."

"Maybe. Goodbye, Captain Annie Dowtly."

The male servant opened the door. Annie bowed to her, a proper old-fashioned bow, and made his way out.

Leaning on the balustrade of the second floor of the fan-tan house, you looked down on the rabble crowding around the table; you looked down on the cashiers and could see into their little drawers as their white hands manipulated a hundred varieties of money. There were Chinese banknotes issued by a dozen different banks: their values were denoted in taels, one tael being an ounce of silver. But in China the tael varied in weight from province to province, like all Chinese weights and measures, so a table of values had to be consulted. Old Chinese silver dollars with the dragon emblem, the new Yuan Shih-kai dollars issued by Peking, and the silver half-dollars minted in Yunnan by Governor Tang, exhibiting His Excellency's bust, were all to be seen in quantity. American dollars and British sovereigns and Portuguese pesos were welcome, and of course Hong Kong dollars dominated the proceedings in terms of quantity. Old American "trade" silver dollars, Mexican silver dollars, and Japanese likewise, of high purity, were exhibited stacked in heaps, to give the place a classy tone. Saigon piastres were scrutinized with sour expressions for the likelihood of forgery and stuffed into a drawer. But it was all money, all legal tender in China, and in Macao, too, and welcome in the fan-tan house.

The cashier's job was not easy. That was why there were so many of them. After every play they flicked their writing brushes in their ink and tallied their take in great books, and their abacuses rattled ceaselessly throughout the days and the nights, for the fan-tan house never closed.

It took about fifteen or twenty minutes for all the bets to be placed. People consulted their elaborate notes on the run of the play; an attendant handed out little charts with columns of zeros, IIs, IIIs, and crosses that related the day's results up to the last play. These signs stood for one, two, three, and four. It was that simple. And the betting itself was only a little more complicated; an assistant croupier placed your money on one of the four sides of the copper plate, on which were inscribed the signs above. Fan-tan was a game where only one of these four numbers could come up; if you won, the cashier paid you four times your stake (less ten percent off the top for the house, which meant plenty of cash handling and abacus clicking — very calming to the excoriated soul of the gambler). But anyone who played regularly usually bet on pairs of numbers, which was called Kwok and paid you double; or Ching, which meant you bet on a single number and made two numbers neutral. If your number came up, Ching also paid you double; if it was a neutral you got your stake back — you could only lose it on the fourth number. Mathematically speaking, Ching was apparently safer than Kwok, and professional fan-tan players usually shot for it.

There was a fourth play: Lim. Here you bet on one number, made another neutral, and could lose on the other two. It paid three times your stake. For mystical reasons, it was said, only people born in the Year of the Rat should play Lim; they would habitually win. Those not so designated would always lose. Every fan-tan player had noted the invariability of this rule of the universe.

The baskets flew up and down, the old *loki* upstairs chanted their clients' instructions, and Annie leaned on the smooth teak balustrade, watching. He fondled Lai Choi San's mah-jongg piece in his left hand. A canary was twittering in the cage that hung in the small window near him, its shutters half-closed against the smoldering glare of the Macao afternoon. The clatter of the street outside was not audible against the mutter of the gambling house. Up here, Annie was among the serious gamblers.

A few tourists, mostly British from Hong Kong, were up there too. Opposite Annie was a chief engineer with a round pink face and shoulders nearly as big as Annie's own. He was a gambling man; he was not fooling around. Next to the Chinese the British are the world's most obsessive gamblers — an odd circumstance that was a pointer to the future of Hong Kong, for those willing to take note of it.

The white pate of the chief croupier glistened like an ancient melon. In front of him lay a heap of copper coins called "cash" by the Chinese, who invented this name. They were the old-fashioned sort with the hole in the middle, so that they could be carried on strings. The chief croupier received signals from his assistants on the progress of the betting. When he saw enough money on the table to justify the effort, he picked up a metal bowl about six inches in diameter with a metal knob on it and used it to cover a bunch of cash. His movement was swift and casual. He shuffled his bowl a little. It was impossible to guess how many coins it concealed.

The croupier waited a few moments, eyeing the players through his implacable lenses. Now were the moments of the final frenzy, as those who had hesitated made their move or faced their cowardice. They were long-drawn-out moments, often under the weight of imminent revelation. Taunted by the sight of the metal bowl with its secret already fixed, the gamblers besieged it with the exhortations of their eyes and, succumbing to illusions of supernatural vision, plunged for excessive sums. Often the stakes on the table doubled or tripled in those last minutes, wherein apparent time stretched relativistically. The chief engineer's *loki* sent down his basket at the last moment with two hundred dollars on Ching. A young, intellectual-looking Chinese further down, wearing a finely embroidered blue gown, bet the limit, which was fifteen hundred.

The croupier struck his bell with the palm of his right hand. A great hush fell, in which Annie listened to the dance of the flies, and the rustle of dresses.

The croupier removed the bowl. The cash were revealed. He picked up an ivory stick resembling a conductor's baton or a refined chopstick and divided the coins with elegant sweeps into three columns. Then with the tip of the stick he drew them toward himself in groups of four. He had between thirty and sixty to deal with as a rule. Long before he had finished, the eyes of the experts had counted them, and voices triumphant or bitter in tone called out the result, frequently arguing, in a frenzy, up to the final moment of truth, when there were four, three, two, or but one of the metal discs left on the table to denote what was true and what was hope.

And that was all there is to it, said Annie to himself as he straightened and dropped the mah-jongg piece into his pants pocket and went downstairs. He caught the next ferry back to Hong Kong, in good time for dinner.

A few days later Annie had got things organized and *The Sea Change* was chugging west and south through Sulphur Channel and around West Point to Aberdeen on the south side of the island.

Aberdeen was the original Chinese village on Hong Kong Island. Its harbor was sheltered by a small offshore islet, and ten thousand junks lived there, for it was still the headquarters of the biggest fishing fleets. Annie liked to moor there when business was slow, for the privacy, and because the charges were only a quarter a day even for a vessel of ninety tons.

Annie had put the diesel in, a Perkins 4, in '25, a year when he had a big score — which is another story. The diesel was a big deal at the time; it gave him a leg up versus the competition, which was the steam launches, when it came to coastal business and puttering about the Canton Delta. Of course, on longer hauls the economy of the wind counted and Annie could compete dollar for dollar on his rates when it came to sixty-ton cargos, which was about his limit, and still finish nicely ahead. And with a crew of four or five boys and an old man (he preferred Malays or Lascars; they didn't mind adapting to Western rigs, as the Chinese refused to do, and Filipinos were too emotional), plus Barney, expenses weren't exactly high even if the hold contained only a few dozen bales of silk or crates of tea or whatever the agent had to offer. (Annie dealt with Crawford and Perry, who didn't mind small stuff and turned a blind eye to a lot of stupid regulations when you got to know them, such as slips and omissions from ship's manifests.) All in all, small was good in many ways.

But Captain Doultry drew the line at opium — not for any reasons of morality, but because the heat was increasingly on when it came to opium in Hong Kong. The whole of China was swamped with the stuff again. In the great inland provinces of Yunnan and Szechwan, in Hunan and Kweichow and Shensi, poppies had taken over vast acreages of rice fields; they were the biggest cash crop. In the cities, it was estimated, over seventy percent of the population were smoking, or popping morphine pills. In Hong Kong the British were increasingly nervous as opium smuggling began to get out of hand. The police, notoriously corrupt though they were at street level (after all, they were Chinese), were finally cracking down. Annie had seen enough of Victoria Gaol.

The boy that Annie called McNab was at the wheel. He was small but far from dumb; he was a Lascar, born to the sea in Borneo, and he even had a good grip on the mysteries of the diesel, which was supposed to be Barney's province. McNab was the brother of Sock, who was about fifteen and took care of the foremast. Annie was good with these boys; he was effective. Sometimes he even paid them. Sometimes he played old and fatherly, sometimes he was brutal and hysterical; unpredictability was his middle name. But he must have been doing something right, for they stuck with him. And the old man, a Tahitian, had been with him for years.

The monotonous sound of a piano being hit one key at a time floated above the bubbly wake. Mount Davis dropped nearly sheer into the water a couple of miles eastward, and to the west rode a fishing fleet, about forty junks strong, clear to the horizon. Annie sat on his bunk sewing a button on his second-best shirt while Barney tuned the piano. The sound of a piano being tuned is irritating to some, but to Annie it was pleasant: it was a symbol of peace, a concession to harmony. This harmony was in turn due, no doubt, to the sweet smell of fresh business in the air. Barney had noticed Annie sniffing, and he knew the signs; when Annie was on the scent, the buttons got sewed back on his shirts. It was like readying the ship for action.

For the first time since he had come out of prison Annie and Barney were at ease again. Maybe it was the motion of moving on the water.

So Annie called out:

"They went to sea in a Sieve, they did,
In a Sieve they went to Sea."

Barney grinned in spite of himself. For long ago, Annie had taught him the non-sense songs of Edward Lear — had even bought him a book with them written out. So Barney had learned to read. And the fellow from Tupelo, Mississippi, sang back in the night:

"In spite of all their friends could say,

On a winter's moon, on a stormy day,
In a Sieve they went to sea!"

They fell silent, and then Annie spoke. He was wearing his glasses. "I don't get it," he said. "She was living in this real bum part of town, but she had this classy little house. She was a real elegant dish."

"You want me to tune her? Well, shut your fuckin' trap," said Barney.

"She had on a white silk outfit — you'd've loved it, Barney. Earrings, jewels. She was really spiffy. And she had a mind like a mongoose." Annie tapped his grizzled temple. His captain's cap looked one size too small for him; he liked the visual effect. "She had an answer for everything. I never met a Chinese bimbo who talked English that good, you know that?"

"I knew one," said Barney. He was pinging endlessly on one high note. "She could talk English better 'n me."

"She's a businesswoman." Annie bit off a thread. "She's not like those rich Chink women who never see anybody. That little woman knows her way around." Annie laid down his shirt. He eyed the cat. The cat's name was Lord Jim. Lord Jim had turned out to be a female, but it never occurred to Annie to change her name. She jumped on his knee, and Annie cracked a melon seed and gave it to her. She liked them, provided they were previously cracked.

Annie had wisely refrained from telling Barney about the money. He was tempted, but Barney would have got upset, he would not have understood. He would have screamed and wailed. Annie was trying to live with his decision. It had led to several lengthy, brooding silences. Even by Annie Doultry standards of unpredictability, any thinking man would have said he'd flipped his lid, turning down a cool grand in gold like that. He could only explain it as one of those hunches. It was a bet. With that explanation, Annie could live with any decision, however crazy. His silences had turned to deep reflections about how Madame Lai Choi San was able to see into a white man's brain box with those H. G. Wells eyes of hers. "What the hell is she up to?" he said out loud to Lord Jim.

Barney cursed elaborately, rolling the words around his teeth and beneath his breath. "Shut de fuck up! How de fuck I gonna do dis an' listen to your dumb mout' at de same time?" He swiveled slowly on the piano stool and glowered at Annie with his yellow eyes. "Okay, you waitin' on me to ask, so I gonna ask you. Did you fuck her?"

Annie shook his head and sighed and tut-tutted. It was not a negative response to this question; it was a little shake of concern at Barney's coarse state of mind. "Listen, don't talk to me now. Never talk to me when I'm feeding the bird — I mean the cat. I just can't concentrate."

chapter 4
Playing Madame's Game

It was time to repair *The Sea Change* — before the dollars melted away. A drink here, a girl there (this was the mixture that Annie later wistfully referred to as a "cocktail party") and he'd be broke again. So Annie bought a good used sail (no. 2 canvas) from a veteran Chinese sailmaker he trusted. He made sure that Barney installed the sail properly and then he went belowdecks — for two days and a night, it turned out — to clean the engine and rebuild the radio. And so it was that *The Sea Change* became its old seaworthy self — and Captain Annie Doultry was broke again.

Annie grinned to think of that tidy, logical development, and then he smiled that kind of inward grin — the sort the world never sees — as he saw a sampan draw up to the side of *The Sea Change*.

157

"Whaddya want?" he called out to the ancient Chinaman, hardly more substantial than the narrow oar he used to make his way in the sampan.

"Cap'n Dowty?" asked the Chinaman.

"You got him."

Whereupon the Chinaman gave a flick to his free arm, and Annie saw a sliver of white in the evening air. It arced toward him and landed in his great hand without a sound. It was a mah-jongg tile from Madame Lai Choi San's game. It was the call that Annie had expected. But he was still not sure whether to be eager or afraid.

"You come alon'?" asked the Chinaman.

"I'm with you, darlin'," said Annie.

The sampan glided through the ten thousand junks, the old man working his oar with great economy of motion. A small boy sat in the bow with his eyes peering out from under his hat, fixed upon Annie, as the light faded from the sky.

Annie did not feel apprehension; he felt a great euphoria. He sniffed the air, ripe with the scents of flowers and fish, and observed with a pleasure that could never wane the mysterious moment when ten thousand junks lit up their lamps almost as one. This time signaled the beginning of the night, and the necessary joss sticks were lit before every shrine on every vessel great and small: the shrines of Tin Hau, the goddess of the sea, and of the Tanka people. The Chinese name for Aberdeen Harbor was Heung Kong: the Fragrant Harbor. Perhaps the pall of evening incense that obliterated the flowers and the fish and the smell of dinner had given birth to this name. But Annie was reminded that the floating city he was now traversing was the mother of Hong Kong. That the foundations of the place were watery was a fact worth noting, and he said so to the small boy in so many words. Swishing silently along the liquid avenues, past the wooden dwellings of the city and its tilted scaffoldings of masts and spars and the raucous laughter of twilight, Annie succumbed to his romantic streak and lit a cigarette.

They rode south down the Aberdeen Channel and past the breakwater into the lee of another islet called Ap Lei Pai, and the steep banks of the main island beyond the ranks of junks gave way to mud flats in the little bay of Tai Shue Wan. This was the edge of the water city, and it was guarded by big oceangoing junks that rode at solitary anchorages instead of gunwale to gunwale. They crossed an open stretch, leaving the water city's sounds, and night fell in earnest. They had been rowing for an hour when Annie saw the riding lights and the bulk of a large vessel loom out of the dark with strange suddenness. Perhaps he had dozed off.

She was the biggest junk he had ever seen, as big as or bigger than the old Foochow traders from northern parts that still turned up in Hong Kong from time to time. But this one was a *mi-ting,* a three-masted merchantman built in the traditional Cantonese manner, though her hull was of solid ironwood, which was a rare thing to come across these days. Perhaps she was very old; it was impossible to tell, for the Chinese had not changed the style or methods of construction of their craft for two hundred years or more, and they knew how to maintain them. Her poop rose twenty-five feet above the water, and Annie noted the massiveness of her rudder, fretted with square holes to increase its mobility, as the old man brought them alongside. She was about the same length at the waterline as *The Sea Change* but much broader in the beam, and Annie had her figured for over two hundred fifty tons as he climbed the rope ladder and stepped upon her deck.

There were few of her crew to be seen.

In a craft this size the belowdecks were quite spacious, and there were lights visible in the hatches fore and aft. A man was at the top of the ladder, a short, broad man with a long-barreled Mauser pistol in his belt and two cartridge belts crossing his muscular chest. He grinned at Annie. Further forward about a dozen men could be discerned squatting round a couple of charcoal braziers eating their dinner. The clink of rice bowls and the cheerful chatter were reassuring. They did not bother to look at Annie. He turned to look aft. There, framed in the light from the low door to the poop quarters, stood the unmistakable figure of Mr. Chung, the writing master, in a white suit luminous as a bird. His spectacles shone.

The other thing one could not help noticing was the twelve cannon, six a side, their chassis rolled inboard and concealed by inch-thick iron plates that slid on cables just above the bulwarks — an arrangement both concealing and protective. Most of the cannon seemed to be ancient twelve-pounder muzzle loaders; but as Annie walked aft he noticed four modern breechloaders, standard seventy-five-millimeter Chinese army field pieces (copied from French Schneiders) set up in custom-made rolling chassis for their new nautical role. But he had no time to observe more, for Mr. Chung was advancing to meet him. From the poop deck the shadowy figures of several men looked down on them.

"Captain Dowtly." The writing master bowed, shining and impeccable. What a tailor this guy has, thought Annie, lifting his hat with equal politeness. Mr. Chung said, "How are you keeping, Captain?"

"I am slightly confused, Mr. Writing Master." Annie looked around with eyebrows a little raised. He felt this was the proper attitude under the circumstances.

"Captain Dowtly, Madame Lai is happy you come see her. She will soon arrive. Please, wait in here."

He ushered Annie ceremoniously through the low door. Mr. Chung himself had to stoop an inch, and for Annie it was tricky. He bent from the waist beneath the low smoky ceiling and was grateful to see benches against both sides of the room; he lowered himself onto one. He was in the tiller room, which doubled as a chart room. The tiller was just that, a beam connected by ropes and pulleys to the rudder below so that one strong helmsman could steer her if necessary, responding like a donkey engine to orders yelled down through the hatch above. It led to the poop deck, which was the bridge of a junk and the station of the *lio-dah,* or sailing master.

An oil lamp swung on a gimbal. There was a chart rack, and an old English compass in a brass binnacle beside the chart table, all this being most unusual equipment for a Chinese junk.* Likewise the Lewis gun in a rack opposite, with another containing at least a dozen magazines. This vessel is a floating arsenal, thought Annie.

In the aft bulkhead two more sliding doors, charmingly lacquered a deep red, led to the owner's and sailing master's cabins. One of these doors slid back and Madame herself entered.

She did not need to stoop. She looked different now, in her proper element. The jade and the jewelry were gone. She wore a tunic and pants of polished black cotton, well cut but not much different from the standard Sunday best of a Cantonese coolie, and she was barefoot like her men.

---

*Chinese junk compasses were ancient affairs, lodestones swinging on a pivot in a wooden box, at best. They had not changed much in two thousand years or more; since the Chinese invented the device, they were not interested in improving it.

A girl came in behind her, apparently a servant, or amah, dressed almost the same, a shawl around her head. The girl squatted on the floor and stared at Annie with nervous, perfect eyes. Her mistress did not sit down. She preferred to move and feel the ocean beneath her.

"Good night, Captain Dowtly. You like some tea? Or some schnapps?" She pronounced it perfectly.

"I'll have both, thank you," he answered. "Excuse me if I do not rise."

She smiled at once. Annie never had any problem making her smile. She apologized for the long sampan ride. Not at all, he said, he enjoyed it, but he was curious to know how she had kept track of his movements with such precision. (In fact, he knew it was an easy matter for someone with her resources, but he also knew that a little flattery never came amiss.) She answered, with one of her little waves, a tiny gesture yet enough to change events.

"I keep track of many, many ships. Big ships, little ships. I will tell you truthfully: I come here to meet you. My vessel, this fine vessel that my father named *Tiger of the Iron Sea*, sail at the rising of the sun this morning from Macao to meet you here."

Her second amah, who was sturdier and

not as pretty as the first, brought them tea and his Stummelpfennig (it was the same bottle — an economical note to her hospitality). As they exchanged politeness, her sailing master came in. Captain Wang Ho was no more than forty, a quiet, good-looking man for whom stooping was also a necessity in the chart room. He was dressed in a Royal Navy lieutenant's tunic, with the two extra gold bars on the sleeve denoting the rank of captain carefully added by one of his wives. His cap was a Portuguese army colonel's, in good condition, complete with white sun protector. He carried his Mauser in its proper holster of leather-covered wood. He was missing several fingers of his left hand and spoke hardly any English. Madame formally introduced him to Annie. The sailing master gave him the once-over without expression and then withdrew.

Throughout all this Annie remained seated on the narrow bench. He rested his hands on his knees and allowed his mind to be relaxed and receptive. But when they were again alone (save for the pretty amah seated on her heels), Annie said: "Madame Lai, I would like you to tell me now: what do you want me to do, when do you want me to do it, and what is the pay?"

She took her sweet time: "Chinese people do not like to talk so quick about business." She sipped her third cup of tea, the Pao-li kind, black as Ethiopian coffee. "But since it is your custom to hurry up in business talk, I will do the same."

She told him that she was the owner and mistress of sixteen armed junks. "*Tiger of the Iron Sea* the most strong but not most fast. I have two very fast junk, bottoms very, very smooth." She made a very, very smooth movement with her fingers.

The movement captivated Annie Doultry. He had an odd urge to feel her hands on him.

"I am a robber of ships," she whispered. "I have robbed many, many ships. That is my business, and it was my father's business, so I know very well how to do it." She smiled. "I am the greatest robber and thief upon this sea." One wave to the south, another to the east. A grand claim, thought Annie. She ignored him, not really looking at him as she explained, her brow furrowed slightly. "I do lot of small business, keep this sea in good order for the fishing people. Before, many pirate people alongside Macao, alongside Hong Kong, but I send them away." The barest smile here. "Many I must kill. I must sink their junks.

So after, all go away, those little pirate people. I take care of fishing people. So they pay me, each master of fishing people pay me. Maybe four, five, six thousand junks I take care of." The old protection racket. Annie nodded politely. She was enjoying herself like any Hong Kong businessman explaining his sphere of influence. It was impolite to interrupt.

Then she said that in 1924 she had entered in the business of robbing the ships of the white man. It was a purely business decision; she was at pains to make that clear. She did not wish Annie to feel that she was picking on foreigners. Then, as if inadvertently, she said: "The *gwai lo* ships have taken the seas and the rivers from my people." She said it offhand, and ordered her pretty amah to bring fresh tea. *Gwai lo* was a lowlife slang term for white people absolutely never used in polite conversation. It was a strange word to hear on Madame's lips; it was, thought Annie, like watching himself in a metal Chinese mirror talking about "Chinks" in the same inoffensive and casual fashion.

Annie was going very easy on the schnapps. For one thing, his last cock-tail-party hangover was just settling in; for another, he wanted to concentrate. It was beginning to look like he would soon be asked to make some pretty interesting decisions — or to place a heavy bet or two, which was a simpler way of viewing such decisions, in Annie's opinion.

She said that last year she had "made robberies" of five *gwai lo* ships. Presumably the *Sunning* affair, in which the pirate Li Weng-chi had been involved, and for which he was hanged beneath Annie's cell window, was one of these. Presumably the fact that it had failed — an infrequent occurrence in these very well-organized piracies — had led to some sort of feud involving Mr. Hai Sheng, "master of sailing on one of my vessels." But Annie knew there was no point in interrupting Madame's flow; she would tell him what she wanted to tell him, no more and no less. She felt it important that he understand how successful and powerful she was in her business. And she was quite terse about it; she didn't waste words or gestures. Each crisp sentence was to the point, and each wave too, infinitely subtle in gradation though they were, like the various waves of the ocean upon a Tahitian beach.

"At the end of the moon which you call June, I will rob the ship *Chow Fa*."

Captain Doultry stroked his beard. He

was seaman enough to hate the very idea of pirates as much as their recent success. But he was an adventurer, too, who could not deny the boldness of the seaborne rogues. There had been fourteen steamship piracies already in 1927. Like nearly every pirated ship since 1919, every one of these fourteen ships was taken by the sea robbers to Bias Bay, a vast, marshy, island-strewn labyrinth about sixty miles east of Hong Kong. At Bias Bay the booty was unloaded, the pirates disembarked, and the dead were dumped in the murky waters.

Bias Bay was a region of small fishing villages. It had been a haunt of pirates for centuries. The chieftains of these gangs, the organizers and financiers of the raids, lived elsewhere. None had ever been traced, much less tried. Who they were was a matter of endless speculation.

Annie lit another cigarette. Madame Lai Choi San paced the chart room of the *Tiger of the Iron Sea.* She did not wish to sit down, although there was another bench opposite Annie's. She said: "Do you know the SS *Chow Fa*, Captain Doultry?"

He said, "Yes."

"Do you know its registered tonnage?"

"About ten thousand tons," he said. "She's British-owned. The Indo-China line, on the Manila–Hong Kong run. Or she was."

"You are a man who knows his business. Did you know this ship carries silver?"

"No," said Annie. In fact, he had heard.

"I think you know. Unimportant. The *Chow Fa* carries silver to Hong Kong maybe four, five, six times in a year. This silver comes from the Loofangs of the Philippine Islands, it is number-one silver. The Hong Kong and Shanghai Bank buys many tons of this metal to make into Hong Kong dollars. On the ninth day of the third moon there will be a shipment of silver. I will rob it."

"You mean, you will steal it," said Annie helpfully. He knew she wished to speak the barbarian language with perfection.

"Ah, yes? I will steal this silver. Thank you."

There was a considerable silence. Madame Lai gazed at her tea. Annie poured himself just a wee dram of Stummelpfennig. "Well, that's very interesting," he murmured. "You are not drinking your tea."

She responded in a rather motherly tone: "Captain Dowtly. Mr. Chung, my accountant, thinks you are an excellent person, a very fine man. He thinks this, and I say it for him. He ask informations about you all around very, very careful. Mr. Chung a very careful person."

"I'm sure he needs to be, working for you, Madame Lai."

"Thank you. So. You are number-one sailor man. You are, how can I say, you are boss of your own heart. I like this. You go to jail, okay, this I like too. The police have make monkey business against you because you no pay them. Very bad people, these Hong Kong policemen, they steal from everybody."

"I was dumb," said Annie.

"Next time, you no dumb." She permitted herself one of her little smiles. "So. Now I do not need to tell you, I like to do some business with you. I want to steal. I am not policeman, I am a thief. How 'bout you help me steal this silver?"

She had great force of character. Her straight-on approach was atypical of a Chinese, and Annie guessed she had learned it the way she had the language. What a power this girl could have been in the world of straight business, he thought. But he concealed his admiration. He sighed and scratched his head under his cap.

"Madame Lai," he said. "Thanks for the kind words. But I think you may have misjudged me. I don't know how I could possibly be of service to you in such a scheme as you mention. I have always had a disinclination to make myself nervous. I like to do a little business, but I like to do it the easy way. Just listening to you, and looking around this vessel of yours, well, I don't need to tell you that I see plenty of evidence that violence is a way of life with you. Me, I've seen enough violence in my time. I have to admit I am not the wild and pugnacious feller I used to be. I incline to the easy life these days. I like to play the piano, you know."

This was a big speech, and a pretty good one tactically, or gaming-wise, and Madame Lai approved of it. It was even partly truthful, which put it into a small percentage bracket among Annie Doultry's big speeches. But Lai Choi San was not blind to the big fat lie that wriggled in its midst like a cockroach in a jar of honey: Annie liked to play the piano, sure, but he had reached a time in life when a man with fingers like his coveted a better class of piano than an old Brinkerhoff upright that couldn't keep its tune for over a week. From where Annie stood, or lounged, a decent piano and a permanent spot to stand it in were still way out on the dim horizon of life's bleak ocean. A halfway decent payday was what he dearly coveted, and Madame Lai knew that as surely as she knew the sixth moon was called June by the *gwai lo.*

"Captain Dowtly. I think you like to get some money."

Annie could see out of the door. It was a low, sliding door, and it was pretty dark and misty, but he could see by the light of a lantern a man being dragged across the deck by his hair. He was naked and tied up in an old Chinese way. There was no sound. Annie's expression did not alter. "How much?" he said.

"I do not know."

Now Annie could hear bumping sounds as they dragged the man down the ladder of the forecastle hatch. Lai Choi San said, "There will be three tons, four tons, of silver bullion. Maybe other things. Many rich men make this voyage always on the *Chow Fa.* Very fine ship, the *Chow Fa.*"

"What I am asking is, how much money will you pay me? That's one. Two is, what do you want me to do? And three is, who is that man your crew are dragging around by the hair?"

"A dead man."

Meticulously he avoided looking at her,

173

but he could feel her freezing over as if in a sheath of ice. "You want talk business, Captain? Or you want to go home?"

"I want to do both, ma'am. Now, just let us be frank with each other, or at least pretend to be frank. You know that I would have to be a very dumb and uninformed person not to have heard a few rumors about the Mountain of Wealth. I always had this mountain figured as a feller, and I don't recall ever hearing the name in Chinese. So what kinda mountain are you? Aside from a beautiful mountain?" He gave her his top-of-the-line grin, for he wanted to thaw the ice.

She replied, "You are exactly correct. I am the Mountain of Wealth."

"Pleased to meet you, Mrs. Wealth."

The ice evaporated instantly. With almost girlish enthusiasm she ran it down for him. He did not interrupt. In her own inimitable way she said that the bullion alone, at fifty thousand dollars a ton, would make this the richest haul ever taken off the China Sea, by herself or by anybody else in the business. This would be by far the biggest ship ever attacked, and the fastest, and she carried a crew of over three hundred. She also carried at least twelve guards, and they were good ones. To take such a ship

174

in "the usual way," as she put it, she would need to get fifty men or more aboard her, and their arms too. The arms were the problem. This was a luxury ship, the Indo-China line was a famous international line, and their cargo- and baggage-searching routines were already thorough and becoming more so as the piracy panic increased. She was grinning ear to ear there for a few moments; it made the rapacious little woman look endearing. But she quickly reverted to facts and the hard nose, Chinese style. She stroked her forehead with her hand. "I think about this business. I think I must have a white man by my side for this great and magnificent act of robbing. And I think maybe you like to do this with me."

Annie was forced to admit that it was magnificent the way she said that. "With me" was the perfect touch; it justified all the evasiveness about how much was in it for this white man.

"You're telling me you want to go pardners with a *gwai lo?*"

"Sure," she said, very casual and open. "I do not like very much you *gwai lo*s, but you are not foreign devils like the China people say. You are white sickness. You are foreign sickness of China."

Annie refrained from comment. Smoothly she passed on to the nuts and bolts of her scheming, and at the heart of it was Annie's skills with a wireless. They were no secret, of course. He had installed one of the first private shipboard outfits in the South Pacific when he put in his three-valve Marconi in '23, and he constantly bragged about it. Now everyone was getting them, and in this part of the world the piracy scare was a boon to the wireless business, with the talk of making them compulsory on all steamships over five hundred tons. For every radio on twenty-four-hour service you needed three operators, but operators were in short supply and got paid a third engineer's wage — which they deserved, let it be said. The Morse code took some mastering, not to speak of the dexterous tip-tapping of it and the maintaining of the mysterious machines themselves with all their pernickety ways. Oddly enough, the Chinese were strongly attracted to this Western offering, and many young men were studying English for this reason alone.

Annie majestically confirmed his long experience and expertise. "I put in a new transmitter last year. An Igranic neutro-regenerative short-wave transmitter. And she's got the optional long- and medium-band transformers on her receiving end. It's a twelve-hundred-dollar setup." He didn't go into the source of all this, which was a certain Signals Company quartermaster in the good old U.S. Marine Corps on Mindanao Island. Nor did she ask.

"There are three radio operators on the *Chow Fa*," she said. "One of them will soon become very sick. I arrange so you will have this post."

"Are you gonna poison him?"

"Oh, no. He is Chinese. I am going to pay him. This way he will recommend you for the job." She beamed her somewhat premature congratulations at Annie. "After, perhaps we will poison him," she said mildly.

He hoisted himself to his feet. His chin bent to his chest and his head jammed against the ceiling, he suggested that they go out on deck for a breath of fresh Aberdeen air. Her hand described a lovely by-all-means gesture in the air, which there in the tiller room smelled strongly of kerosene.

Annie leaned on the port bulwarks and gazed at the whispering lights northward up the channel beyond the breakwater. A bunch of Madame Lai's crewmen were already tucked in for the night on mats laid out all over the foredeck, and their snores droned into the rigging and supplied a rhythmic bass to the tune of the offshore breeze, as the bagpipe's drone does for the melody of the chanter, the ivory-mouthed pipe the piper's fingers play.

She sat upon the breech of a seventy-five-millimeter Chinese Schneider with her hands interlaced across her kneecaps. The number-one amah, who could not yet have been sixteen, sat at her feet with her eyes still fixed on the vast *gwai lo* man with the pudgy little blue cap on his bristly head. The number-two amah brought out the schnapps bottle and the porcelain cup and stood in the lee of the mainmast like a stocky sentry.

Annie said, "Suppose we do not come to an agreement? Do I get poisoned too?"

She gave him a very calm look. "Oh, no. I trust you, Captain Dowtly. I trust you. We have meet, we talk about gambling, talk about dog's lifes. You wish to do business, you gamble one thousand dollar that I will trust you because to trust you is pretty damn hard. So, I trust you."

"Where did you learn to speak English?"

"In Sacred Heart College mission school of Macao. My father send me. Now he dead 'n' gone. He was not a Christian, but he velly fine man, fine Tanka man. He like his daughter — read, write, arithmetic, English language. He velly modern man. A great, great man, great Tanka man of modern China. And great robber of ships."

"Mrs. Wealth — I hope you don't mind me calling you that? It's a first-class name; your pa would have approved of it, believe me. Anyway, I want to explain something to you. The risks you take are what you're used to. Maybe you don't care about getting your neck stretched in Victoria Gaol. But mine is precious to me."

He rubbed the back of it; he was just a titch nervous and gave in to the impulse, to hell with the impression it made. To hide his shame, he raised an eyebrow at the seventy-five. "This is the twentieth century, ma'am. You heard about the *Irene* piracy, didn't you? Where a submarine intercepted her when the goddamn pirates — pardon me, please — were bringing her into Bias Bay, and shot her up and set her afire? I think it was eight of those boys got strung up after that fuckup. Well, I guess you didn't have nothing to do with that one; it sounds like it was a disorganized effort. But I got to say" — he eyed the ancient twelve-pounders farther forward —

"you got a ways to go when it comes to modernizing your methods, Mrs. Wealth. You need a wireless aboard this tub for a start. What'll she do in a full breeze? Six knots?"

"We make ten knots very easy," Mrs. Wealth replied, all beady-eyed.

"My ass. Pardon my French." Captain Doultry felt on firmer ground now, or afloat a mite less queasy at least. "You're lookin' to take a big ship with a dozen good British officers here, and you know they've been waiting and waiting for this, they're jumpy. That vessel is a very well-protected vessel." He felt the sweat under his beard now. Am I trying to raise the ante on this deal, he thought, or am I trying to scare the shit outta myself? "How the hell are you goin' to get your fifty tried-and-true assassins aboard her anyway?"

"Not fifty. Twenty. You are worth thirty men, Captain Dowtly."

He had no ready reply. She had a trick, not of deflating her opponent at the critical moment, but of inflating him. Extra wind in the sails instead of less.

She was not amused. "Captain Dowtly, you are a man of knowledge in your profession. But if you are always right in your judgings, then we have not been meeting, because you would not have been living for one half a year in a British jail." A barb in the tail of this little dart, there was: the British. He did not miss it, nor did it miss him. The fucking limeys! What a pity it is, thought Annie, for the tactics of this evil little dame that I am a man to whom revenge is an empty and meaningless word. God bless good King George! Still, to fuck him up his royal arsehole would be a deep pleasure all the same.

"I had a lot of company in that jail, lady. There was a hangin' every Saturday before the cricket match and most of those mugs were pirates." She wore a bored expression. That was good.

"The fact is I'm standing here on the deck o' your fine junk and you're asking me to do this job with you. You want to try judgin' your way out o' that one? The bottom line is the bottom line." He could see her brain like in an X-ray picture filing one or two of these bottom lines away for future use.

She stood up. He drew himself to his full height and weight and they faced off in the dark, the little amah at their feet, Mr. Chung watching specterlike from the poop deck and a surprising number of hard faces peering at their mistress and her guest

181

from various perspectives up and down the broad-beamed war junk suspended in the mist somewhere south of the eighteenth century. The dragon's ghost was present; the great beast's breath was on the water.

She said: "I can take this ship *Chow Fa* without the help of any man, white, yellow, pink, or blue. I am the mistress of sixteen war junks and a thousand brave men, and if they all fall dead in the closing of an eagle's eye there is one thousand thousand stand behind who will serve me. I will take the *Chow Fa*. I will put a hundred men with naked knives among her fine officers and I will wait behind an island and spring out like a Tiger of the Iron Sea and fire my guns into her belly. I have velly, velly number-one gunners, you will see. I will kill the guards, I will kill the passengers, and I will hang the bowels of her captain from this masthead above you. You will see, Captain Annie Dowtly." Her tone was not overvehement, but her heart was in her intentions. It wasn't a speech — it was a movie!

She turned away from Annie and called a name into the darkness. There was a scurrying of feet and a man hurried into the poop quarters and a short man naked but for a red loincloth emerged from the midship's hatch. She clapped her hands briskly and spoke harshly: she looked in an evil frame of mind. Annie lit up another Woodbine as the number-one amah disappeared like a night moth.

Two more men came up from the hatch dragging a big bundle. The prisoner was a big guy, and his hair was long and done in an old-fashioned pigtail, as all Chinese wore their hair following the law of the Manchu dynasty until its overthrow in 1911. His neck was tied to his feet at the back and his wrists too, and he had been beaten with rattan canes, as the laws of China prescribed for felons — and the British laws too, in Victoria Gaol. However, it was perhaps beyond a single beating; for the man looked like he had received a great number of strokes over a period of days. There is no point in describing the state of his back. After one glance Annie decided there was no purpose in looking at him: whatever happened, he was already a dead man. So Annie turned away and admired the lights of Aberdeen Harbor. And he noticed on the very top of Victoria Peak a new light, a red one; on the radio mast of the new wireless telegraph station, the most powerful one east of India. He decided he might ride up on the peak tramway and pay a visit and talk shop with the ex-British-navy signals sergeant who was in charge of the station.

Annie heard various sounds on the foredeck behind him, but he did not turn around. Captain Wang Ho emerged from his sleeping cabin, which was next to Madame Lai's in the poop, and it sounded like he was officiating, giving orders and so on. Most of the crew seemed to be waking up with moans and protests, but those sounds quickly changed to cheerful ones when they saw there was going to be some fun. Then abruptly Captain Wang Ho silenced them. Annie heard the sound of shallow breathing, like a sick dog's.

Then he heard Lai Choi San speaking quietly and rapidly in her language, and curiosity compelled him to turn his head.

The man was lying on his side all trussed up as Madame Lai's crew listened to what she told them. A fat man with two Lugers bound to his torso with bright flowered sashes and wearing a pair of British army ammunition boots was holding the prisoner's pigtail, keeping his face turned to his judgment. The man had lost his eyes to the imagination of his torturers, but most of his mouth was still there. He listened carefully to the words of the woman who had punished him, and who he hoped would soon release him from these unforgiving circumstances.

Lai Choi San called another name. A little wiry character with an air of importance and several knives attached to his various belts listened attentively to her instructions, then went to the prisoner, grasped his left foot, braced it against his knee, and hacked off the middle toe, which took only a few moments. Then he tried to stuff that toe in the man's mouth. The prisoner did not wish to open it, so the little guy used his knife to pry it wide and had no difficulty getting the toe in. The man objected to eating his own toe, but the little guy spoke to him. What he threatened him with was anybody's guess, but the threatened one changed his mind and tried to chew his toe. A raw toe is damned hard to eat even for a strong man; this fellow was in a bad way already, so it was even harder going.

After a minute or two of the spectacle the audience started to show signs of restiveness; and Madame Lai herself was very bored — Annie could see it in her demeanor. She spoke sharply to the little wiry guy, whose name was Ti Tsai, and he bowed formally to her, then turned to a boy standing there with a long bundle wrapped in red cloth. The boy solemnly unwrapped a sword. It was a very fine weapon in the Mukden style of the Empress Dowager's personal guards, with a curved blade of great sharpness.

The red-sashed man tugged on the hair of his prisoner, trying to haul him upright, but he kept sagging. In Cantonese Tsai said impatiently, "That'll do, that's okay," and with his sword measured his swing casually and then delivered a scythelike blow to the victim's neck that almost severed it. Bright Sash laughed and must have said "Try again, pal," for the little man, with an irritable look due to his small loss of face, did try again, with a swipe that not only finished the beheading job but came within a millimeter of eviscerating Bright Sash. There was much guffawing and merriment among the crew as Tsai held up the head and blood gouted from the expiring arteries of its owner, causing those nearby to spring away and merrily shove each other about as children do fooling with a lawn sprinkler.

Annie sat on the portside cannon where Lai Choi San had sat. He picked up his bottle from the deck and poured himself a bracer. Lai came over to join him at once with a brisk apologetic little air, as if she had been called away to the telephone and could now get down to business again.

"I am so solly," she said. "This dirty dog was once one of my men. In our talk we call him 'brother,' you understand. He do business with some Russian persons, he give informations, velly, velly fatiguing story. But result is one other brother is shot four times in opium raid. He die later. Now this one" — she nodded at the darkening pool of blood that was all that remained of him — "has been sent to next world without eyes, without one toe. He will come back in form of a blind worm. That is the belief of my men." She had the gall to giggle daintily to detach herself from such barbarous superstition. "Would you like some more tea, Captain Dowtly?"

"I don't think so," he said.

They entered now into a terminal region of negotiation the likes of which your average board chairman knows nothing.

"I am a human being," she declared with great sweetness.

His beard quivered. "You won't get mad if I get the giggles, will ya?" Yes, of course she would get mad. "Okay. Let us get back to how much. For me." He tapped his bent nose.

"I have not decided. You must think now, I must think now."

"I think we've both done all the thinking it takes, lady. If you're gonna deal, deal now, or I have a notion that my pride may part us permanently." Jesus God, what choice invention is this? he thought. A man's pride! Where did he keep this domestic creature? In his scrotum? In the sweatband of his cap, like Barney, among a multitude of other IOUs? In the tarnished metal of his mirror?

She decided to take an initiative. "Our custom is to divide what we take. This is our custom for one thousand years. But I have not thought."

"I think you have thought. I think you have some tiny little idea. I can see it deep in the depths of those scintillating eyes of yours." He paused for a piercing look at them. They had no backs, they were all shiny black-and-white surfaces. "How about fifty-fifty? Half for you, half for me?"

She laughed uproariously. The little amah smiled like a marigold, and Annie could hear a faint chuckle coming from the poop deck. He turned and looked up at Mr. Chung.

"Mr. Chung," said Annie, "you have a penchant for floating insubstantially behind me and to my right. The only person who has my permission to stand there is the black man on my boat. You got that?"

Annie turned his back on the poop deck again, but he could hear the writing master strolling over to the far rail. He has lost face, thought Annie; I'm gonna have to watch that individual. To Madame Lai, who was still smiling — she seemed to enjoy seeing Mr. Chung put in his place — Annie said: "Even steven, honeybunch. For less than half I ain't excited."

"There is a law among us," she replied. "We are wolves of the sea, and as everyone knows in the forests of Szechwan the wolves have such laws also. I am the leader; I take one-third of all that is taken. The rest is divided equally among my men; but the law says that my captains shall have sixteen shares, my sailing masters and my chief gunners seven, my *tou-mu* get four, and also my — how say *to-kung?*" She made a pulling gesture as on a tiller.

"Helmsman," said Annie.

"Yes. So . . . to you I will pay one hundred shares."

Annie could have laughed too, but he thought it more effective to knit his brows and look at his watch and murmur lightly. "Lady, I have no intention of puttin' my interests in the hands of your accountant, Mr. Chung. But as a matter of interest, what is the total number of shares likely to be?"

"Maybe two hundred men I shall use. Maybe three hundred share."

"After you take your share off the top?" Now he laughed. His high and throaty titter awoke a gunner lying a yard away in the lee of the seventy-five she'd been sitting on, and he growled like a dog. "Mrs. Wealth, this talk of ours is an example of the Chinese wasting time with their obsession for haggling. That is not modern. Also I am getting goddamn hungry. You know and I know that I will not get involved with you for less of the action than you're taking yourself. Okay? One third to you, one third to me, and the rest to the boys." Annie smiled whitely at the grumpy gunner. The young man spat and rolled back under his gun.

"I cannot give you so much. My people would not allow it." She was taking refuge in the democracy of her institutions.

Annie said, "Madame Lai, I want to go back to my boat."

"Go," she said.

She bent over the side and hollered for

the sampan man. He was still parked down there. "I am sorry, Captain. I am sorry that I will make a last offer. I give you one fiver."

"You mean a fifth? Off the top?"

"Off the top."

"Thanks, sugar plum, but the only fifths I'm interested in are the ones with schnapps in 'em." He put a leg over the rail, his foot feeling for the top rung of the ladder. "You sure are a tough cookie, Mrs. Wealth." Then he disappeared from view.

She went to the side and looked down. Annie's weight was making the ropes creak, but he was a graceful man around boats and he made his descent like an expert. He sat down on the center thwart of the sampan and looked up and waved. The old man was looking up too, waiting for the go sign.

"I'll take a quarter," said Annie. "Off the top."

"One fifth," she said.

"Goodbye, Mrs. Wealth" was his reply.

The go sign was not perceptible to Annie, but the old man got it and pushed off into the stream. Annie waved like the gentleman he pretended to be, a little wave like a queen saying goodbye to some far-flung colony, and the sampan drifted out into the stream as the old man leaned on his oar. They were a good twenty feet abaft of the junk and the darkling mist was fast obscuring both parties when Madame Lai's voice rang musically but raucously too across the current's breast:

"You like to play fan-tan for your quarter?"

There was a pause. To Madame Lai's ear the oar splashed twice, and diminishingly, and to Doultry's eye the night had swallowed the *Tiger of the Iron Sea* as he scratched his beard and murmured to the sampan man: "Why not?"

The sampan man paused in mid-stroke. His oar dripped in its wake and then he turned and sang out in his high voice the three syllables in Cantonese that mean "Why not?" Then he dipped his oar with swift strong strokes, spinning his craft around in little more than its own length.

Lai Choi San sat upon her heels on the poop deck. In the light of a storm lantern held steady by her sailing master, Captain Wang Ho, she poured from a linen bag a pile of copper cash, worn to blackness by the indomitable game. Mr. Chung, the writing master, was lighting one of his cheap Japanese cigars. Captain Doultry sat opposite Madame, his legs outstretched on the deck in a grand V, the battered toes of his brown Oxfords pointing at the shrouded stars and his back taking its ease against the mizzenmast, since he was not accustomed to sitting on decks. The mizzen's unreefed sail flapped gently, and Madame Lai picked up her captain's tin rice bowl, inverted it, and slammed it down on the cash. Some were trapped by its rim, but she shuffled the bowl for a moment as the croupiers do to include or exclude the undecided coins.

"Speak your bet, Captain."

She removed her hand. Annie eyed the bowl and meditated on its secret. A cockroach marched into the circle of light, circumnavigated the field of conflict, and exited stage right.

"I'll go for Kwok on one and four."

Madame Lai took one coin from those remaining and placed it to the left and likewise three more to her right. That is the way they tallied bets in the fan-tan played in the temple yards and street corners of Macao. "I win," she said, "with two or three." Then without further delay she lifted the bowl.

Not many cash seemed to have been covered. She extended her immaculate forefinger to commence the count, but her opponent made a little clacking sound with his tongue and offered her a yellow Venus pencil stub unearthed from his shirt pocket. She accepted this without comment. With its blunt point she separated the cash into the required twin lines and rapidly began the count: four, and four, and four, and four, and so forth.

There were precisely fourteen cash remaining when Mr. Chung coughed delicately and Annie's eye came to the conclusion that he had lost. Then there were ten. Then six, and he knew it for sure. He tapped the side of his nose. Her pencil wand removed four more.

"Ah. You have win!" She looked up with a solemn face. On the desk before her lay one coin.

Mr. Chung stooped involuntarily and peered at it. There was no doubt that this shrewd accountant had also observed fourteen coins, and ten, and six. But he said not a word as Madame Lai picked up the solitary cash and dropped it between Annie's legs. It rolled up to his crotch and nestled there, not even falling over.

"You get one quarter of business, Captain Annie Dowtly," she said lightly. "But I keep pencil."

chapter 5
The Hall of Righteous Heroes

As he rode back to *The Sea Change* in the sampan, a warm and diaphanous drizzle began to fall, and Annie reflected on the business of the six fan-tan cash that should have become two but became one. She must have palmed one of them, and it was remarkably skillfully done. But the motives that decided her to let him win were equally intriguing. Possibly if he had been winning she would have cheated too, and ensured her own victory, not for greed's sake but simply to reverse fate, irrespective of whether it favored her or her adversary: to stand the *gwai lo*'s fortune on its head, to show who was boss. The will of Lai Choi San, not the laws of arbitrary chance, may have been the urge that swayed the woman.

Another possibility was that Madame Lai just wished to make the *gwai lo* captain feel pleased with himself. How much this decision, or whim, would cost her in cold cash would not be known for a few weeks yet — but she was determined to have him.

Back on his boat Annie found Barney lying in a state of grace on the quarterdeck, blowing up condoms like pearly balloons. Three of them floated from Annie's flagstaff, bobbing in the warm drizzly breeze, and a fat brown girl sat on the helmsman's seat admiring them. Annie retired to his bunk without discussing the night's events with his first mate, who was far too blasted to have followed them anyway.

The next day, which was Thursday, they loaded up with twenty-six tons of fireworks manufactured by Lin Huang Chang and Son, Aberdeen, and set sail for Canton just before sundown. They reached Whampoa docks the following morning and discharged their cargo, and Annie visited the offices of Crawford and Perry, his agents, to see what was cooking. The year-long boycott of British shipping organized by the Communist unions in Canton had fizzled out the way these protests always did in China. Too many people were losing too much money to keep their political consciences well fed, and since the Reds had been divorced by the Nationalists there had been nothing but the hook of patriotic pride to hang the boycott's hat on. The Chinese were patriotic in a deep and mystical way, but not in a day-to-day business way.

Still and all, vessels carrying other foreign flags like *The Sea Change*'s weather-worn Stars and Stripes were in a favored situation. There was a choice of cargo and destination, mostly silks destined for Singapore and Indo China. But Annie hemmed and hawed and settled for a small load of cooking utensils and similar hardware meant for Macao, only a sixty-mile trip. Barney screamed and howled, since the money was peanuts — how could a man turn down good long hauls in mild weather when the business was there for the taking? All Annie deigned to tell him was that he had an important date in Macao on Monday evening, a business appointment with a "big" before the "business." Then he abandoned Barney and went into Canton to have a chat with a person connected with the retail arms trade. The deal with Madame Lai was as yet a mirage on the horizon of Annie's mind; it could very well prove to be a nightmare from which he might want to wake at a moment's notice. So Annie soberly made the necessary inquiries about alternatives: not silks and fireworks and electric fans, but the stuff with the big profit margins — machine guns and spare parts for Chiang Kai-shek's battery of American-built twelve-pounder mountain guns, of which parts Annie happened to know a sizeable stockpile existed in the Philippine constabulary's armory just outside Manila.

Ah, Manila! That beautiful apology for a city holds a permanent concession in the wide domain of my stars, thought Annie. But why? Why Manila, Manila all the time, past and future, coming and going, when Manila was the last place he ever wanted to see again in this lifetime?!

On Sunday evening they docked in Macao's modest harbor, and on Monday after lunch Annie visited the Yung Chung fan-tan house once again. Mr. Chung was there, chatting with the manager, to whom he was related, and greeted Annie most warmly. He was wearing an English straw boater and a navy-blue blazer with brass buttons and very wide gabardine pants of the most delicate beige, breaking voluptuously over black patent-leather pumps with little purple bows on them. Annie was wearing his second-best silk shirt with its strange assortment of buttons and a pair of baggy, tiny-checked French chef's pants he had acquired in Seoul and which he knew suited him to a T. He had trimmed his beard and dusted off his cap. He did not bother to pack his Walther; the weather was too warm.

Macao is an island only four miles wide. They rode together in a horse-drawn buggy along the Praia Grande, the seashore drive; past the governor's palazzo; past the Ma Kok Miu, the temple of A-Ma, the sea goddess, after which Macao was named; past the old Barra Fortress and the great floating fan-tan casino called the Sun Tais; and up a little alley between high walls.

There was a gate in the wall with a bell pull. An eye looked through an iron shutter, and then the gate was opened by a man who wore odd black boots and had difficulty walking, though he was not old. He bowed to Mr. Chung. As the writing master conducted Annie through the garden to the house he said cheerfully, "This man a velly number-one gunner. But he shot up in fight, he lose he feet. Madame Lai look after her people. She fix up him, makee him special boots from Jobson's, Queens Road, Hong Kong."

The garden was exquisite in the fashion

of old Chinese gardens, with rocks and trees of archaic shapes. They crossed a pool of lotuses by way of a humped bridge and reached a small house half-hidden by the vegetation. The corners of its eaves curled upward, its gutters issuing from the mouths of green bronze dragons.

She was wearing a pale violet robe this time. It was traditional in style, like the white one, but more frivolous, embroidered with a labyrinth of flowers. They looked like jasmine, like hyacinths. It was high-necked, and beneath it she wore white pantaloons. She was not the kind of woman who would have been seen dead in a cheongsam. This afternoon her jewelry was all jade of a deep blue-green color, save for a sapphire in one of her rings as big as a wren's egg. The sapphire was cut in such a way that it did not sparkle but glowed. She walked with him by the pool. The trees shaded them, it was not particularly hot; but she used her fan constantly.

"This is a very nice garden," Annie told her.

"I do not bring to my house people for doing business."

Annie told her in an elaborate way how honored he was.

For business, she said, she used the apartments in a house next to the Yeng Chung Gambling Company, of which she owned a piece. She had plenty of connections in Macao. She said her father had had a kind of official title; he was an Honorable Protector of the Fisheries or some such thing. It sounded like a proper gangster-style title.

Her house was very fine. It was a traditional Chinese house in that it was really an arrangement of pavilions with little courts and the garden all around it; but it had Macanese touches: it was several different colors, though predominantly rose-tinted, and the windows were uninhibitedly Mediterranean, with much expensive glass in them. Inside, stuffed Portuguese furniture mingled with the rosewood and black lacquer, the divans and the screens and the porcelain; and grandiose portrait photographs of rich-looking relatives were proudly hung beside the great silken waves that soared in the paintings of the sea that the family taste seemed to favor.

There was a library with many books. Madame Lai waved at it and said, "This is a room of poems." It seemed unlikely to Annie that she had read them, but she was a creature of contrasts. He heard the voices of children, but he was not permitted to see them. He asked her politely if she had sons or daughters; she said, "We gonna do like *gwai lo*s. First we make business, then we will speak about other things."

There was a bower in the garden of white stone between two willow trees, and in it was a birdcage with a large gray bird. She fed the bird pieces of coconut. "There is one more thing, Captain Doultry. You understand how we people, the people of the Yellow Banner, how our hearts feel about ones who betray their brothers — people who betray their own people. You must think very careful about this."

Annie had been waiting for this ever since the big pigtailed man's middle toe had been offered him as his last meal. He reflected that the guy had probably been kept alive a day or two longer expressly to make this point on a prospective *gwai lo* business partner.

"I think I'm pretty damn careful about plenty of things, Mrs. Wealth," he replied, looking the fat bird in its purple eye. "But I don't bother to think about betrayal. It is not in my nature." If she bought that one, she would buy anything.

She looked at him sideways. "You are a white man. Man of white race. Are not you betraying all this?" A wave here. "This sea of whiteness?"

Annie permitted himself a chuckle. Helping himself to some of the bird's coconut bits from Madame's little basket, he said, "There's only one race a guy can betray, and it's the two-legged one. I don't count baboons. By my lights most of this race is lousy no matter how you color it. But I don't think I've ever betrayed it out-and-out. I don't believe so." She said nothing. "You ought to know, honey," he added a mite testily, "what I've been doing — you've had your stooges following me around ever since I got out of the pokey."

The gray bird opened its burnished beak and made a raucous sound. "It is best," said Madame Lai, "if you become one of us."

"Best for you? Or best for me?"

"It is best."

The organization was called the Hall of Righteous Heroes of the Yellow Banner. It was a sort of triad society or tong, and it was connected with or descended from the Hall of Heaven and Earth, which was founded by Chang Pao, who was the adopted son of Madame Cheng I and also her lover. Madame Cheng I was the wife of

Cheng I Sao, called the Emperor of the Seas. He was a pirate.

At the summit of his power it was said that Cheng I Sao commanded seven thousand war junks. He thought seriously of attempting to overthrow the Dragon Emperor, Chia Ch'ing. In the West, Napoleon Bonaparte had crowned himself emperor of France, and in the middle Nicholas I was the emperor of Russia.

Anyway, as Lai Choi San, the Mountain of Wealth, told the story to Annie, Cheng I Sao's principal fortress was on the island of Lantau, which is next to Hong Kong. In a war with some other pirates from Hainan, the Emperor of the Seas captured the boy — he was fifteen — and became enamored of him. Not only did the boy become Cheng I Sao's most beloved lover, he had also adopted him as his son, naming him Chang Pao.

Cheng I Sao was killed in battle. To honor him and no doubt to please herself, his widow had in turn taken Chang Pao as her lover. He was twenty-four, and already the leader of the Red Squadron. Madame Cheng I had succeeded her husband as Empress of the Seas, and she and her young and beautiful lover had extended the power of the Hall of Heaven and Earth over all the seas of China.

"Chang Pao is my ancestor," she said.

They were in her house, taking tea and eating puff cookies exactly like those sold in the alley next to Stoffer's Bar and Grill. It was hardly a coincidence: Madame Lai was thorough, and Mr. Chung had spies everywhere.

She made one of her waves, up toward the yellow sky; it was nearly seven o'clock. "The father of the father of the father of my father was Chang Pao. He became the husband of Madame Cheng I but he had many lovers. He was a Tanka person. I will show you his tablet one day. Chang Pao was my most honorable ancestor." She passed Annie the cookie plate and he availed himself of another. "However, he did not live very long. Madame Cheng I became tired of him. He was in his bed with a woman and ate some little cakes. Chang Pao died from the poison in them. It took several days to destroy him, and even the most powerful opium could not put out the fires that burned him from inside so that his flesh became black and fell off from his bones."

Some family, thought Annie. Shaking his head sympathetically, he helped himself to another puff cookie.

"You will become one of our brothers," she said. It was not a request.

"Does that mean I have to call you 'sister'?"

"No," she said. "But I will also be your brother."

Annie did not go for mystical stuff. He had been around shamans in Mindanao and voodoo personages in Haiti and never had anything but grief from these associations. He yawned and picked up the bronze mirror she had given him to play with because he had told her he was interested in mirrors. He looked at his dim and shimmering reflection and adjusted a curl of his beard.

"Madame Lai," he said wearily. "You're pulling my leg. I never met a Chinese in my life who considered a white man anything more than what you might find behind a pig."

"Never mind," she said with a tetchy wave. "Not important. This is business. You will make very serious swearing of blood. This is same as *gwai lo*s signing paper. But more final."

"In that case, I'll be happy to sign, sweetheart. I'll go through all the hoops, but I'm sure you're wise to the fact that the only swearing that counts is swearing on our very serious old-fashioned greed. I trust your greed, and you can trust mine." He raised his teacup to her gallantly.

She was not taken with his light approach; this was obvious from her smile, which showed all her teeth. "I am not greedy, Captain. I trust swearing. We say: to break the Law of the Hall is death; and to follow the Law of the Hall is death. I trust those words."

Annie nodded seriously. He did not feel it was the time to question the attractions of such a proposition. The Chinese often tended to be frivolous about death.

The mirror was a bronze disc eight inches in diameter, with its face polished and refracting the color of a sea the instant before dawn. In the center of its back, which bore an obscure greenish patina, was a round knob with which to hold it, and around the rim were the twelve signs of the Chinese zodiac, which also corresponded to the points of their compasses. Around the knob prowled the Animals of the Four Quarters: to the north, a black tortoise, around whose body was coiled a snake, and which was called the Dark Warrior; to the east, a green dragon; to the south, a scarlet bird; and to the west, a white tiger.

Annie liked the mirror. He liked its weight, and the way it reflected everything as if in the shadow of its own years of elapsed time. It reflected his face with the most perceptive insight. Lai Choi San told him the thing was made in the Han dynasty, "before the birth of your Christ."

Barney knew something was up, and it was something to do with the Chinese woman; and Annie decided that was all he was going to know. Barney would have gotten scared, he would have made a terrible fuss, he would have had no faith in the outcome. Barney had seen Annie's schemes come to grief any number of times; and all he wanted was a quiet life, the pride of being first mate on such a fine, prideful vessel, the satisfaction of bossing the various boys, the security of feeling Annie could afford to get him a new set of false teeth if and when necessary and a little Edward Lear now and then. He wanted to trust Annie and to look forward to an indefinitely protracted old age beside a fireside of dignified reminiscence, with a good piano in the front parlor.

But Annie made these modest plans seem speculative to say the least. Annie was crazy. The crazier a scheme was, the more likely Annie was to be attracted to it. A man of fifty-one!

No wonder Barney was losing his hair.

They were moored to a ramshackle quay alongside where the Hong Kong ferry berthed, dining tête-à-tête on deck, for it was a fine evening. The old man had cooked up some fish and shrimps and rice Tahitian style, the icebox was full of Tsingtao, and a bottle of excellent Portuguee rosé wine was on the small folding table spread with a red-and-white check cloth. A domestic scene. Annie tasted the wine, filled Barney's glass, and laid five hundred dollars in crisp Hong Kong bills beside Barney's plate. He said: "That there's a little something on the wages, son. I'm gonna be leavin' you for a while to your own devices. Here's a letter giving this vessel into your charge until I come back. Stay clear of the clap, and remember, sixty-weight oil, not eighty, okay?"

"Shit," said Barney. "Where'd you git that dough?"

"I got a little front money. On some personal business." This was true. He had collected that thousand clams' worth of gold sovereigns from Mr. Chung again. As Annie now carefully explained to Barney, this money was a legitimate binder on a business deal, not a bribe, or a tip more like, which in the Chinese view of things put a person in a position of subservience, or of obligation. "You gotta wise up on Chinese psychology, Barney. You got to understand the ins and outs of my moves, boy."

Instead of applauding, Barney just had a bunch of dumb inquisitive questions. Annie responded to these with mild disgust and facetious or insulting answers, and Barney gave up quickly. He assuaged the feeling of loneliness and yawning insecurity that opened before him with passionate, whining pleas for more money: the main hold pump needed a new diaphragm, the boys needed a few bucks, Sock's sister was getting married in Singapore and a silver bracelet had to be mailed, and so on. Annie came up with another fifty; he had it already folded in his pocket. He told Barney to stick to silk and maybe prime tea to the Straits Settlements, direct to the small ports that the steamers didn't serve. No fuckin' opium, or it would be divorce.

"An' no fuckin' guns neither," said Barney. "And you land yo'self in the slammer again, Annie, I am sailin' dis mudderfuckin' boat o' mine straight back home direct to New Orlins an' up dat bayou. You ain't never gonna lay eyes on me or her ever again, mudderfucker."

"Barney," said Annie, "don't you go worrying your head. I'm tired of getting bad grades at school. I'm tired o' standin' up in the corner, and I sure as hell never want to see the insides of a jail again. I'm tired of gamblin'. I got a lot of other things to think about."

A glimmer of light appeared on Barney's horizon. "Annie, dose words gladden my fuckin' heart. Why don't we take dat run on down to Bombay? Wid dat load a linens? Dem piece goods dat keep her light in de water? An' she fly? She fly like a flyin' fish, Cap. De wind still blowin' dat way, dose nor'easters gon' ketch her upside her quarter an' we gonna make two hundred mile a day cross dat Injun sea, Cap." His eyes swam; he filled his mug to the brim with that primrose wine. Annie always got called Cap when Barney's heart sang a song of the sea. "Dere ain't no gamble to dat, Annie. Dis de first time in a year dat I hear you talkin' sense."

Annie gave him a soulful look. "Yeah. I'm tired, Barney. I don't know. I'm just tired of taking big risks for short money."

"Annie, we gettin' too old for dat shit. We gonna clear an easy thousand bucks inside of a month wid dose piece goods, an' we gonna run back to Rangoon wid a load o' chutney or sumpin' nice an' easy. An' stay in dat part o' de world a while, where we got some respeck. De world west o' Singapore."

Annie didn't say anything. Sometimes Barney touched him in a soft place. It was true, the people westward of the China Seas were a lot nicer to Barney than the Chinese were. The Chinese didn't understand black people, or like them one bit.

There were wide regions and long voyages that Anatole Doultry and Bernardo Patrick Hudson could keep company upon with hardly the need to speak a word to each other, save for the occasional argument over the merits of Bix or Louis as trumpet players.

Annie got ahold of himself. "A thousand dollars?" He studied the bruise on his left middle finger's knuckle, flexing it to remind himself of what Fred Olson had suffered for that paltry sum. "Barney, that wouldn't keep me in chewin' tobacco."

"Since when did you chew tobacco, mudderfucker?"

"I'd go squirrely, chum. Going back to the trading life. You go on and run that cargo o' sheets and drapes down to Bombay, and you make goddamn sure you keep 'em dry. I'll fix it up with the agents. But you better get back here 'fore the end of May, boy. You better."

"Where you goin', mudderfucker? Where you gonna go?"

"I don't know yet."

The one tidbit that Annie did let on about was that he might visit Tientsin. This was untrue, of course. But Annie knew that Barney knew that Marshal Sun Chuan-fang was reputedly holed up there (Tientsin was up near Peking, five days by steamer up the coast) making some new deals, fitting out a division of refugee White Russian troops and probably talking to the Japanese about this and that. So when Barney got wind (as he surely would sooner or later) of the fact that Annie had shipped out with a wireless operator's ticket on the SS *Chow Fa*, he would put it down to another fucked-up arms deal out of the Philippines and Annie trying to save face. Give Barney something to work out and he would work it out according to Annie's known proclivities. Barney would feel a cunning satisfaction and hopefully not go hunting for other motives, stirring up Chinese mud with his big feet en route.

While they were on a second bottle of

213

the wine, Annie leaned across the white table to Barney, who had gotten all lachrymose and nostalgic, and said: "Barney, there's one important thing I want you to do. Are you payin' attention, darlin'?"

Barney's jaw, the edges of which were sharp-angled like some axe-hewn carving of African timber, was resting on his knotted hand and his moist eyes were staring at the thunderous rays of the Guia lighthouse as they swung balefully above their heads and echoed off the steely clouds lurking around the horizon.

"I should of married dat chile in Samoa," said Barney, "Sara Bamey. She was sweet as butter. She was tender. Her skin was tender like a baby's butt. It shined beautiful. Her breath smell like Carnation milk. Dat's how tender she was."

Annie allowed a suitable pause. Then he said, "It's only one thing, but it's a number of times, Barney. I'm gonna rely on you." He patted Barney's other hand, limp on the table. "I'm gonna rely on you checkin' on the radio there with the Hong Kong wireless telegraph office regular every day at around this time, and see if I've left a message for ya. And I'm countin' on you to be within a day's sail o' Hong Kong first week o' June. 'Cause early June you gonna

214

meet me somewheres in this neck o' the woods. I'm gonna count on that. I'm gonna bet my life on it, Bernardo. This is a bet that's gonna pay me some pretty long odds, so don't let me down or I'll come lookin' for you with a machine gun, pal."

"*Yo'* life? *Yo'* mudderfuckin' life? What de fuck dat worth, man? Yo' life ain't worth a plugged nickel. Dat dere bet, it better pay dose long, long odds, my man, or we ain't never gonna squeeze us no juice outta dis Chinaman setup till de cows come home."

The following evening Annie was picked up from the quay in front of the Ma Kok Miu, the temple of A-Ma, the sea goddess, and taken out to the *Tiger of the Iron Sea*, which was anchored way out offshore from the firecracker factory. He carried his medium-size suitcase and a couple of blankets rolled up in an oilskin bag and his black slicker over his arm.

There was a lot of activity aboard the junk. Half a dozen sampans were tethered to her, and supplies were being stowed. As Annie stepped aboard, a cradle was being winched over the side carrying several familiar-shaped metal boxes, which his connoisseur's eye identified at once as seventy-five-millimeter ammunition for the Schneider cannon. The boxes even carried the familiar stencils of the Chinese arsenal at Foochow. A sound, or commingling of sounds, approached across the fading water, accompanying a sampan carrying splendiferous lanterns and a priest from the temple of A-Ma. A number of his assistants were letting off firecrackers and sounding the sonorous gong that announced an avatar of the goddess. The priest (who was called a *hsiang-ku,* because he was a servant of the sea goddess) was robed in yellow and wore a pointy hat and sat facing an effigy of A-Ma, or as the Tankas called her, Tin Hau: the goddess of the sea and of fishermen, too, for it was that particular function of hers that they worshipped and to which they paid their dues. It was the junk's own effigy of this lady that was being returned to her shrine aboard the vessel after spending a day of ceremony and prayer at the temple (a day that cost Madame Lai top dollar, but that was to be expected). The box that sheltered Tin Hau was about two feet high and covered with red drapes that blew in the breeze that blew to Annie's nostrils the perfume of her approach, for pounds of incense and joss sticks were being burned aboard the ceremonial sampan, as befitted the departure upon an ocean voyage of a great vessel like *Tiger of the Iron Sea.*

She wore the Yellow Banner at her masthead. It was a vast sheet of old gold silk with black dragons at its pennant points, and a number of scars from shot and shell that had been lovingly repaired by the women of the men who sailed her: their Righteous Heroes.*

The voice of the gong echoed across Macao with the fall of night, and thence to the Lappa Hills, which brooded above the city. The box containing Tin Hau was carried up into the junk and put back in her shrine in the tiller room. Annie glimpsed her face; she was made of pear wood and sat there like a goddess should, wearing a quiet smile and a perceptive expression. The monk beating the gong followed her and more incense was burned and Annie's balls contracted a fraction as deafening

---

*Now these women, wives of all statuses, concubines and sing-song girls, were leaving her. In port there were always visiting women; but unlike many owners of war junks and traders, and all the fishing fleet, Lai Choi San allowed no women to voyage on her fleet save the sailing master's, and of course her own servants.

volleys of firecrackers exploded on the temple sampan just a few feet away from another boat loaded to the gunwales with gunpowder and small-arms ammunition.

It was at the climax of these proceedings that Madame Lai appeared from her cabin. She looked serene, lofty and detached. Two or three of the junior monks, ragged as beggars, chanted a song of great peculiarity, but similar loftiness, as Madame Lai lighted a single joss stick — no doubt a high-quality one — and put it in the square bronze cup of the shrine. Inaudibly she murmured her own prayer. Then she laid some jasmine blooms beside the cup.

The new moon rose to the southeast as the *Iron Tiger* (which is what her men called her) lifted anchor and was towed out of the anchorage by a boatload of sailors singing a song of their own, the inevitable gong announcing each stroke of their black oars. Then in a freshening southwest breeze Annie watched her sails climb. They were gold in color, made of a fine canvas of cotton and jute, but it was a somber, muddy gold that did not compete with that of her banner. To hoist the mainsail they used a windlass with four men on it, for the battens of these big lug sails (six

218

a sail in Kuantung vessels) were of massive lashed bamboo fifty feet long.

Madame Lai did not reappear from her cabin. Annie leaned on the poop taffrail, paying close attention to the working of the ship ("boat" did not seem an adequate word, he had to admit that). There was a lot of casual talking and joking among her seamen that would have appalled the master of a Western vessel, but they were such experienced men that their efficiency was not impaired. Pools of gold light swung across her decks from the lanterns hung on her masts. These decks were dark with tung oil and were caulked with that white caulking of remarkable strength and elasticity that the Tankas called *chunan.*

A couple of miles south of Macao, Captain Wang Ho went about into the wind on a southeast heading. The moon and the light upon the sea were of an extraordinary greenish color, and in this dizzying light Annie now saw a wonderful sight. Heading straight out toward them from round the lee shore of Macao came a canoe paddled by forty men. She was a *dragon boat,* a war canoe near sixty feet long. Annie had seen one of them being careened on some island and remembered how he could see his face in her upturned bottom, so polished and smooth was its surface.

The canoe must have been making a good fifteen knots, plowing through the choppy seas like a beaked serpent, the waters arcing from her stem in a luminous spume. The power and rhythm of her paddlers reminded Annie of the Polynesian crews who always made a man stand and watch with awe as they raced back from the fishing grounds, dividing great seas with their art and their courage.

Captain Wang Ho trained his big night glasses on the canoe, Bausch and Lombs they were, and suspiciously like those favored by heavyweight masters in the British merchant marine. A moment later the junk hove to and waited for the message, for it was a message that the canoe was bringing to her.

She invited Annie into her cabin.

It lay aft of the tiller room behind one of the sliding doors of red-lacquered camphor wood. It was small, but most lavishly decorated with carvings of wood, and had two brass lanterns that gloomed through a haze of sandalwood incense and tobacco smoke from Madame's little silver water pipe. The owner's bunk took up most of the space; it was a remarkably comfortable-looking bunk, more of a divan in fact. Junk bunks tended to be narrow and Spartan, but Madame Lai was no ordinary *lao-pan* (as an owner of ships was called). She sat cross-legged on this bunk; the young amah was asleep on the floor. There was a large brass-bound chest against the aft bulkhead, below the shuttered poop windows, which gave onto a stern walk reached by another sliding door, just as in a seventeenth-century European man-o'-war.

Madame Lai said, "Sit down, please." Annie sat on the sea chest. The cabin was not much over five feet from deck to ceiling. She said, "The British navy blow up my house this morning. My house in village of Hai Chan. In Bias Bay."

She looked extremely annoyed. It was understandable. Annie wondered if he should maybe remind her he was an American. She said: "I have plenty houses. But these British very bad people. They send two cruisers, this airplane ship, blow up many, many houses of fishing people. Fifty junks, all blow up. They look for pirates, but all they find is poor women, children, old men. And they have not ask okay of Chinese government. Dirty British pigs."

"What Chinese government?"

221

She ignored the question. She was mad at the British. "I hate this name Britain," she muttered, lighting her pipe with vengeful puffs. "In the time of my ancestors, the British bring opium to China. Very cheap opium. Chinese always weak for opium, always the emperor fight bad peoples to stop growing of the yellow poppies. But British ships too strong, Chinese people too . . ." She made a crazed, vague gesture. "Opium destroy China."

"I thought you admired strong people," said Annie, eyebrows raised.

"I hate this name Britain. I spit poison on this name."

In Macao, Madame lived a few streets away from the official Portuguese-government opium factory that exported annually millions of dollars' worth of refined opium to "licensed" Chinese dealers. What happened to the stuff after that was not Macao's business. The Germans had assiduously created a vast market for up-to-date morphia and heroin, and the Japanese had set up a heroin factory in their concession at Tientsin. But Madame Lai was not in a mood to listen to apologies for the British.

Annie personally had no use for opium. Viewed dispassionately, it had obviously devastated the crumbling civilization of

China that most of its educated citizens had become collectively hooked on an anesthetic and hypnotic drug. But they desired this drug. Perhaps a great collective pain, or despair, had provoked this appetite. Anyway, the limeys had gratified it, ably assisted by the Yankees.* Business was business. Great Britain was the first nation to make pushing dope a national industry, but not the last.

Annie asked her what she knew of the Bias Bay raid. Very little, as yet; simply that the British government was fed up with the pillage of their ships and was prepared to raid Chinese territory if necessary to make a show of their indignation. They had evacuated the inhabitants before destroying their homes; they were careful not to

*In fact the first non-Indian opium shipped to China was Turkish, back in 1809, in the Yankee brig *Sylph*. But the American Civil War had interrupted American efforts to secure a piece of the Chinese market. However, American traders — the *hwa-ke,* or "Flowery Flag Devils" — hung on to a piece of the action, as did the Portuguese *se-yang kwae* (or "Devils of the Western Ocean"). Samuel Russell & Co., from Connecticut, ran a major opium business in Canton, from 1816 onwards.

hurt anybody. A rather pretty little house of hers occupied by poor relatives had been blown up. It was merely an irritation. Aircraft carriers sent against fishing villages and the burning down of these villages and the destruction of their fishing vessels might have a symbolic effect, but not a practical one.

However, the raid was not a good omen upon this day of launching a piratical enterprise that would dwarf all that went before. She did not say this in so many words, but Annie knew it was in her mind. There were a bunch of joss sticks fuming away in front of the little shrine in the cabin wall with its minuscule red lamp. In the shrine were two funerary tablets of black wood; one very old, one not so old. They were the earthly symbols of Chang Pao and her father.

But then, who cared about omens? Annie did not believe in them. He told her he was very tired and wanted to take a nap. He left her smoking her pipe fiercely and chewing out the little amah because her tea was cold.

Under a green moon she sailed.

Captain Wang Ho's heading was east by south, making for Lantau Island, as Madame had been good enough to inform him without elaborating. Her mood was so poisonous that Annie had not pressed her for details.

Annie was impressed by the way the vessel beat to windward, just a few points off the wind on each tack, coming around neat and easy without wallowing. Western sailing men always talked about clumsy junks, but Annie, who had watched them carefully, had never seen anything clumsy about their sailing manners. They only looked clumsy when they were riding at anchor. The Chinese style of rig had been ingeniously developed over many centuries of coastal sailing on seas notorious for their erratic winds, their treacherous shoals, and their devastating typhoons. A junk's sails sacrificed some efficiency in light air to their great strength and handiness when conditions were tough. So too with the model of their hulls: sea-worthiness took precedence over speed. A flat-bottom New England scow was their closest Western relative, but the Chinese innovation of the huge retractable rudder and a mizzen sail that the helmsman used like a sort of airplane fin were most sophisticated solutions to nautical problems. Another thing that impressed the seaman in Annie was the rigorous structural design of the hull, divided as it was into four or more totally watertight compartments by heavyweight hold bulkheads. It took a hell of a lot of hull damage to sink a junk. It was odd that in the West nobody had seriously adopted this system until ironclad battleships were developed.

Captain Wang was not communicative. Neither he nor his helmsman, a formidable and intolerant-looking character, seemed inclined to look directly at the *gwai lo,* which was okay with Annie. He was given the run of the poop and the tiller room but was politely discouraged by Madame's number-two amah, who seemed to be following him about to keep an eye on him, from going forward of these areas or belowdecks.

It began to rain and a spring squall abruptly blew up, the wind veering and blowing hard onshore up the West River delta. Captain Wang donned an Imperial Japanese Navy oilskin; he seemed to favor the international look. Annie watched him deal with the blow (it must have been about force six or seven) in a most casual way. They dropped the mainsail in a jiffy; the way its battens accordioned allowed for a swift, practical shortening of canvas.

Madame Lai did not appear again. The seas were choppy and the wind gusty, but the junk rolled very little and stayed pretty dry. After a couple of hours Lantau Island loomed out of the lunar haze dead ahead. The squall had blown itself out by the time Captain Wang slid his vessel into the lee of an islet off the big island's north coast called Chep Lak Kok. The cliffs dropped sheer into the frothing seas, and on the north point the tiered roofs of a Trappist monastery were symmetrical against the moon.

Annie had never bothered to make a landfall on the north coast of Lantau. The island was sparsely populated with fisherfolk despite its size, and inland among the hills there were villages that had never seen a white man. The place was a legendary hangout for pirates before the British came, and still a well-known refuge for fugitives from Hong Kong law. Annie remembered Madame's story about her honorable ancestor Chang Pao. The ruins of his fortress still stood at Tung Chung on the main island. As the junk dropped anchor in the little bay west of the monastery, Annie concluded that tradition was still strong in these regions.

It was a little after midnight. Some lights

were bobbing in the bay on shrimp boats, but the village called Cheung Sha Lan that straggled down to the gray sands seemed dark as any pirate's lair, though it was only twenty-odd miles to Hong Kong, as the sea eagle flies.

It was still raining and Annie was wearing his old sou'wester as Captain Wang and his number-one officer led their guest up the muddy lane that was the main street. Even the pigs and chickens were asleep. They passed small shuttered shops and a place where opium smells came with dim light from a doorway, passed a diminutive but well-kept temple, and arrived at a house with stone walls and a gate with firing slots in it. There was a yard with a sleeping bullock and the alluring perfume of a kitchen that reminded Annie that a bite of supper would be appropriate.

They left him in a small room with a brick floor, sparsely furnished. A girl who would not look at him brought him a bottle of warm rice wine and an elegant cup. The girl was dressed like a peasant. Then she left him, too.

A short time later, as Annie was getting adjusted to the wine, Lai Choi San came in without knocking, followed by her strong-looking number-two amah. Annie was putting his legs up on the divan and trying to make himself comfortable with a couple of rather hard cushions. He made a polite motion to rise but she stopped him and sat down on the chair. Her sleek head was wet from the rain and she was wearing her black cotton seagoing outfit and a pleasant, almost compassionate expression.

"How about a little chow?" said Annie.

She shook her head. "You cannot eat. A man cannot eat before he is given the ring of the Hall. You drink wine, wine very good for the heart." She patted hers. "But no eat. You must forget your stomach." If this was a joke, she gave no sign of it.

Annie complained vociferously. He said he'd thought about it and saw no sense in joining up with this Hall of Righteous Heroes. "I'm not one of you. And I don't want to be. We can do some business, but why do I have to join the club? This is a one-off deal, honey. I'm not going through with it."

"You will," she replied mildly. "You will. Because you want money, a great pile of money. Also you must, because my people expect it. They will not accept you otherwise."

"I will not."

"You will." She said it so quietly.

He drank his rice wine. She did not join him; she just sat there reflectively, observing his face from time to time. Annie remained silent and gave the appearance of relaxation, though he was not relaxed at all.

"I'm starvin'. I want a bite to eat, and then I want to get some shut-eye. Tomorrow we got a lot of plottin' and plannin' to do."

"You are not starving. You eat when bored, or uneasy."

She was looking at him with a contemptuous and narrow look, her head back, her chin up. "You do not know about starving. Your children have never starved, your children have never eaten mud to fill their bellies, all swelled up." Her hands described the belly of such a child. "I am a rich woman now, but I have been poor. In the time of the great famine I have seen my father kill a farmer and both his wives so that his own family can eat. From another man my father take away one small boy, two girls, he ask thirty dollar to send back children. One child, ten dollar. The farmer no pay. My father cut off one finger of this boy, six year old, send to this farmer. The farmer pay ten dollar, say he sell his last pig. Say, keep these daughters, O Pirate, they my gift to you. If I take them back, I will have to sell them so that my son can live."

She stopped. Annie waited. The interesting part of the story was just coming up, he assumed. But she did not continue. "There have always been people starving in China," said Annie. "Way before the White Devils came."

"True. But they starved with a small pride. They were betrayed by their emperors and the rich fat ones: betrayed by Chinese, not by foreign devils."

She was getting into one of her emotional states — one of her xenophobic states. Perhaps it was just the blowing-up of her "unimportant" house in Bias Bay, but Annie had now witnessed the widening of her broadsides to include all foreigners. Annie felt expendable, to put it mildly. Madame Lai, despite her admiration of modern China, was as trapped by hatred for the rest of the inhabited globe as any feudal Chinese aristocrat. She believed that the outside world had destroyed China, by conspiracy or accident. In a number of ways she was quite correct. But the fact that China had aided, if not willed, this destruction was one she could not admit.

"You're wasting your time, hating the foreigners," said Annie pleasantly. "Since when have strong nations had pity on the weak? The white nations are tough and greedy people. And they're organized. China is not organized. China is full of tough and greedy sonsofbitches but they're all out to save their own asses and fuck the next Chinaman. You got to gang up, girl. You got to find something to believe in. You are the most cynical and hoity-toity people on the face of this earth, bar none."

Strong words, but undeniable. What could she say? "There is no one in this enormous country of yours who cannot be bought," said Annie, who was in a fair position to intuit such things. "The foreign devils did not have to fight Chinese to take what they wanted. They have bribed governors and merchants and big shots here for hundreds of years. You are a country of five hundred million people who have been destroyed by the guys who are supposed to be running the country. Right now there are well over two million goddamn sojers stumblin' up and down the Heavenly Land fighting each other in the mud, most of them fried on opium. You are a country eating off of its own body, like that bozo in the Greek story. Eating his own liver, right?

And all you can do about it, rich or poor, is to blind the pain of it with opium."

She did not contradict him, but she said, "You do not admire Chinese people."

"There is no Chinese people," he said. He had drunk three-quarters of a bottle of rice wine on an empty stomach. "There's a helluva lot of Chinese, but there is no Chinese people."

"You are the same as all of them. You are a *gwai lo*. You came to the Heavenly Land with a hand open, in friendship." She mimicked a foreign handshake. "But in the hand behind the back, you carried a poisoned knife. You cut, cut, cut at the flesh until you reach this liver" — her hand on her side. "You poison this land, poison, poison, poison with gold and opium. Now the *gwai lo*s sit like vultures on the body of the great Dragon and pick clean its bones with your sharp beaks."

With a tiny twinge of guilt, Annie's finger stroked his nose, his warrior of a nose. There is nobody, he thought, more racist than a Chinese in one of their manic depressions. "I am no particular fan of any particular breed o' human being," he said patiently. "We worked over this territory before, honey. Can you name one bunch that I should admire?" He waited patiently for her to say "American bunch," but she did not. She was retreating from all this petty invective into her old cunning. Annie was ready to sneer at and condemn the good old U.S. of A. with the rest of them. And the Scots too — if only she would take a dig at the fuckin' Scots! But she refrained, though Mr. Chung, the writing master, no doubt had ascertained long ago that Annie was born in the bitter northern land, in the lee of Dunedin's great rock.

The rain roared down on the tiles above like an endless roll of malevolent drums.

"What *do* you admire?" she asked him. He did not answer for several moments. How did she learn how to load her questions with such words? He was looking at the emptiness of the porcelain cup in his hand. Around its blue rim exquisite herons stood among lotuses.

"I admire the Chinese," he said. "More than I can very well account for. But you are all full o' shit." He looked her in her narrow eye with feigned despair. "Why are they all so full o' shit, those particular people — white, yellow, black, and blue — that I admire, and take off my hat to?" And with that he removed his cap, warm and dry as it was from his sou'wester's protection, and placed it gently upon her sleek head.

Guided by a man with a lantern, they went up a lane that entered the hills. Captain Doultry, walking with his legs rather wide apart, was accompanied by eight men in all. Several carried Mauser rifles, others the long-barreled Lugers and Mauser machine pistols that were considered the finest sidearms in the world and were highly prized in China. But there was something ceremonial about the way they carried these weapons, the preference they had for wearing leather and canvas bandoliers two and three at a time, fully charged with ammo despite their weight, and knives of large sizes. These were senior men, more than one well past Annie's age, and they carried themselves in a special way. They bore an astonishing variety of scars. Some wore caps that they had once worn in some Chinese infantry battalion, or that they had taken from slain soldiers. One or two wore the hard little straw hats belted with leather under the chin that Tanka men had worn for centuries. These hats could absorb great blows, even from swords. The *to-kung* of the *Iron Tiger* was a tall and powerful man with arms as thick as Annie's own, from many years of work at the helms of heavy junks. Around his shaved head he wore a red cloth bound with silk rope. This headgear was favored by a number of the crew, in several varieties of the color red, particularly the chief gunners. To be the master of a gun for Lai Choi San was a role in life's movie that seemed to demand a bravura performance. These men were very proud, and talked boldly, and spat great spits. Dogs barked in the darkness as they passed.

Annie walked behind the lantern man. Somewhere ahead a gong began to sound. They came to a place where the path entered a canyon, where there were a temple and other buildings of stone, and a door was opened.

Annie sat upon a mat against the stone wall of a room entirely empty save for the lodestone hanging from the ceiling in its north corner. The stone was a big one, set in a square wooden frame around which the twelve points of the compass were signed. It hung about two feet from the floor, from a fine cord. Annie had been there half an hour and had noticed a very small rotation in this instrument, which was used in the Chinese science of feng

shui, or geomancy, to determine the ener-
gies and currents of the earth, the spaces it
contained, and the spaces contained within
living things, most importantly human be-
ings. It was a difficult and arcane science,
but many of life's most important decisions were based upon it.

Annie could not account for the rotation, which was of no more than three or
four degrees and to the east. Perhaps the
rotation was in the entire room, he thought.
However, he was now in a gay and debo-
nair mood, the alcohol in his brain leaving
him no option. Outside, a rooster started
to crow. The sky beyond the bars of the oc-
tagonal window had assumed the color of
freshly cast iron, like the ocean's color before a typhoon.

The rooster crowed a second time, and a
third. The silence that followed disturbed
Annie unaccountably until he realized that
he was awaiting the answering calls of
other roosters, of which there were no
doubt many in this as in all Chinese villages. But no answers came.

Three men entered the room. They had
left their arms behind them and were carrying bunches of white feathers from the
tails of full-grown cocks. One of them was
the *to-kung*. He went over to the feng shui

lodestone and examined it. Whatever it indicated satisfied him. Perhaps, thought Annie, it measures my virtue; or perhaps my ruthlessness; or perhaps the percentage of alcohol in the blood that I am soon going to shed. He had heard about these ceremonies.

Then the geomancer himself came in. He was wearing black robes of great ornateness. He was not old, nor were his eyes piercing; they were dull and looked nowhere in particular from beneath a very broad forehead and a skull cap with a red jewel in it, like a court official's in imperial days. Upon his neck was a black mole like a great beetle, from which sprouted three hairs several feet in length that blew in the breeze of his decisive movements as he bent over to examine the lodestone. But he did not look at it: he held his fingers very close to it, and it was only then that Annie realized he was blind.

The geomancer said nothing. They led Annie from the room.

They crossed a walled yard. They entered a very old building of greenish stone, by way of a thick and heavy door opened by a gatekeeper, a small, strong-looking old man with a big stick with a knob of bronze that was a demon. Annie's three escorts each gave this gatekeeper a feather. As they crossed a vestibule with wooden pillars, the door groaned and was locked behind them. Ahead was a long room with a low ceiling whose beams were carved with incomprehensible beasts, beneath which the five other men who had come here with Annie were standing naked to the waist, wearing sashes of silk whose yellows varied from the color of lotuses to that of old camel dung. There was a table whose surface was lacquered red; upon it lay incense burners, an axe with a great crescent blade and a tang like an eagle's beak, and a tray on which lay nine knives and a *kuang,* or bronze jug, whose mouth was the mouth of a cat.

Annie stood at the end of the table, swaying slightly as he surveyed the scene. At the far end stood a shabby-looking but dignified *hsiang-ku,* or priest of Tin Hau, the sea goddess. He wore the usual yellow robes, with a shaven head and long fingernails and a long threadbare mustache (which was highly unusual for a priest). The eight men, presumably officers of the Hall of Righteous Heroes of the Yellow Banner, stood four on each side. They laid their feathers on the table, and Annie noticed that each was wearing on his left

239

hand a ring with a square black stone in it. The rings were iron, save for the *to-kung*'s, which was gold. In front of Annie was an iron cup with a handle like a serpent biting its black rim. Annie looked around and said, "Time for another drink, I guess?" Nobody responded.

It was a ceremony of great peculiarity that in the aftermath Annie Doultry was hard put to remember much about. He was given a cup and it was filled from the *kuang* with dark and warm liquid, and as he had surmised he was told to drink it. The concoction tasted of wine and blood, but he swallowed it all, the ordeal made easier by the fact that his stomach was more than willing to compromise; it demanded something, anything, to ease its emptiness.

A door was opened. Two men entered and took Annie out to a walled space with a great fire burning in a sort of iron brazier. Men were seated and standing all around, most of the crew of Madame Lai's junk among them. A gong six feet in diameter hung between two wooden pillars. The *hsiang-ku* struck it — "caressed" is a better word — with a hammer wrapped in yellow silk until the gong started to sing in a voice that seemed to come from the bowels of the earth.

Annie now realized that the potion he was digesting contained something other than blood, alcohol, and opium, all of which he had anticipated. His brain was fragmenting beneath the chisel of some powerful drug and reassembling itself in an alien configuration. He began to be afraid.

The *hsiang-ku* was addressing him in Chinese, but an assistant of his, a young boy whose name was Ch'en, said intimately to Annie in serviceable English: "Each one time you answer, must answer *'hou'* — only *'hou.'*" This was a common, familiar word that meant agreement: "yes" or "fine" or "okay."

The *hsiang-ku* asked him the questions. Each time Annie answered loudly: *"Hou!"* Soon the men around him were answering with him: *"Hou!"* they said in single harsh voice that echoed like the gong in Annie's head, and he felt assured that he had perfectly understood the question.

He could now see only a narrow tunnel leading into the metal of the gong, bright as if fired to its melting point.

A basket was placed close to his eyes within this field of vision. The *hsiang-ku* opened it, and a white cockerel of great size stepped out, looked Annie in the eye, and crowed mockingly. Its crow was repeated by the voice of the gong, and then by all the cockerels in the village. It was a tumultuous sound, and Annie shut his ears, and his eyes. But they made him open them, and he was given a knife, or dagger. He stood with his legs wide apart, his fear evaporating in a great wave of assurance as he looked at the knife. Its hilt was of ivory, its blade bright steel. Knowing what to do with it, Annie gripped the cockerel by its thick neck and cut short its triumphant mockery, throwing its head upon the ground.

The priest's assistants held the creature's body and caught its lifeblood in the same cup Annie had drunk from. Then they eviscerated it with knives, as the men shouted *"Hou! Hou!"* — Annie's voice along with them, filled with shameless conviction. The *hsiang-ku* received the heart, which appeared to be still pulsing with its own life, upon a bronze dish. He spoke to it, commanding it, and then, without needing to be so instructed, Annie ate it. It tasted extraordinarily delicious. Perhaps the drug gave it such a fine flavor, or perhaps Annie was so hungry he would have relished anything.

The *hsiang-ku* drank from the cup of

blood. Then he was handed a white feather. The priest opened his mouth, thrust the feather into his own throat, and then drew it out, red with blood. He eyed Annie with great sternness. Annie had no difficulty now in understanding precisely what the old bastard was saying. With a light heart he opened his mouth and the *hsiang-ku* thrust the red feather into his throat, rotating it cunningly.

Instantly, Annie vomited. Two of the priest's boys were holding a basin in expectation, but nevertheless the proceedings must have been extremely disgusting. Annie vomited from the depths of his deep and powerful belly, and was surprised at how much he seemed to have drunk. The extraordinary thing was that the rooster's heart was not among the effluvia.

Two men supported him. Now Annie saw through the burning bronze of the gong and perceived an endless wasteland of mud. He understood that he was alone in this waste, and that time is endless. Then time stopped, and he was convinced he was to be there forever, surrounded on all sides by these bleak horizons where the abominable wastes met a sky of asphyxiating fire: an unbearable sky. Annie cried out. He still held in his hand the knife, but though he wished to cut his own throat he did not have the strength.

The sky that Annie perceived with drugged, demented eyes must have been the dawn. They took him back into the long room; that is to say, he found himself there, seated in a chair facing the giant *to-kung,* Madame Lai's helmsman. The man had discarded his red bandanna; his hairless head shone like the flat muscles of his chest and arms. With his right hand he took a knife from those on the table, resembling the one in Annie's hand, and held it in the fumes of an incense burner. Then, holding out his left arm to Annie, the *to-kung* knifed himself where the deltoid slid under the triceps. The blood trickled down his hairless arm. Without hesitation the seven other men took up knives from the table and in turn did the same thing. Annie saw that one of them — the wiry little man who had beheaded Madame Lai's prisoner — had a great number of small scars upon his shoulder. Another had a left arm wasted by the work of a machine gun and cut himself upon the forearm.

Annie rose to his feet. Although he felt steady as a rock, the room and the men watching him rotated around him like the rim of a wheel as he undid the buttons of his second-best shirt and removed it. His white skin, which he took care never to expose to the sun, reflected the lanterns admirably, and the men's eyes studied his body and were naturally impressed by the massiveness of it, by the great thickness of the steep sloping shoulders and the unusual breadth of his torso, like a cylinder embroidered with curly hair (a curious thing to Chinese eyes), and the general treelike verticality of Annie's physical being. A two-hundred-and-twenty-pound man of six foot two is a rare sight in southern China (although there are such men to be found in the far north of the country, among the Mongol peoples).

The *to-kung* spoke, and young Ch'en said: "Now you swear. In your speaking you swear to answer Law of Yellow Banner."

Annie held his knife in the incense and then sliced his arm carefully in the proper place. As his blood witnessed his words, he said: "I swear to answer this law of yours, which I guess is the law of honor between men, and no fuckin' point in spellin' it out. I will not betray you guys, or your Yellow Banner." Then as a poetic afterthought he looked the *to-kung* in his bright eyes deep in their bone and said, "To break the Law of the Hall is death." He did not feel like adding the second part of Madame Lai's quotation, though; "To follow the Law of the Hall is death" made it seem too much of a one-sided proposition.

When Annie awoke in the small room with the red brick floor it was approaching evening again. He assumed he had slept since daybreak. He remembered nothing about the finale of this exhausting ceremony, but he noticed that on the second finger of his left hand he was wearing an iron ring in which was set a square piece of black agate engraved with a sign, or a word. He examined it carefully. He felt very weak, but not in the least hungry. The small wound in his upper arm was closed and not even sore. He was lying on a woven mat on the brick floor covered by one of his blankets. The weather was fine and airy. His shirt was folded upon the solitary cherrywood chair that Lai Choi San had occupied.

The girl who had brought him the wine the night before came in and carried dishes of wild woodcock braised with plums, rice, and sweet cakes. This repast struck Annie as a masterpiece of culinary art. His appetite returned with exquisite little pains of salivation in the machinery of the jaw, and he ate everything, drank tea, and tried to feel normal. But it was difficult. Later the girl took him to a kitchen yard and washed him with hot water, assisted by one of the temple cooks. The girl was an attractive young thing and took a lot of time and trouble with her duty, rinsing each of his balls individually, but Annie did not try anything funny, not even joking around. The sun set on this solemn scene.

Back in the room he lay down and immediately fell asleep again.

When he awoke, he saw a lantern on the floor and beside it a chart.

It was a British Admiralty chart of the South China Sea, and Madame Lai Choi San was sitting on her heels in her coolie fashion measuring off distances with a pair of navigator's dividers that she held in her unforgettable fingers as if they were chopsticks. Annie watched her with considerable amusement for some moments. Without looking up, she said: "This is the way from Manila to Hong Kong."

"Yes. I see," Annie replied.

"In June the South China Sea is often calm. The cold monsoon of Tai Hung is tired; he stays only to the west of Taiwan.

The southern monsoon has not yet gathered his strength."

The number-one amah was sitting in the corner preparing tea. She brought Annie a cup. It was jasmine tea, his favorite. She brought him his Woodbines, too, from his shirt pocket. He liked Wills's Woodbines; they were narrow and pungent, a typical low-class limey cigarette. He extended his left hand complete with its bruise, its cigarette, and its black ring and said: "What does this mean? This sign? This word?"

"This word mean Great White Bear." She used the chart to indicate the Far North, with one of those flourishes of hers that were music to the eye. "From the seas of ice. Great White Bear. Mean you."

Annie tried to look expressionless. But he felt at home with this name. It was a large name, and it had nature's dignity and nature's honor, but no more. It was absurd. It was appropriate. But like all names it had limitations; it had a deceptive side. "I do not like the cold," he pointed out to her. "I don't like cold countries."

"Cold country in your *gwai lo* heart," she said, and laughed ringingly. She was obviously in a good mood.

Annie felt more or less sane again (or as sane as he had felt before), but his ears were still sensitive; he winced at that laugh. She took pity on him. "White Bear," she said. "You must put this ring in secret place. No people can see this ring. But you are Righteous Hero now. I tell my men: 'Decide. You must decide,' I tell them, 'if this foreign *gwai lo* is a man to trust.' My people. My men. You understand?"

"Sure. And I guess nine times out o' ten they agree with you, no?" murmured Annie.

She smiled at that, and made a gesture that meant sometimes yes, sometimes no, but with the emphasis on the affirmative. "They are men," she said lightly. Her tone was at once respectful and dismissive of those men who served her. She may have been their brother, but she was also their mistress.

Annie was struck at this time by her womanliness. He saw himself, the whole scene, as if in a mirror. He saw himself lying half-naked under his blanket on this floor of this stone house on this precipitous and baleful island; on the floor of one of her innumerable houses, in the lamplight. His heart may have been a cold country, but his endocrine system lived in a warmer climate. The stuff they had given him was complex. Her sleekness of head, the narrowness of her back, the great beauty of her neck and forearms had an effect on him. But of course he did not let this biological state of affairs show in any way. The blanket covered it. "No," he said. "Why should I understand?"

"Yes, you understand. There is a law of Yellow Banner people. Small law, but very, very hard. You understand very good."

"The only law you follow," said Annie, "is the one that lets you be as ruthless as you want."

So saying, he removed the ring and put it in an empty matchbox that once contained a cockroach and that he still carried in his pants pocket. She laughed at him again.

"Your men eat rats," said Annie. "I saw one of your famous gunners gutting two rats on your fo'c'sle. Last night. All you boat people eat rats."

"We eat cockroach, too. On empty sea, empty stomach eat anything." She was laughing her head off. "Rats very, very good. Tomorrow we have rat dinner, special for you. Damn!" She slapped her knee. "I see Frenchy people in Shanghai eating frogs, eating snails. Damn rats taste better. So tell me, Captain, what is your law?"

The little amah filled his teacup. "My

law," he said, "is to avoid ending up in the pot with the rest of the rat meat." She loved that. She laughed so much she nearly fell over.

"Rat meat! Rat meat! No, you no rat meat," she stated reassuringly. "You are okay now. You are White Bear now. You eat your rat meat, but you will not be put in pot." And then with the abruptness typical of her, she stopped laughing, her face uncrinkled, and she eyed his own fixedly. "You are a Great White Bear. But you are not animal. We are not animals. We are social people, Captain Doultry. We have responsibilities."

"Well, you don't mind if I get my share of laughs out of it, do you?" He laughed too mildly to make his point. She did not understand what he meant; her small brow furrowed. "Your share? Of laughing?"

"Yeah, my share. How about you?"

Her hands wore no rings. Her fingers touched the jade of a comb in her hair. "I laugh. Oh, yes. I laugh."

Annie, his head propped on his fist, secure under his blanket, a Woodbine balanced on his untrustworthy lower lip, watched her steadily. Her fingers touched her hair, stroking it upwards gently at the back of her neck, where it was very fine.

251

"Perhaps I have neglected myself," she said abruptly. "Perhaps I have passed beside some of pleasure of life. But I do what is right thing to do. I have responsibility. To my father, to my people."

"Your father is dead. Your husband is dead too, no?" It was a guess, but an easy one.

She told him that her father had become a slave to opium. When he realized that he was compelled to withdraw into the land of dreams forever, he had made his eldest living son the leader of the Yellow Banner. A year later this brother was dead, killed "with his slippers on." The second son took over. He lasted three years and died in a typhoon with all his crew. The Old Man, her father, was still alive then; he had lived long enough to see his third son "lose his soul." A Jesuit father who taught at the mission school (Father Texeira, his name was) had taken a great hold on the boy's mind. He had become a Christian. He had entered the Jesuit seminary as a novice. He had become a monk.

The Old Man, after being asked for and giving permission for his last son to enter (like himself) another world, had emerged for the last time from the small cabin — it was only a *tou-mu*'s little box — aboard the

Tiger of the Iron Sea, where he had remained for four years attended only by his opium pipe and a single servant, and with a great effort of the will reassumed command of his war junks, which by that time had been reduced to seven in number. And aboard the *Iron Tiger* he had brought his daughter (his favorite daughter, for he had several), whose name in those days was Secret Jasmine. She was nineteen, and had undergone an extraordinary education for a Tanka girl; but her father had always been attached to her, and had this vision — though he was a very traditional man — of a modern China. Probably it was an opium vision. He had intentions that she should marry a rich man, an educated man; although he had let the business slip, the Old Man was still wealthy, still well connected to those serpentine Macanese and Shanghai organizations, the tongs, that arbitrated the divisions of things, of territories, spheres of influence and seas, in the Chinese underworld during the final days of the Empire. At the College of the Sacred Heart she had learned her lessons with such energy that Sister Agnes had spoken to her father about her future. Fearful that she would go the way of his youngest son, the Old Man had taken her away from the school forever. "For thirteen moons," she said, "I sailed with him upon the *Iron Tiger,* and never one time I go on the land."

There were two other males, one old and one young, a nephew and the son of a lesser wife, in the running for the overlordship of the Hall of Righteous Heroes of the Yellow Banner. But her father told her what was in his mind, and his word and his will were law, of course. So this young girl had opened her heart to the sea, and also steeled it against certain aspects of the business from which the Old Man had not attempted to shield her. He explained that there was both an art and a morality implicit in the practice of violence, toward ends that he defined in a positively Confucian manner. "He say to me in the thirteenth moon, before he die: 'You are the one with the strong heart and the clever head, my Secret Jasmine. Now you must take a new name.' "

Thus she had become the Mountain of Wealth.

She had also taken a husband. It was her cousin, the nephew. She did not care for him. She had put him away from her, but he had insisted on coming back and making trouble. Then he had suddenly died. She had taken another man. She had three children — two sons, one daughter — by this man. Later he had gone away; it was said he had gone to Mei Kwo — America.

"Now I have twenty-six war junks. And two sons, twelve years and seven years. How old are your children, Captain Doultry?"

Annie tried to remember. "I have a son who is a Frenchie. His mother was French; she took him back there." He tried to concentrate. "Last I heard of him he was in the army, the French army, in Algeria. And I have another son." It was too exhausting, Annie did not want to discuss the subject. He could not remember how old they were or even where they were.

Madame Lai must have realized this, she was a wide-awake girl; but nevertheless she said: "I am sure you have a daughter."

"Yes." He yawned. "Yes, I believe so. Could be wrong, o' course. She must be four, now." Suddenly his feeling of fatigue lightened. Feeling Lai Choi San's eyes upon his face, he wished to maintain his detachment from the whole subject, but abruptly he found himself all aswamp in a wave of sentiment. He felt confused, but found his escape in a low chuckle.

"Where is your home?" she asked. "Where is your woman?"

"My boat is my home. I am a boat person," he replied. "My boat is my wife too."

"Where is your daughter?"

"My daughter is in America. If you ever go to San Francisco you must look her up."

"I will never go to America," she said, her eyes never wavering from his face. Maybe she perceived that he was lying, who knows? Annie was not a fool. He was not the type of man to tell a Chinese pirate where his children were. But she had no hard feelings about that; she did not hold it against him.

If you asked Annie what his feelings were about Madame Lai Choi San, he could not have told you. He would have answered, but he would have made it up as he went along. As long as it was not present as a serious thought before he uttered it — or let us say, as long as it uttered itself — without reference to any visible points of truth, Annie was happy to say it. Of course, sometimes he made up answers that turned out to be true.

But he did not trust her. He was sure of that.

"You are thinking," said Lai Choi San. "You are thinking: I do not trust her."

"Yes," Annie replied. "And no."

"There is one thing that bind you and me," she said. "One more after first one, greed, and second one, the swearing on blood. What is third one? I tell you. It is love."

The directness of her expression took him aback. Annie was at a loss for words. But she qualified her statement.

"I mean, you and me, we have same love. We have same love. For same deep water. Deep water. I am not a lover of the great rivers, I do not love the land. I love the sea."

"Someone told me," said Annie, "that there is no Chinese word for 'love.' "

"That is not true. Very stupid thing to say. There are many words mean love." Annie was studying the bottom of his teacup. "What do you see in your fortune, Captain Doultry? Your future?"

"It looks like cigarette butts to me."

Her amah was asleep, curled up on the floor. Lai Choi San extended her foot (which was naked) to get some service, but Annie made a movement to dissuade her. "No more tea for me, darlin'."

"What is this 'darlin'?"

"It's just a figure of speech." Let her work on that one. Annie devoured her with his eyes; at least this is what he said to himself. He said: "Annie, you are devouring this Chinese doll with your eyes." He immediately saw her as something to eat; that is the point. She was appetizing. Would she object if she knew what was going on in his mind? Probably not in the least. Calling her a "doll," she might have objected to that, though. On the other hand, she was profoundly aware of what cannot be better described than her own animal magnetism. No, *mechanical* magnetism; she was a beautiful piece of machinery. Her power-to-weight ratio was formidable, her structure delicate and highly stressed. Her movements were deft and authoritative without being brutal: a balance that Annie had never quite achieved in his own person.

The chart on the floor had rolled up on his side. She leaned across it, picked up one of his shoes, and used it as a paperweight. "Hold corner here, please," she instructed Annie. He did so, with a finger, willing to be her slave. She had that dry, pungent smell, a spicy smell, a mixture of natural and artificial perfumes, manmade and female-made. Annie's nose reacted with a profound sensation of pleasure, and his cock echoed its brother organ with everything at its disposal. The blanket moved, visibly writhed, and although Annie tried to move his leg to conceal it, he was unsuccessful. She saw it happen; she seemed to be looking right at the blanket when it happened. But she pretended not to notice.

Annie did not feel the need to speak. She sat there quietly beside him, admiring the chart as if it were a thing of beauty. Her back was close to him, to his leg, or more precisely, to the inside of his right knee. He was lying somewhat on his left side in the posture often seen in pictures of classical Roman characters at feasts. It was a favorite position for Annie. His left hand was a prop for his cheekbone, and the weight of his head and its computations. He adjusted his position so that when the time came to make his move, it would be languorous but inexorable. "Yeah," he said at last. "When you are upon the sea you don't have to decide anything," he said. "There's nobody to bother you. Except Mother Nature, when she humps you."

"What means 'she humps'?" asked Lai Choi San.

"When she fucks you," said Annie.

"When she gets up and fucks you. Then you don't have to think about anything except getting fucked, and staying alive to tell the tale."

On this profundity he reached around her body, so compact, with his right arm, placing his hand upon one of her breasts, and held her tightly. In his arm, she felt as small as a child. Just for a moment he held her, or hugged her, and then relaxed the arm and let it lie there around her waist so that she could push it away easily, like an enormous cobweb — if she wanted to.

She let the arm lie there and said: "Well, Captain, that seem like a pointless life to me. Waiting to be fuck by Mother Nature."

No point denying it was intriguing to hear her put it like that. She was permitting herself to talk in that loose, dirty kind of way in which the Chinese often talk to friends and family and people on the street. It was a stupendous language, as rich with obscenities and gutterish phrases as it was with possibilities for sublime images and metaphysical metaphor.

"Mrs. Wealth," he said. "I don't think it's a pointless life. I've got my music and I got my . . ." A pause here, empty as the store of the man's possessions. "I got my freedom. My life is better than some, maybe not as good as others. If you look around, I don't know, it's always astounded me seeing what people kick into a pile and call life. I don't think it's so bad, what I do. I do it for myself, it's all mine. There are no footprints on the sea."

"Sure, no footprints. The sea is not made of sand," said Mrs. Wealth. "It is water. But water is a mirror." She lifted the map. Underneath lay the bronze mirror, the mirror with its twelve points like a lodestone or a compass, which the peoples of the dynasty of Han called a Cosmic Mirror. It lay facedown, its knob responsible for a bump under the chart of the sea like a tidal wave. She picked it up and looked at herself in its dark depths. "Before the people in the Middle Kingdom make mirrors of metal, they use only water. Water in a bowl of copper make mirror for the face. No footprints, no prints of face. Just you, but inside out. Yes?" Her "yes" was accompanied by a pass of her hand in the lamp's light that mirrored the mirror's inversion of two of the three dimensions of whatever was revealed or seen.

She lifted Annie's hand from her waist and placed the mirror in it.

He put the mirror on the floor without so much as a glance and replaced his arm around her, touching her breast again through the cotton with the tips of his fingers. He did not want to get into a Chinese discussion about mirrors. He accepted that she was more of an adept among universal metaphors; it was a Chinese specialty. So he said: "Mrs. Wealth, among the lovers you have mentioned *en passant,* as the Frenchies say, was there ever a Foreign Devil?"

"No."

"You never made love with a *gwai lo?*"

"No. But I have kill a few," she said in the same light manner. Then abruptly she placed her hand on his, pressing it against her body. Her palm had an electrical dryness to it; the shock was immediate. "I kill *gwai lo*s," she went on. "I kill running dogs of *gwai lo*s. I kill Chinese running dogs. I kill hoodlum. Hoodlum of the city of Shanghai. Hoodlum, hoodlum." She liked that word. To say that sensations of sexuality made her think of killing may be over-simplifying it. "Chiang Kai-shek," she said, her voice soft but metallic. "He pay number-one hoodlum gang of Shanghai to kill Reds. They kill five thousand, ten thousand Reds. One day maybe I kill Chiang Kai-shek."

Annie was stroking her breast with the

greatest tenderness and respect when she made this remark in a voice that exuded husky eroticism. He could feel her shoulders shivering. He was not interested in her political opinions. He was horny as hell. He wanted to fuck her brains out, and his own too. It was lust pure and simple, with all the spices of fatality upon the dish. He thought: They musta put an aphrodisiac in that revolting brew. And he was suddenly in the grip of a loss of confidence; you could not call it fear, but it crawled over his skin from the groin upward like a lizard which, arriving at his ear, spoke to him distinctly: "What the fuck are you doing, Doultry? Before you're through, this dame will be using your balls as earrings. Set in jade, naturally."

And naturally, this changed the course of things.

"Are you afraid?" she asked him.

"Maybe just a hair," he answered. And perhaps the fact that for once he told the truth disappointed her.

"Yes, Captain Dowtly," she said. "You are afraid. Too much afraid. Well, I must learn to understand you. And you must understand me. We gonna be good friends. But in my heart — no, I say 'my life'; you do not understand heart — in my life love and business are two things never must cross. Never, never. Please take 'way your hand."

He did what he was told. He had no option; her primness was so absolute she sounded like a nun. Her eyes were on the chart; they flickered over it. It occurred to Annie that maybe she could not comprehend it. Then he apologized silently for such a thought, in case she was reading them.

"Madame Lai, I would not fool you in matters of the heart. To me, the heart is this big red pump up here that drives the rest of me. I am a man whose love is part and parcel of his body — of which I have a lot, so I do not believe I am short on love. I would like to be your lover because to my eyes, my dishonorable eyes, you are a thing of beauty." Here he lapsed sweetly into song:

> "Oh you beautiful doll,
> You great big beautiful doll . . .
> Let me put my arms about you,
> I could never live without you."

Well, she could not help smiling. As he sang these verses in his light and pleasant voice and in perfect tune, his face shone with sincerity. He looked his best. Lai Choi San may have thought so too; she had a refined sense of timing, for she turned and walked to the door. There she stopped again and bowed to Annie, holding her hands in the old-fashioned way. He was on the third verse as she exited, leaving behind her chart and her mirror, but followed by her maid with the tea things, to whom Annie blew a generous kiss, which made this charming young person turn away her face in confusion. Her mistress may or may not have observed this event; with Madame Lai you never could tell.

chapter 6
Typhoon

To Manila from Hong Kong by steamer was a two-day passage. The northeast monsoon was blowing steadily and the junk made a landfall on Cape Bojeador, the northwest corner of the isle of Luzon, on the fourth day, April 27, late in the afternoon, having averaged a good eight knots.

Though nothing in particular happened during these four days, they were important ones. It was at this time that Annie began seriously to weigh up the potential of the deal. It boiled down to this: if there was as big a silver shipment in June as Madame Lai promised, the most stringent security possible would be planned by the Indo-China Steam Navigation Company. Several of their ships in the coastal trade had been hit by pirates; it was a big, rich company, and they were wary. What was equally certain was that Madame Lai's plan to capture this 10,000-ton, sixteen-knot ship, the *Chow Fa*, had a calculable probability of success. The third sure thing was that he himself, Dandy Annie, was the sine qua non of it, if not the deus ex machina. What he would need to do was hard, but he was a hard man. The sum of his calculations, which occupied all four days of the voyage, was that the overall chances of pulling it off were something over seventy percent, but less than eighty — say, three to one on. So in the end, at those odds, he had to say, "Annie, you're on."

He was given an after cabin on the upper poop deck, right above Madame Lai's and Captain Wang's quarters. The *tou-mu,* a small and perpetually angry man who could be called the first mate, had the adjoining cabin, and the chief gunner the one opposite. For four days Annie lived side by side with his Chinese peers, so to speak. These cabins, the officers' quarters, were five feet high, four wide, and hardly long enough to lie down in; it was like sleeping in a packing case. Annie was amused to meet the cockroaches, a fine Chinese seagoing breed with a sense of humor. They were the top dogs among a large selection of bugs — not to speak of the friendly rats, whom the crew fed until they were fat enough for the pot, and a weird little species of mouse not worth catching, for it was not worth eating.

He wanted to be close to these forty-four thieves in all their lowness, their depravity, their callousness, and their good-humored camaraderie. To help, he even pretended to share their absurd superstitions. For example, when the northeast breeze suddenly died, simply switched off, when they were still within sight of the coast, everybody knew this was one of those abrupt calms seasonable in these latitudes in April, and would soon pass. Nevertheless, there was a lot of chanting, and a paper boat decorated with gold tinfoil and red paper prayers was set tenderly upon the sea, upon the lee side, by the executioner. A gong was beaten in a slow, undulating rhythm as the paper boat rode the swells, drifting south on the current.

Then a puff of wind caught it and blew the shining toy like a bird across the chiseled water. Then another filled the sails of the *Iron Tiger*, and they were on their way again.

The crew were filthy in their habits to Western eyes, but no worse than most of this world's landsmen. They never washed themselves, but they spent half their lives scoured by nature, in seawater; they were pickled in salt. Their skins were magnificent maps of the weathers they had seen, mahogany in color. Their faces could tell stories to make your nose hairs curl. However, Annie felt comfortable among them, for they were seamen, and like all seamen they were bad-tempered and emotional, but tolerant and more broad-minded than dwellers on the land — more down to earth, in short. For example, they pursued the lice in their patched and scanty clothing with constant good humor. When they knew Annie was looking they would sometimes eat the unlucky ones just to shock him; for, of course, he did not conceal his revulsion — why should he? It amused the crew. He was a clown. So he became clownish, a Great White Clown of a Bear. It was quite hard work, but Annie was a pro, after all, and the Tanka seamen enjoyed his act. They laughed and offered him puffs of their pipes and parts of the fish they caught. They fished all the way, there were always hooks trawling, and two days out, beyond the coastal grounds, the catch became plentiful.

The difficult one was Tang Shih-ping, the *Iron Tiger*'s chief gunner. The word had got out (probably leaked by Mr. Chung) that Annie knew about guns. Annie did nothing to aggravate this rumor;

he kept his distance from the seventy-fives and the endless cleaning and general parading of firearms. They were as crazy about guns as a bunch of Mexican bandits in a movie. But Annie kept feeling the weight of Tang Shih-ping's eyes on his back. This man had spent his life married to a harem of cannon; he was a veteran of twenty-four years of warlord wars. His current love affair was with Madame Lai's four seventy-five-millimeter imitation Schneiders.

Then a young man, a strong but not very bright kid, brought Annie a copy of a Colt 1911 army model that had been rechambered for nine-millimeter Luger Parabellum ammo. With expressive sign language he explained how it was jamming and fired a few rounds to demonstrate. On the fourth it jammed.

Annie knew at once what was wrong and he knew how to fix it. He even watched the kid disassemble the gun with sympathetic eyes. Then he told Ch'en, the one who spoke English, "Tell this guy I'm sorry, but I only sell guns. Buy 'em and sell 'em. I don't understand too much about how they work."

Tang Shih-ping came over. He pondered the problem thoroughly, laughing very loud, and saw how the feed pawl designed for a fat .45 cartridge had not been filed down enough to engage the svelter European slugs every time. Annie slapped his back and congratulated him. By the time they reached Manila he was getting along fine with this bunch of boy scouts, and the chief gunner had lifted the pressure of his eyes and was being civil.

Lai Choi San did not speak directly to Annie for the first thirty hours or so out of Lantau Island. As Victoria Peak slipped beneath the horizon's haze dead aft of them, she inhabited her own world in the manner she was accustomed to and ignored her guest completely. Annie had heard of this stratagem; he had read about it in books — stories about eccentric English dukes who never spoke to their guests until the third or fourth day of a country house party. Madame Lai had a similar attitude. That was okay with Annie; he was not bored.

He didn't mind being dirty. He was adaptable. But he was particular about the kemptness of his beard, the way the seamen were about their hair. Now, there was a barber aboard who could shave a head in a fresh gale in ten minutes flat, and so naturally Annie asked for a trim.

It was late afternoon, and the whiff of supper was on the breeze from the charcoal stoves, and most of the crew turned out for the barber's show. Annie sat on the stool. He had wrapped his head in a scarf, a green willow-pattern strip of weathered silk, in the style they favored. This was to protect his head hair, which was growing out in an erratic and shaggy fashion. However, he did not wish to get a short back-and-sides from this barber. So he used his bronze mirror to indicate: the beard, please. A trim.

The barber studied the beard critically from all angles. Eventually, after receiving much advice from some of the spectators, he indicated to Annie with his fingers: twenty cents. This was way too much, and Annie was not prepared to be made a mockery of over anything so serious; so he protested. There was a discussion, and it was not a mere formality. They settled on sixteen cents. The barbering itself did not take long, though. The barber gave the beard a classical Chinese cut, with two points.

Madame Lai was looking down on the scene from her lofty perch on the poop. She smiled, but she did not laugh; so none of the crew laughed, either, as Annie studied the results in his mirror, leaning back against one of the old-model cannon. His fingers felt his points. He gave the barber sixteen cents and a two-cent tip and then arose and went to where young Ch'en was painting the carved part above the fo'c'sle bulkhead, a carving all in repetitions of a symbol called "well-being" (which, turned backwards and called by its Sanskrit name, *svastika*, was being utilized by the demented but charismatic young leader of the National Socialist Party in Germany). Annie said, "Excuse me, Ch'en," and took his paint pot from him and dipped the points of his beard in it. It was red paint.

The effect was tremendous, and since it was now okay to laugh, they all did, Madame Lai's animallike sounds conspicuous among them. He had sacrificed the integrity of his beard to make her laugh: his beard had been many shapes and sizes. It was more of a chinpiece than a beard. Even the malevolent little *tou-mu* laughed, a harsh honk of a laugh. But it was all for her that Annie did it. He liked to watch her laugh, and the great exhibition of her mouth, ornamented with gold, with Chinese goldsmithing. But the two of them did not come near each other; they were never alone.

However, on the poop in the great glare

of noonday they did have a conversation. It was after the morning when the wind had left the sea for those few hours, and they were heading east-southeast with the warm dregs of the winter monsoon coming dead on their port beam from down the Straits of Formosa (or Taiwan, as the Chinese called it). It was evident that she was making for the Pratas Islands. Madame was sitting in her usual place, on a chest along the port rail with one or the other, or often both, of her amahs at her feet. Captain Wang wandered about smoking and arguing about racehorses with the helmsman in the tiller room below. It was odd how everyone within Hong Kong's spell, or region of influence, talked about racehorses and bet on them.

Madame Lai never talked to the *to-kung*. She talked only to Captain Wang. He did the rest. But this evening she told her number-one amah to tell Annie that she hoped he was not too tired to join her for a cigarette. She would like to try one of his cigarettes, was the message.

Annie lit it for her. The number-two amah was sitting beneath a black parasol. Annie said: "You're on a heading for the Pratas."

"Yes." Automatically her eyes flicked at

274

the sky. "Small wind tonight. And big moon. I know Pratas Islands very well."

Annie did not comment. He knew of no Western shipmaster who would wish to come within five miles of the Pratas at night in any weather. In uncertain weather, make that twenty miles; that was Annie's rule, and he was not conservative.

He looked at the sky too, and the surface of the sea. He sniffed the airs with his notoriously sensitive olfactory system. "If you ask my opinion, if I had a barometer I'd wager she would be falling. There's heavy weather up north, and she has half a mind to head this way."

The sun shone whitely. Lai Choi San said, "There is a Tiet-Kiey coming from far. She is coming from the island of Bataan, and Captain Wang and I agree that we will cross her path. We are going fast; she will pass behind. But she will leave us with a strong wind from the north, for Manila."

Annie was about to ask her where she got her information, since she had no radio; but instead he walked over to Captain Wang, who was talking to the helmsman, and asked him with polite signs if he could borrow his glasses. Captain Wang obliged at once. Annie turned them due east, in the direction of Bataan, four hundred miles away. The horizon was clear, hazy, benign. Then he felt Captain Wang tap his shoulder and point, a degree or two north and well above the horizon's haze. And there, shimmering in the objective of these powerful glasses, way above puffs of sea-green cumulus, was a coil of vapor that must have been at stratocumulus level, a good six vertical miles above the waters of the Luzon Straits and the island of Bataan.

"What is this Tiet-Kiey?" Annie asked Madame Lai.

"Is name of Iron Whirlwind," she said. Annie had never heard it called that before, but he knew all about typhoons. He was familiar with the rage of that old man who was the wind, the rage that measured itself weight for weight against earthquakes, against volcanoes, against Mont Pelée, against Krakatoa, against the great Bull upon whose back the universe rests. When the arena is as wide as the waters, and a pirate and a liar sit jointly on Nero's stone bench, one might expect to see an act of violence from that old man of a majesty to give full resonance to the word "catastrophe."

"Madame Lai Choi San," said Annie, "I

think your master of sailing, or *lio-dah,* or whatever you call him, is a pretty competent guy. That's my impression. But it would seem to me a wise move to take a long tack to the southwest right now, and let this fine nor'east breeze take us as far away from the skirts of that typhoon as we can get, and as far away from the Pratas reefs likewise. To try and cut across in front of her is plumb crazy."

"Captain Wang not my *lio-dah,* he my *tou-jen* — he my head eye. Under the Yellow Banner, we call sailing master 'head eye.'" The head eye himself was at that moment relieving Annie of his Bausch and Lombs, though apparently he did not need them to see the Dragon's Breath advancing upon them. "He say, my *tou-jen,* that we can cross in front very easy. Go straight, straight-straight. We go by leeside Pratas Islands, we catch piece of wind behind us blow us all way to Manila by tomollow for breakfast."

With this, Madame Lai yelled with laughter. It was the signal for the little number-one amah to giggle and clap, and for Captain Wang to smile, and there came an echoing low-register belly laugh from the helmsman.

The ripple of laughter spread symmetrically forward, touching the humors of the crew as they trimmed the yards and began battening down the main hatch and made fast the cannon with extra chain and hawsers to the decks. A number of them even discarded their hats, throwing them down the fore hatch. And the junk heaved forward with the wind abeam of her in a great reach to the east.

It struck Annie as a possibility that this softly hysterical gesture of laughter was directed at him — in a nice way, of course. Madame Lai and her head eye and his crew had agreed — for it was a democratic crew, like the best pirate crews — to race the Iron Whirlwind, for the hell of it. Perhaps they viewed it as a question of face. It was a matter of mood, anyway, for nobody was in a particular hurry, and Manila by tomorrow evening would be perfectly satisfactory. But Annie said no more in the way of contrary advice, or wisecracks, either. If they were gonna go, they were gonna go.

Then the hump of a black dragon eighty miles wide and high as the stratosphere arose out of the east and advanced upon them. It followed the lustful coil of its tongue, which was spun away from the Iron Whirlwind by its cyclical momentum. The ocean began to turn the color of glassy iron that Annie had last seen in the bronze of the round mirror. A vast swell began to move vertically, like the rocking of the sea's cradle. There was little wind but this on the water's skin as the exhalation of the Tiet-Kiey seemed to move like a razor against the surface.

The helmsman held her on a straight reach, her sails all set with a golden defiance as the sun fell away to leeward as if to get out of the way. And where the advancing tongue of black vapor caught the sleeping light, it turned a vivid yellow.

Annie figured if the wind veered and backed from northeast to north, it would mean the front edge of the depression was on them. Typhoons are like cyclones: their winds whirl around a center of low pressure often no more than ten miles across. In the Northern Hemisphere, this whirling is anticlockwise (and in the Southern, the other way). So with experience it is not hard to figure where the typhoon is; but in a wind-driven boat, by then it is often too late. The winds on the wheel's ruin come in fearful gasps. Storm winds like these are called "squalls" by seamen, but a typhoon's squalls often blow at velocities of a hundred miles an hour, even on its outer edge.

Annie put on his oilskin, tied his sou'-wester under his beard, and adopted a gloomy expression. For he knew what to expect; and as he looked east he could see the first squall coming across the sea surface like a wedge of blackness fringed with spume. Captain Wang was ready; his men were at the yardarm hoists, and they let the mainsail rumble down with a clash of bamboo and were tying her down as the wind hit her beam-on, leaning her over and burying her foreyard in her bow wave. They dropped the mizzen sail too, and Captain Wang let her run before it under the foresail alone, and that was three parts reefed. But he wanted to keep a scrap of sail up if he could. You cannot keep a sailboat's head into a typhoon wind, for it veers so quick it can put you over, if it has a mind to.

A great swell lifted the boat, a swell with a rim beaten to a froth of desire; and then, as it carried them, the vessel leaning way over as if bent by fear of the wind, this swell grew into a vast wave which curled over the junk's windward bulwarks and rolled her over almost on her beam ends before she slid down the water's black face into the trough that had opened to receive them. Annie could hear nothing but the waves roar, but as he hung on he could see the face of Lai Choi San grinning like a demon as she clung to a mizzen stay; and as the water broke over her and the little amah hung on to her, the woman appeared to be laughing.

The junk rose from the water, but you could hardly tell it, for a wall of rain hit them horizontally from out of the squall. The helmsman was trying to keep her stern quarter to the mounting seas, on a broad reach with that little patch of straining foresail pulling her head down and driving her stem high to take the weight of the following seas. This old junk's ironwood hull was built with a strength that only an iron boat could match. She lived in a world of metal names, in a world where the Whirlwind and the Tiger were antagonists cast from this same black metal that the Chinese admired but hated. This was the Iron Sea that she had been built to survive. She creaked and groaned like a beast in a cave of water, and the seas swept over her midships as she heeled and pitched under and then nosed out of the water, resisting the oppression of the elements.

Madame Lai was still perched on her heels on her rope chest, neatly jammed in the corner of the poop on its high side, so she could duck under the wooden wall of her home when the big seas came over. She was hanging on to the mizzenmast stays, her hair uncoiled and unleashed, streaming in the wind like the mane of a small, crazy horse. Annie braced himself with his feet against one of the battens on the deck placed there for the purpose. He wished he had removed his brown Oxfords; he wished he had thought to bring his rubber boots. He hung on to the brass mounting of one of the gingall guns; the gun's barrel, brass and ringed with brass snake's tails, was tied down and served him as a grip for both his hands. He had lived through many winds worse than this, but he hated it like he hated fear, and for the same reason. This may sound glib to some, but that is the way it was. So he tried to detach himself from it; he held this strong thought in his mind: This bitch is just trying to impress me. She walked into this. She did this to me on purpose.

Well, so that is how Madame Lai used the Iron Whirlwind, to suit her purpose, instead of it using her — which had of course happened more than once, for she had spent half the years of her life on junks on this sea. She was yelling something at him in Chinese, "I did it on purpose. Look what I did!" was probably what it was, for she had a wild, triumphant look about her, like a Cecil B. DeMille heroine, only you could tell it was sincere. She was an arrogant bitch, but that was part of her attraction.

The wind dropped suddenly, like the whine-down of a cannon shell; and this is a horrid moment always, for you could hear the roar of the next squall, the next wall of air, five miles away as it rushed toward them. It took under four minutes to reach them. Captain Wang, who was still there at the front rail of the poop, yelled at his foremast crew to get the sail down to the last batten, which was only two feet deep. This they did. The deck under them was tilting, bow up, pointing at the impenetrable sky, for the junk was riding up the face of one of these immense swells, and for a few moments Annie could see clear to the horizon, behind them. He could see the front of the wind approaching like a stripe of white foam across a landscape of gray and featureless hills. But this impression cannot have lasted more than a few instants, in the mounting roar of wind and water blown to divergent molecules, before the next squall hit them.

The *tou-mu* was with the men reefing

the foresail; his amazingly piercing voice was the last thing Annie heard. Then the scrap of sail they had left aloft split with a crack like a gun, and the bamboo gaff bent almost double before it snapped. The typhoon in the thick naked masts and wailing in her shrouds and rigging carried her forward across the Iron Sea. Madame Lai reached out her hand and grabbed Annie's hand and screamed in his ear: "We go! We go! We go more fast than Tiet-Kiey!" She held up her arm, wet black cotton streaming in the wind, as the junk heeled violently, for it had veered again; it was howling out of the northwest now.

As Madame and her captain had predicted, the typhoon's cauldron was indeed going to pass astern of them; all they were taking was the outer edges of the wind's wheel. The *Iron Tiger* had crossed its path sufficiently to avoid the central vortex of the thing, which would pass at least thirty miles astern of her. But she was too deep in it to do much but run before it. Of course, she was running in the right direction, which was presumably keeping Madame Lai and her crew in such a gay mood. They let her run. The *to-kung* had two men with him on the tiller capstan, and Captain Wang was hollering advice down the hatch to them, for all they could see down at main-deck level was water and darkness ahead.

Now they were in the teeth of a hurricane. It held one note, a steady call like a pack of elemental coyotes, but with a hollowness to it, not the shriek of pain of some winds Annie had been forced by circumstances to listen to. And Annie remembered that he had heard some Chinese seaman call seas like this "the white hounds of the hunt," which was a fair phrase. He was amused to notice the little amah still in place like a barnacle, curled up and jammed behind her mistress's narrow back, narrow but hard. The crest of a sea had just traversed them, partly under and partly over her hull, but the vessel was still bow-down for a moment, as if perched on a hill fit for a telescope. Annie's eyes, filled with annoyance but also admiration, were on Lai Choi San, for she was worth watching. So he saw her see what lay ahead and was so fascinated by her behavior that he continued to watch her, as she got to her feet, her small hands fisting up the mizzen stays, and flung out a hand in that inimitably imperious way of hers, pointing with an expression of diabolical glee in the only significant direction — that of the wind, and the vessel, and its occupants. Then from the lookout forward came a banshee screech that Annie felt rather than heard. He looked around to see what it was all about, and what he saw scared the living daylights out of him.

Stretching as far as the eye could see, which must have been no more than two points on either bow in these conditions, was a snow-white ridge like the ridge of a mountain range seen from some Himalayan plateau. It was the mountainous surf breaking on the reef of the Pratas. Then, as the sea moved on, the junk slid into the trough, and the sight was gone. But in Annie's mind his eyes remained fixed on that ridge of white foam a mile or two ahead, for it was apparent that there was no sea room to pass to windward of the reef. It was maybe only ten miles long, but now the typhoon's vortex was passing astern of them, thirty or more miles back but dead astern; and with each squall of her passing, rising to a pitch every five minutes, a cyclic wave of winds was bearing on them from a more westerly direction. There was no way to get a scrap of sail up and try to beat against it; they could only fly before this violence. So they were flying down upon that reef which had gutted more hulls and sailor men than any other thing of nature in the China Sea. A vessel could survive a typhoon, but driven upon the Pratas she would surely die.

Annie, his back to the weather, caught the downward wail of a great gust in his lungs and hollered up at the ear of the Chinese woman: "We are goin' on the Pratas, sugar."

She looked down at him. She could not have heard him, but she gave him a smile. Annie knew then that she had lost her marbles. "You stupid broad! You motherfucker! You did it on purpose!" he howled at her in a voice she could not hear. But all the same she shook her head, and she tried to wave so violently she almost lost her grip and was nearly blown away.

"*Iron Tiger* fly!" she screamed vaingloriously.

Captain Wang was hollering to the *to-kung* down the hatch, but the latter had seen what was coming. Four men were on the windlass that hauled the rudder up; its blocks and tackle were shrieking silently as they raised the great slab back up into its special cavity in the junk's ass, till it had only a foot or so of purchase in the water. The orders would have been the same in any language, in any ship being driven by a typhoon onto a reef of black coral. Every now and then they could glimpse it, closer by the minute, as the waves breaking on it sucked back from it: a broad and jagged reef that rose normally only a couple of feet above a calmish sea. Like the wall of a fortress, but without symmetry, the reef protected a lagoon studded with crags of black coral that sailors called "nigger heads," which you could see clearly, since the lagoon, though ripped with little waves, was only a few feet deep and seemed calm as a mill pond by contrast with the roaring ocean outside. But when a ship struck the Pratas reef, it was not just once: she would bounce off or be sucked off after the first impact and then thrown again and again against the coral. Even an ironwood junk would disintegrate in a very short time; and though safety was only a few yards away for her crew, they were commonly beaten to their deaths as much as drowned in such conditions.

"I shall go over the side before she strikes. I will survive this insane and inept adventure," Annie said quietly to the wind, as he saw through the blinding, gloomy whine of air and spray Madame Lai lashing herself with a line to her mizzen shrouds, paying no attention whatever to her *gwai*

288

Io victim. And with his naked feet planted wide her head eye was yelling in his own language to his helmsman the only thing a ship's master could say under such circumstances:

"Steady your helm, pal."

"Steady it is."

"Keep her dead afore it!"

The junk was sucked into the last trough before the last rising sea that would break her on that reef. "Well, here goes," said Annie, and got ready to jump, for she would be going in with the velocity of the breaking wave, a good thirty knots, which was like a car crash for shock and would break all hell loose. But as the black reef rose in all its awfulness above their bows, and Annie hauled himself up on the teakwood rail by way of the gun mounting, he felt himself rising as in an elevator at the Waldorf Astoria, with the boat rising under him as the great wave took her up, and up, and up. So Annie hung on, and did not jump, for he was not a slow thinker. The wave rose higher, much higher than the reef, and the *Tiger of the Iron Sea*, all two fifty tons of her, rose with it. Then her prow fell, splitting that great breaker in two, and shot her forward clear onto the top of that wall of coral. Her hull hit it, coming down fast but still level, flat on her keel with a dull, grinding crash. She shuddered from stem to sternpost, buried in a cloud of spray, which fell away, and Annie looked down on the flat, shining rock on which they were lodged, square across it on the junk's broad bottom, near flat too, but rocking slowly but vastly from one bilge to the other, side to side, shuddering like a living beast.

He experienced an uncanny sensation of yawning nothingness, in which the groaning of the hull seemed distant. Her bows were tilted up; ahead there was nothing but blowing skies, emptiness, and foam — besides which, Annie's head instinctively turned to look backwards, and he saw Lai Choi San, hanging from her rigging like a lemur, looking back too, and her yell announced what all could see with great clarity: another vast breaker, tall as a house, climbing against blackness and foam-bearded water behind them, falling upon them.

Annie bent over, holding the bulwarks with both hands as the sea's crest fell upon them from thirty feet. It fell with the sound of water heard only through water, pounding him into the deck, and behind it came the mass of the breaking wave, shoving the junk forward across the surface of the coral, but giving the hull enough lift to save her from a gutting, and then lifting her again like a coconut shell and throwing her across the far edge of the reef. She teetered there like a great log for an interminable moment before toppling into the white foam on the far side of it.

The tail of the wave thrust her forward out of the surf's chaos across the lagoon, the big vessel spinning on her axis like a toy. On either side those fierce knobs of coral rose from the lagoon's floor, whipped with spray. But ahead was a channel along which the rinky-dink waves of the protected water swept the junk, pitching quietly, but intact, as the wind howled through her masts and rigging, unwilling to let her go.

Annie stood up. Captain Wang was down too. He seemed to have hurt something, but he was grinning with a pride that one could not deny him as he looked up at his mistress. She was meshed in the rigging like a black bat, her hair still coiling on the wind, laughing in that noisy Chinese way that Westerners sometimes mistake for hysteria. Her small amah had disappeared (under the rail forrard and down the hatch into the tiller room, as it

291

turned out). But Lai Choi San was not worried about a little thing like that. Annie loved her and wanted to murder her.

A warm, wet wind blew from the north in the wake of the typhoon. It was the residue of the Iron Whirlwind, but it imitated the northeast monsoon, so steady was it. Madame Lai smoothed back her wet hair and pointed back at the reef, upon which waves were still breaking monotonously, a reef that was a few feet lower just in this spot, and a little flatter on top, and a pool and a channel three fathoms deep to catch the hull of a junk just right and see her safe across.

"This one place," said Madame Lai, pointing back. "At this one place, my father's brother bring his junk across in a big storm. Many, many year ago. Before, others have done it. This place called Gate of Angry Sea. Today I take this passage too." She looked disastrously proud and pleased with herself as she said this. Forrard, her men were shouting with pleasure at life's renewal. Some were singing.

She had every reason to feel pleased, thought Annie. His limbs were fatigued; his left hand was still clenched on the teak taffrail. His throat felt hoarse; he figured he had maybe been shouting his opinions and feelings. But now he just nodded slow in Madame Lai's direction as the lagoon current shoved them gently down the channel between the nigger heads. The helmsman's mates were lowering the creaking rudder again, to take charge of her.

They dropped anchor in that lagoon and rested there for three hours or so, shaping up the ship and repairing and rigging the foresail. The typhoon had blown on down the South China Sea. Night fell, and though the wind still gusted and the surf boomed on the Pratas reef, the stars appeared, and gave light enough.

The reef, which was roughly elliptical, surrounded a little hump of sand thick with weather-beaten shrubs like giant cabbages, and a few acutely leaning palm trees. This was the island of Pratas. Convolvuli overgrew everything and steeped this graveyard in their rank perfume. In this bower of flowers, wreckers and pirates had built a temple to Tin Hau: a temple to the goddess of the sea built from wood, from the figureheads of doomed ships, wreathed and carved teak stanchions and balusters, brassbound rails, cabin mirrors, bird's-eye maple paneling, and even the plate and pewter of many a ship's saloon. And when the stocky figures of the wreckers and fishermen were not attending her, her servants were a tribe of ship-wrecked rats, along with the gannets and the sandpipers.

As the men of the *Iron Tiger* poled her slowly past this little temple in the light that was issuing from beneath the sea's edge, they sang a song in praise of their goddess and beat three gongs in an incomprehensible rhythm. They lighted great flaming bundles of joss sticks and flung them into the sea that rippled onto Pratas Island. At precisely the moment demanded by aesthetic sensibility and their profoundly frivolous religious rites, the moon broke over a clear horizon to the west and arose like an empress of silver, the servant of Tin Hau.

chapter 7
"Shut That Damn Door!"

At dawn Captain Wang piloted the junk out through an eastern gap in the reef and proceeded in fair winds for another two days before making a landfall on Cape Bojeador on the northwest tip of Luzon, the northern island of the Philippines.

The big junk slid into the fishing anchorage at dusk, but she was too conspicuous for Madame Lai to hang about. Annie was taken ashore with his suitcase and driven by motor taxicab to the Hotel Oriente, a comfortable spot for well-heeled visitors that he had often dreamed of gracing with his presence. Here Mr. Chung joined him, by steamer from Macao, a couple of days later.

Annie thought quite intensely, though only intermittently, about Madame's almost catastrophically impulsive decision to outrace the typhoon on their crossing. Or

295

was the decision, rather, to take advantage of the Iron Whirlwind so that she would be compelled to leap the barrier reef of Pratas Island? Was this a debt of honor to an ancestor? (In China, the only true debts of honor were to ancestors.)

Annie decided that it was a pattern of circumstances that Madame would no doubt have considered fortuitous that enabled her to take the gamble she did, to bet her ship and her life against the elements — and win. He remembered clearly the only great conversation he had with her on the subject, as they sailed southeast, leaving the Pratas behind them. "You were lucky," Annie had said.

"Of course, a little luck. But I know my vessel. I know my men. I know of that place where the reef is flat and there is clear water beyond."

"Madame Lai, you are capricious. There is no reason to take such a risk in a boat on this sea."

"There is reason," she said. She was back on her silver water pipe, having abandoned Woodbines. "When there is good fortune in the wind, it must be used — even if there is no profit. The signs tell my astrologer, and Tin Hau tell me, that this is a fortunate voyage. I like to show my men, show my ship, that when I have good fortune, I will always win, because I am strong with the spirit of my ancestors."

How logical, thought Annie with empty, wasted cynicism. "I have no faith in your idols," he said. "And I do not believe you have faith in them either, lady. Your religion is a mixup of gods and goddesses borrowed from all over. It is a bunch of malarkey, a damn game. I have no religion, no more'n you, but I don't play games with idols, either."

She nodded seriously. She puffed her pipe softly. "It is true, I play game with my idols. You know why? Let me tell you: better to show the sea we are children. Better to show . . ." She waved at her sails, the white sky, the universe.

"You think your goddesses like bein' offered little bits o' silver paper? Pretendin' it's money? Silver dollars, hard an' heavy?" Annie had always wanted to get a direct answer to this question from a truthfully inclined Chinaman — or woman. But it was no good; she would not get a logical handle on it. "Yes, they like," she said gaily. "Because they know it is all a game of children. The Queen of Heaven see very well that we are foolish as children. And that we are afraid of her. And that we are poor, but not stupid. Why throw real silver dollar to bottom of sea? Hunh?"

Annie did not know how to answer this. He yawned prodigiously. She leaned across and rapped his knee with her pipe to wake him up.

"Better to play game, Captain Dowtly, and not hide that we are children. The will of heaven is not so severe, so cruel with children. What is the name of your small daughter?"

"Maima," said Annie. "Maima is her name." He felt pierced.

Anatole Doultry, a ship's master of his own trading vessels for fourteen years, returned to employment in the merchant marine on May 10th, 1927, as senior wireless officer of the SS *Chow Fa.* Madame Lai's plan to install him in that position was enacted with an impeccable precision that astonished Annie, though he tried not to let this show to Mr. Chung, whom he saw frequently, or to Mr. Ting, a resident of Manila who looked after Madame Lai's business in that city, and who arranged the abrupt illness of the junior wireless operator on the ship, a young man named Chou Ah So.

Chou Ah So was an intelligent person.

He was from a solid Hong Kong telegraph-operating family and had attended the government school for wireless telegraphy. After the nine-month Asian operator's course and much practice in English, he had passed his exams for a coastal certificate with honors. Chou Ah So was a fine example of the new generation of young, bright, technically minded Chinese of the Crown Colony who had acquired modern skills and were welcomed in the international labor market of the shipping industry. The world of radio was expanding rapidly. Young Mr. Chou — he was only twenty-four — got along well with his British bosses, and why not? Nevertheless, Mr. Chung's diligent investigations had picked him out right away as a negotiable property. Chou Ah So's cooperation, his information, and his sudden sickness (cholera was suspected) cost Madame Lai's war chest less than three thousand dollars.

The *Chow Fa*'s scheduled route was Manila–Hong Kong–Shanghai and back, with occasionally a stopover in Amoy. She was a fine Birkenhead-built vessel from Cammell Laird's yards, launched in 1921, oil-fired, twin-screwed, and turbine-powered, of 10,000 registered tons, and 395 feet overall. Her geared Brown-Curtis turbines developed 6,500 horsepower; her cruising speed was sixteen knots. She was a well-found, handsome ship with twin funnels and accommodation for 210 first- and second-class passengers in addition to her four cargo holds, of which one was refrigerated. She regularly carried eight thousand tons deadweight of cargo, for Manila was one of the world's most rapidly expanding ports, and Filipino-Chinese trade was brisk.

Timing was of the essence. The *Chow Fa* normally laid over for ten to twelve days in Manila, where her bulk cargo was loaded. If one of her three wireless operators had fallen sick en route, or in Shanghai or Hong Kong, her master would have carried on with the two remaining. But in Manila there was no excuse for this. Three men were regulated to handle a twenty-four-hour radio service. So in Manila, a sick man would be replaced. The fact that Annie Doultry had a long-standing international operator's certificate and plentiful experience made him an obvious choice as soon as the company was informed, by Chou Ah So himself, that Doultry was in Manila and looking for a job. The fact that he was a white man and a well-known name in seamen's circles would have clinched the matter. His brush with the law on arms-smuggling charges was not held against him in his trade, especially in Asia, where white men stuck together and a smuggling rap was trivial. It also turned out that an old acquaintance of Annie's had recently joined the vessel as first officer. His name was Stoddart McIntosh. Annie had shared a passage with him of seventy-one days, between Brisbane and San Francisco, on the clipper *Thermopylae*, carrying two-and-a-half-thousand tons of wool. That was in about '98, or '96, Annie thought — before the twentieth century dawned upon us, anyway.

Annie had been third mate on that full-rigged legend of a ship, the *Thermopylae*, and McIntosh, who was a few years older, was the second. They remembered each other, though they had never met again after Annie paid himself off in Frisco to head for the Klondike.

"So you went over to the stinkpots after all, Stoddy," said Annie as he looked over the *Chow Fa*'s accommodations with this small and red-nosed old salt from Aberdeen. "You said you never would."

McIntosh said: "The grub's good on this

tub. This here's yer cabin." He went in and opened a locker door, for all the world mine host at a country inn. He plumped himself down on the bunk, testing its springs for his old shipmate, and looked up at him with a squinty, ruddy face from under his rather grubby cap.

"Ye've no got any slimmer, me lad." He was smoking one of Annie's Woodbines. "I have a family in Melbourne. I have three fine girls. I was master of the *James Dollar*, you know. She was a four-master of Robert Dollar's, big iron bark, Port Glasgow she was built. We was shippin' sugar from Hawaii, but they could not make it pay, so they laid her up."

McIntosh stepped out on deck and looked at the port of Manila and the forest of grimy funnels abeam its eleven piers. "If you can't beat 'em, join 'em." The scene was alive with the iridescence and perfume of coconut oil, the fumes of the great engines, the prowess of American empire building.

Annie did the trip twice, Manila–Hong Kong–Shanghai–Hong Kong–Manila, nine days out and eight back. It was easy work. His job was in fact plain wireless operator and his pay was forty-two dollars a week.

There was nothing unusual about certain sailing ships' senior officers, even masters, who had not managed, or wished, to move with the times, seeing their later years out in minor sinecures aboard steamships — especially in Asia. Annie had moved his official address to the Seamen's Institute in Manila. He figured that Barney would never think of looking for him there, at an address synonymous with reduced circumstances and broken-down sailor men.

By the third trip, he had gotten to know the *Chow Fa* thoroughly, end to end. He liked McIntosh more now than he had thirty years back. The man remembered a lot of things about the old days that Annie had forgotten (a deliberate forgetting or not, how could he remember now?). But Annie figured he had better buy McIntosh a drink and listen to him ramble on. He figured it would be wise to gain his confidence. It was part of the plan.

They went to a bar near the port on Escort Street. Annie remembered Manila when the street had not been there. McIntosh just drank beer; his stomach was giving him problems. Annie had a couple of schnapps with lemon juice — the barman called it a Krupp's Cannon — and as Stoddy talked about San Francisco, Annie's memory suddenly started up and he saw it all as if it were yesterday.

It was a strange sensation for Annie. But then, he felt he had not been quite the same since drinking all that shit with Madame Lai's boys; he put it down to that. Stoddy McIntosh was talking of the graybeard that had pooped the *Highland Glen* in appalling seas west and south of Cape Stiff. It was in October; and those omnipotent sea swells were running up against Cape Horn and wearing down its black and icy rocks with their revenge, sixty feet from the froth of their beards to the immense troughs of their malevolence.

Now Annie could see it. He could see that sea drawing back like an immense hand. As the clipper rose from the trough, he could see through a mist of water like it was on the Pratas reef, but a lot colder, the wheel of the *Highland Glen* shattered into a shepherd's star and the boats too, all matchwooded, and the deckhouse hatch stove in, the helmsman thrown forty feet forward by that gray hand, hollering from his broken thigh and holding on to a stay for his life as the sea tried to take him. She was swept from poop to stern. Two men had gone with that one, and the foretopmast a few minutes later, everything blown to strips that flew like the white pennants of the devil's own ship. But sixty-eight days later they berthed in Liverpool, still in one piece, and unloaded twenty-five hundred tons of copper ore. Annie remembered it, now. He saw it all, clear as a bell.

In China, things were getting crazier and crazier. The Fourth Division of the Nationalist Sixth Army, heavily Communist, had occupied Nanking, and General Cheng Chien had encouraged his troops to loot all the foreign consulates, businesses, and missionary institutions. The U.S. consul had signaled the American destroyers *Noa* and *Reston*, and they had shelled the city from the river, placing a barrage of shrapnel into the streets. HMS *Emerald*, a big British destroyer, was attacked by rifle fire at her berth and a blue-jacket killed, so she opened up on the town with her 4.7-inch guns. The Communist newspapers claimed thousands killed; the Foreign Devils said not more than a few dozen. A week later, in Shanghai, already occupied by Generalissimo Chiang Kai-shek's Twenty-fourth Nationalist Army corps, the great leader had struck at the Communist militia that were running the city's streets armed with Mausers and machine guns, and killed as many of them as he could. The battle raged in the alleys for days. The hard-core Red cadres holed up in their union buildings and factories and fought to the bitter end.

But to Annie, playing dominoes with the chief engineer of the *Chow Fa* (David Mogden was his name) in the wardroom first night out of Manila on May 29th, though all this was happening in their port of call it seemed remote and irrelevant. Trade went on, the British and American navies were out there, and the seas were not China's domain — the West had seized them. Besides, it was a quarter to eleven, sleepy time down south, and Annie might not make it to Shanghai. He had personally watched the loading of four and three-quarters tons of silver (in four hundred-pound crates) at Pier 9 a couple of hours before they cast off. Plenty of passengers had come aboard too, but Annie had paid no attention to them. His mind was on his work.

The third officer of the *Chow Fa*, the "pidgin snatcher," and easily the most obnoxious, was a young man called Peter Storch. He was one of your cartoon-character stiff-upper-lip Englishmen in all respects but one: he was an Aussie from Port

Adelaide. His impeccable white tunic was ludicrously belted with a regulation Royal Navy webbing belt and holster, in which was stuffed a huge Colt cowboy-style long-cartridge .44 revolver. This was about the most powerful sidearm you could get hold of in those days, before magnum loads. Annie had the feeling young Storch was a bit of a fanatic. He was a nitwit, too.

Right after breakfast, an hour before departure time (which was 10:00 a.m.), Storch was out on the job, looking for "pidgin." He was junior deck officer, and being called the "pidgin snatcher" reflected one of his duties. Now this word "pidgin" was a sort of Chinese slang for "business," and it had also come to refer to small quantities of deck cargo that were snuck aboard a ship by the stevedores in return for bribes, but were not on the cargo manifest and were thus transported for free. To combat this practice, it was the pidgin snatcher's duty to keep an eye on deck cargo being loaded, last thing before departure. This was when the steerage passengers were boarding too, and confusion and argument about what was legitimate "baggage" and what ought to be called "cargo" was usual.

Storch took pleasure in the exercise of authority; and what is wrong with that?

With his big pistol strapped around his dapper white waist and his clipboard with the official cargo manifest, he strutted about the tween-decks cargo area poking into bundles and indecipherable cardboard boxes and disturbing the crates of chickens that Chinese working people tended to carry everywhere. Most of the arguments he got into were with women — old grandmothers, little girls — for it was usually the women who looked after the family baggage.

Annie was on deck too, leaning on the rail of A deck. On the dockside of Pier 9 below, four of the *Chow Fa*'s Sikh guards, aided by a couple of Filipino police, were checking the boarding steerage travelers for arms. But it was a fool's job, and everyone knew it. They did not search the women, for example. And if arms were going to be smuggled aboard, they would be there already, hidden in the general cargo or the official baggage room. No professional pirate in that day and age would risk an earnest pidgin snatcher's discovery of handguns hidden among the chickens or shotguns up an old lady's skirts.

At 8:15 two large vans came chugging up the pier preceded by two cops riding a motorcycle sidecar and followed by a Ford with a couple of guys from a bank. The cavalcade stopped alongside number 2 hold, forward, but that was not where the van's contents were going to be stowed. They used the ship's own cargo hoists, not the new electric cranes of which the Luzon Stevedoring Company was so proud, to load the silver.

Madame Lai had been right about the silver, too. It was not on the official cargo manifest. It had been scheduled by Butterfield and Squires, the agents, for transport on June 10th, the *Chow Fa*'s next departure. This was a security measure designed to confuse piratical intelligence systems. Bullion and specie were rarely transported on the dates scheduled, and if they were, this also was considered a security measure, because of the rarity of such conformance between plans and practice. But Madame Lai's intelligence gathering was equal to all subterfuge. She had known when the real silver would leave, and she was right.

It was in wooden crates weighing nearly four hundred pounds apiece, so logic indicated to Annie that they contained six ingots of silver. There were twenty-eight of the crates. Annie counted them as his own personal check; for Madame Lai had said there would be over four and a half tons, and Mr. Chung and Mr. Ting had confirmed this. So there was.

The twenty-eight crates were lowered to the main deck and thence manhandled on trolleys to the strong room. This was right under the bridge deck-house; it was within the "citadel," in other words. A large room with no exterior ports, the citadel had two sets of steel doors as its only access. The silver about half filled it; there was some other stuff in there, too, passengers' valuables and so on.

Annie went down and watched them stow the bullion for a while. First Officer McIntosh was there, with the purser, Harry Stokes; it was their duty to be present. Annie shared the time of day with them before wandering off, but his mind was on his work.

The import and export of silver was a big and very mysterious business in China. The Chinese economy was held by many to be based — if it was based on anything — on silver. This had always, for the Chinese, been a much more significant metal than gold, both practically and mystically. The Chinese ounce of silver, called the tael, was the basis of all serious transactions.

Oddly enough, hardly any silver was ever mined in China. But the accumulation of it had been considered of primary importance by the Dragon Emperors for five thousand years. The first Opium War was fought against Britain principally because of imperial concern about the huge outflow of silver to pay for the drug. China was the world's largest market for the cool white metal, the Metal of the Moon. Gold was never in the same league, in Chinese eyes.

In Manila silver was stored, specifically for Chinese tastes, in ingots of 1,000 Shanghai taels, or about 62 pounds apiece, and a fineness of 999 thousandths. Each of those giant bricks was worth wholesale around 1,600 Hong Kong dollars, or 800 of the U.S. variety. Seen in a great luminous stack, as Annie saw them in his mind's eye, they looked extraordinarily beautiful. In fact, this eye of his took care to keep that fine image shining like a light upon the map of his moves as he plotted them upon the ceiling of his little cabin, from his prone position on the bunk. And Annie liked to think it was good American silver, not Mexican stuff, that lay in the strong wooden boxes in the *Chow Fa*'s strong room, on the main deck, right underneath the wireless cabin, which was right next door.

The other two radio operators, both Chinese, occupied a two-berth cabin on the port side. Annie's was to starboard. Chou Ah So had been the senior operator, responsible directly to Captain Bristow, the master of the *Chow Fa,* for all operations of the apparatus, as it was called. Both transmitter and receiver were Marconis, the former a Poulsen arc 12-kilowatt instrument, the latter a three-valve job. The radio cabin was midships, between the operators' cabins, all three opening onto a transverse corridor. The cabin was a dark, windowless little room with a humming ventilator, evidence of the odd idea of some experts that seclusion, or even pitch darkness, was conducive to superior Morse telegraphy.

On the forward side of the corridor were the junior deck officers' and the third engineer's cabins. Above were the master's, chief engineer's, and first officer's comparatively spacious accommodations. Atop all were the bridge and chart room. These three decks, or floors, of the "deckhouse," as they still called it, were referred to as A deck, upper deck, and bridge deck; and they constituted both the nerve center and a Caucasian enclave, the heart and mind of the ship. This area could be completely cut off from both the first- and second-class passenger accommodation sternwards (with its dining saloon sumptuous with oak dado and French gray panels, and central lighting well surmounted by a stained-glass skylight, and its smoking room with "cottage" windows and frieze panels of scenes of an English hunting field). It was also cut off from the main deck below, where the steward berthed forrard and the steerage passengers (who often numbered up to a thousand, but never were listed on a ship's official "passenger accommodation") had their great and smelly dormitory in the after regions, the ass of the ship.

It struck Annie as amusing that three Chinese had come to share this so-called "citadel" just because they could operate a radio and could be had for less wages. But they were obligated to share this privileged accommodation because they were an absolutely indispensable part of this command structure, referred to in the Piracy Commission Report as the "citadel concept" of defense against the Wolves of the Sea.

Stoddy McIntosh had demonstrated the

setup the morning after Annie had joined the ship. There were heavy steel bullet-proof doors with observation windows on the main deck and on A deck; and steel grilles forward and at the bottom of the companionways leading up to the bridge, and even along the open sides of the vessel adjoining the superstructure. There were extra grilles on both doors to the bridge and even hinged, half-inch steel "dodgers" that could be swung up or out to cover officers on the bridge from small-arms fire that might be directed from the fo'c'sle, where most of the crew (Chinese and Filipinos, numbering about 120) were berthed.

McIntosh issued Annie his regulation sidearms: a nice Smith & Wesson patent .38 revolver, the hammerless model, in a web holster with belt, plus three dozen rounds. Annie stuck it in his waistband like most of the officers did, who were always cursing the things as if ashamed of them. Also, they were boring to have to carry around in the heat and all, but the latest Piracy Prevention rules were adamant about this. Every officer had a Winchester .300 repeating rifle in his cabin, and there were six more in a locker on the bridge together with enough ammo to hold a battalion at bay from this improvised fortress, this "citadel."

It was expected that pirates would bribe crew members to facilitate operations. That is where the traditional Indian guard system had its relevancy. The Indians of Hong Kong were there to work for the British. They never had anything to do with the Chinese except in the capacity of police, prison guards, soldiers, or security persons on ferries and railways. They were almost all ex–Indian army men, and their loyalty was taken for granted. It is amazing, but there is no record of any Indian army men betraying their employers in Hong Kong.

The guards aboard the *Chow Fa* were Sikhs, like the warders at Victoria Gaol. For Annie it struck a sweet chord of memory's sad song to see them walking stolidly up and down, their Greener riot guns on their shoulders as if they were army Lee-Enfields. Their turbans were white, immaculate, enfolding their immense lengths of hair and beard, parted at the chin's apex and hitched up smooth and neat behind the ears. The twelve of them cooked at allotted times in the ship's galley. They had tremendous fish curries and pilaus with tinned peas. The Chinese cooks were greatly inconvenienced but had to put up with it.

"Have you ever studied the science of psychology, Stoddy?" asked Annie.

"I heard of it. But I never put my mind to studyin' up on it."

"The Chinese have no psychology," said Annie. They were in the wardroom, drinking lemonade. Annie was going on duty at 9:00 p.m.; he had elected to take the night watch, and no one had objected. "That is why they cannot trust each other, or anybody else." What an absurd statement; he made it in solemn jest, no doubt.

"They believe in devils. They are heathens," said McIntosh. He filled his pipe — he was going to go to bed after this one. A cool breeze puffed in the open door to A deck, and the sea shone, though the moon was not up yet. It was starlight, pure and simple. Neither of these characters was oblivious to the beauty of the scene.

"The Chinese," said Annie, "are a subject of interest to me, Stoddy."

McIntosh grunted. They did not interest him, but then he was a dull man, dull but solid, and he had never gotten to know a Chinese woman properly. In fact, the Chinese tended to like a man like Stoddart

McIntosh, a man with no imagination and no belief in devils, a chap who believed there were causes and effects, a system of natural laws, God-given or not being an unimportant issue.

"You know what they believe in? The power of the will." Annie said it with emphasis. "The various wills of Nature being no different from a man's or a devil's, just a wee bit more powerful. Now, you and me, we have a will. Is there any laws as governs it?" There he goes — it's Scots he is speaking again. "Can you answer me that, Stoddy?"

"There's laws to human nature, Annie."

"If you believe that, you are a psychologist, Stoddy."

This pleased McIntosh, though you would not have guessed it from his expression.

Later on, Annie said: "If there is one thing they have any worship for, it is absolute capriciousness. It is blind fate. It is chance. Maybe that's a natural inclination in all of us, red, white, yellow, and blue — what d'ye think, Stoddy? To worship that blindness? Is there something to that thought?"

"I like a bet once in a while myself," the old shellback said. "But they say there are laws to it too. To a bet, I'm speakin' of, the odds of it. Or there would be no book-makers."

"Very true, Stoddy. Very true. I'm up a blind alley, pal, and no mistake." Annie shook his head and went out on deck. He leaned upon the rail and removed his cap, letting the breeze blow about his face and hair.

Peter Storch, the third officer, was in charge of the night watch beginning twelve midnight, and Annie went up to the bridge to say hello before going on duty, as was customary. The ship was nearly fourteen hours out of Manila and the weather could not have been better. Storch was in the chart room making his entry in the duty book.

The helmsman's relief was already on the bridge. Annie said to Storch: "There's a new station started in Shanghai playing music for dancing, sir. You want to pop down and have a listen? Reception is excellent tonight."

The "sir" was ironic, of course. Annie was not attracted to Third Officer Storch; but it was not the man's fault, it was nature's. Storch thanked him politely and smiled emptily; he had no appreciation for the limpid romance of the airwaves.

Annie went down again to A deck. He went into his cabin and closed the door. He took the gun they had given him from his belt, unloaded it, and dismantled it. He unlimbered his Swiss Army knife, too, and with its aid bent the firing pin of the revolver several degrees. It was difficult to do, but afterwards you could pull the trigger and the thing would not fire, because the pin just missed the cap of the cartridge.

Annie stuck the revolver back in his belt and then opened his suitcase and got his Walther and stashed it in his special undershorts. These were very old-fashioned ones, with a drawstring in them instead of elastic, which was ideal for supporting a neat-featured automatic just beneath the beer barrel. Its muzzle rested reassuringly on the wide root of his cock, the whole ensemble invisible under his voluminous, Doultryesque seagoing pants of khaki drill.

From his suitcase Annie also took out his bronze mirror. (He assumed it was his, temporarily anyway, for Madame Lai had not asked for it back.) Annie had a look at himself. In the shady cabin, whose porthole gave on the deck beneath the promenade, the light was perfect for the mirror.

Needless to say, Annie had retrimmed his beard all by himself. He had sacrificed its formidable points, not for aesthetic reasons, but to look like a sea captain again, rather than some Mephistophelean Chinese demiurge. To tell the truth, he had liked those bristly points, even though there was a residue of red paint in them that looked like ancient bloodstains. But he could not at this time afford to strike awe and terror into the eyes of one and all, given the ticklish circumstances of his mission.

He put away the mirror and went next door to take his watch.

Mr. Peter Justice, one of the *Chow Fa*'s two junior wireless telegraph operators, was only half Chinese. He was a pleasant, educated, soft-speaking man who reminded people of the actor Warner Oland — without his malice. He did not know his father, who may have been anything but was probably a seaman. The reason why his mother (or he himself?) had chosen the name Justice was a question that apparently nobody had ever asked, except Annie. The half-caste wireless operator had said: "It is not really a name; it was a hope. A vain hope."

Peter Justice accepted a couple of Annie's ever-handy Woodbines as he signed off, and informed his relief that he had just sent the midnight "negative" signal to Cape d'Aguilar, Hong Kong, and also signaled the Chinese wireless station at Canton on 1800 meters for test purposes. He said he got a very weak receive signal from Canton. Peter was a thorough man, always eager to test transmission conditions.

Annie said good night to Peter and settled down at the desk. There was always that rancid, acidic smell in the wireless cabin from the emergency batteries stacked in the corner.

He flipped the Morse key. It had a brass bar, a spring with tension adjustment, a gap between its points, also adjustable (one-sixteenth of an inch was the professional average), and a black knob of Bakelite. It was an instrument of elegance and strong meaning.

Annie put on the headphones. He twiddled the dial to see if Swatow was there, at 1800 meters. Swatow had been run for a while by Marshal Sun Chuan-fang; it was part of his domain. When he withdrew, the Nationalists had taken over; and after that the station was on and off the air with whimsical irregularity. The Communist factions used it as a symbol of anti-Imperialist intransigence. But Hong Kong was coming in, loud and clear. Most of the traffic was with merchant ships, acknowledging position reports and relaying passengers' telegrams to the post office. First-class passengers had cottoned to this quickly: sending business telegrams to and from ships had a touch of class, a whiff of modernity; one day, they said, people would have wireless telephones in their Buicks and Bentleys.

Now for the adjustment of the gap. A small ceremony, but important: the gap between the delicately spring-loaded contacts of the key. Annie adjusted it by twiddling the set screw, by the feel of it, the touch, the smell of it. This gap is a string of the maestro's violin, the flex in the gold tip of the poet's pen, the rhythm of the slave's great punkah fan in the sultan's library — in short, a thing of personal persuasion, but potentially earth-girdling echoes. Annie altered it by one hundredth of an inch. Closer, a closer gap than Operator Peter Justice could handle. Annie liked a tight key. He could send twenty-five words a minute. Maybe that's what kept his forefinger in such nimble shape and rhythmic condition.

The Sikh guards changed over every four hours, like the ship's watches, but on the half hour, to avoid insecure confusion. They had their own odd system of rotation; but it meant six of them were always on duty, day or night. A corporal called Jamal Singh, who had once been a corporal of Spahi lancers in a Punjabi cavalry regiment, was their senior man. He was not young — none of them were young, and all of them were tough — and he had done duty on ships now for three or four years. He had survived the piracy of the *Tung Chou* in 1925 and took his job seriously. But Sikhs always took their jobs seriously; they are extremely conscientious people. The Hong Kong Police Anti-Piracy Unit had become a well-organized institution and encouraged a small immigrant movement of retired Indian soldiers to the Crown Colony to fill its ranks, which numbered nearly two thousand by '27. But this impression of efficiency, of the Empire rising to an emergency, was marred by continual arguments of a paranoid nature raised by the China Coast officers' union over questions of authority: to whom did the guards owe their first allegiance — the captain superintendent of police or the captain of the ship they served on? The question was never finally settled, from a disciplinary point of view. But the facts of their valor in action spoke for themselves. The pirates always went for the guards first, and an amazingly high proportion of them were killed or wounded. It was the captain's decision when to surrender a ship. Unless or until he did so, the Indians fought till they were shot down.

A security system is only as good as its men. But the system of the system is important; its tactics and cunning are relevant. Experience had proved that the moment of greatest vulnerability was the moment now imminent. Annie consulted his Rolex. The guard was about to change.

The prime weakness had to do with accommodation. Until someone designed ships that had space for a detachment of Indian guards berthed in the officers' quarters, they had to be housed with the crew, in the front, or (as on the *Chow Fa*) with the stewards and kitchen staff at the back. Berthing the Chinese wireless operators within the locked steel doors, behind the grilles, in the "citadel" of the bridge deckhouse had already bent conventions and accommodations way out of shape. There was simply no room for the guards, too. So, when their watch changed, the reliefs had to come in and the duty roster had to go out. Through these steel doors. On the *Sunning*, the *Seang Bee*, and a dozen other ships, this was the moment when those bastard pirates had chosen to rush the bridge behind a hail of bullets.

Annie left the door of the wireless cabin open. Via the transverse corridor, he could hear the clump of the men's boots as they positioned themselves. He had watched their moves; he could visualize their bearded, solid wariness. They did not reveal which door they would use, port or starboard side, until the four relief guards marched up and positioned themselves outside it, their Greener guns across their chests. Behind the door, one man would unlock it — there was no keyhole on the "unsafe" side, as they called it — while two of his buddies covered him from behind the steel "dodger" at the foot of the steps to the bridge. The fourth man remained at the top, by the grilled gate of the bridge itself, covering those below. Beside the Sikh would be the officer of the watch — Third Officer Storch tonight, with his .44 in his fist, hoping in his heart of hearts for some action.

Annie listened to the polite orders of

Corporal Singh, who was going off duty. He listened to the boots and the clanking of the gates, the going in and the coming out. There were some cheerful exchanges in Panjabi, and then it was all quiet again on the *Chow Fa.*

Down a floor, on the main deck, a similar routine took place at the upper forward doors to the engine room. This was the unpopular detail with the Indians, stoical though they were. The heat of the engine room was an engineer's burden, but it had to be shared by the guards, in rotation of course. However, there was a general feeling that the rigorous protection of these nether regions of clanking steam, though vital to the ship, was superfluous from a strategic point of view. The wireless room was now the vital target; if a raiding party could not neutralize it instantly, an SOS would bring the navy. Of course, it took the navy a little while to move; but when it moved, the captured ship would be moving too, with their chief at the wheel and his boys all over the ship, looting it. To have His Majesty's Navy after you was no joke, even for a Chinese pirate.

Annie sat in a dozing position with his earphones on, listening to Hong Kong. At about 9:45 the cabin boy brought him a small pot of coffee. Annie was just taking his first hot sip, his tongue protruding about a quarter-inch, its nether side on hot enamel, when there came a tap on the door, and Harry Stokes stuck his head in.

"Hallo, Annie," he said.

"Hiya, Skroff," said Annie, peering up from his slumped position. "Skroff" meant "purser," Harry's job. He was an accountant, like Mr. Chung. But Harry was a solid, law-abiding, friendly, and industrious faggot of about thirty-five, with a boy in every port. Now, Annie had taken pains to be friendly but also to keep hisself to hisself. Getting chummy with individuals was not part of his plans; in fact, it could be an impediment, as Harry's presence in Annie's wireless cabin was now proving. Annie cursed himself, literally saying, "Fuck you, Annie," quite loud. He had got into a habit of talking to the Skroff in the dining saloon, of having cups of tea with him and McIntosh and discussing show business. Now look at the spot he was in.

"I thought I might take pity on you, mate. In your solitude," said Harry Stokes, easing his way in.

Annie eyed him.

"Shall I have my coffee brought in?"

327

asked Harry. He had an *Everybody's* picture magazine under his arm. He was a very nice-looking man, with fair hair and a slight cast to one of his eyes, almost unnoticeable except when he looked dead at you. Which he did; he looked at people like that — and they were taken with the unbalanced look of those magnificent, round blue eyes. He was a tough cookie, though, and never passed up a chance to smash people in the mouth. You couldn't help liking him.

Annie said nothing. He slumped there in front of his little desk with all the radio paraphernalia on it, and the fire extinguisher on the wall and the fan humming irritatingly, and sipped his coffee with a very tired expression on his face.

"You wouldn't happen to have a Woodbine on you, would you, old boy?" said Harry.

"Fuck off," said Annie.

"I beg your pardon?"

"Fuck off, you fuckin' fag," said Annie. "Before I smash your face in. You ever try gettin' into my pants again, I'll tear your prick out by the roots and make you eat it."

Harry looked at him as if he was crazy. This young, powerful man, in the prime of life and condition, was too astonished to get mad. He raised his eyebrows and said, "Well, aren't you in a mood? Gee whiz!" Then he smiled, faintly embarrassed perhaps but no more than faintly, and looked vaguely around the cabin. There was a pinup of some dolly or other stuck on the bulletin board. Just this one girl, a brown-haired bitch. She caught Harry's sour eye.

Meanwhile, Annie sat there. He rubbed his temple with his finger, gazing into the face of his dial, the dial of the face of his electric machine. He seemed to fill the available space. So Harry left, quietly closing the door behind him. He was strongly attracted to Annie, but he realized this was a strange man.

Annie listened once more to Hong Kong. There was a big Japanese ship, the *Manshu Maru*, reporting her position off the Pescadores and lousy weather with fog. Reception was spotty. Fog is good for evil-doers, and the Hall of Righteous Heroes of the Yellow Banner, of which I am one (thought Annie), is no exception. Here we go.

He switched on his transmitter. It took a few seconds to warm up. Then he tuned it to 1350 meters and transmitted the message, "Humpty Dumpty sat on a wall." He repeated this a couple of times and then listened in. Sure enough, a signal came back from the yonder.

The cabin boy tapped on the door and came in. He asked Annie: "You likee more coffee? Plenty more topside."

"No, thank you," said Annie, writing meaningless words on his pad. The boy left. Annie unhitched his headset and hauled his Walther out of his pants to check the safety. The trouble with Walthers was you could never just feel whether the safety was on, with a finger slipped into the waistband of the undershorts. Then he replaced his weapon in its niche, got up, pulled the transmitter partway out of its rack, and dexterously removed a small but vital component with a screwdriver. Dropping this thingamajig in his pocket, he opened the door and wandered out.

There were the two guards there. They were leaning there in the shadows, one of them against the rail, having a chat. The deck was reasonably well lit. Both men glanced at Annie, though there was no need to stiffen; they were always pretty stiff-looking, even when taking it easy. And though there was no need, one of them twirled his mustache. Then the other, cradling his gun like a child, walked away forward. That was the system: one on the bridge at all times, one at each main gate on A deck, and one walking about checking the forward gates and so on. So, being experienced sentries, they traded places and talked about sex. The Sikhs are a sexy bunch of people. The one who walked away looked Annie in the eye (Annie, standing in the corridor's entrance, surveying the scene like an admiral) and saluted him smartly.

This was very gratifying to the radio officer. He saluted the man back. Then, as guard number one disappeared, Annie went to the rail, leaned out backwards over the sea, and fixed his eye upon the foremast.

There was a running light up there, but that was not the point: he was interested in a more mysterious radiance. Gathering his brows with an expression of ungovernable rage, he swore at the radio antenna. Just a wire, a length of naked wire strung a hundred and twenty feet between the foremast and the number-one funnel. About midway, a second wire descended to the bridge and thence by an interior route to the wireless cabin.

"Fuck you," he hissed. "Fuck that bitch!"

He glared at the guard — Mohan was his name, stocky, big-nosed, very Semitic looking despite his handle: "Which of you bums has been fucking with my aerial?" The thick, sweet finger pointing upward; the eyes violent, vituperative, vengeful.

Mohan was used to being sworn at, but Annie was something else. However, the Sikh retained his composure and looked calmly upwards. The aerial, as the limeys called it, or antenna, was plain to see, reflecting the running light iridescently. Mohan did not know what the hell Annie was talking about, and made this plain by saying briskly, "No, sah," with a don't-ask-me expression.

Annie clumped up the steps to the bridge.

The Chinese quartermaster at the wheel and his number two could sense the irritation in the footsteps and avoided his eye. Peter Storch was out on the wing of the bridge staring at the featureless night through binoculars exactly like Captain Wang's. Annie went over to him and said, "There's something up with the goddamned antenna. I mean aerial." He pointed with his screwdriver.

From the bridge the overhead wire was a lot closer, and the input wire came down to a junction box bolted to the wheelhouse itself, just by the door. This Annie proceeded to attack with the screwdriver, muttering to himself, while young Storch looked on, asking mindless questions. He didn't know a thing about radios, a point on which Annie had satisfied himself days ago.

"It's shorting out," said Annie. "I can't get a signal." He poked at the junction box's brassy interior. "This is okay. Everything hunky-dory this end." He replaced the cover. "Got to be an insulator. The mast end or the funnel, what do you think, Peter?"

Annie was staring at the funnel. In the reflected light from the promenade deck below, you could see the glass insulator where the aft end of the antenna was secured to the front of the stack a couple of feet from its black-painted top. "Peter," said Annie, "I'm going to check that insulator. It could be cracked."

"Ah, Doultry," said Storch. "Tell me this. Could it be sabotage?"

Annie gave him a dark look as he descended the steps. "Could be, Peter. There's at least one chance in a million it could be sabotage."

Annie strode to the steel door exiting to

A deck. "Open up, open up!" he said loudly to Mohan. The other guard, the big one, was there too. "Wireless kaput," Annie announced. "Kaput, savvy? Kaput topside."

"I speak English, sah," said Mohan, extracting a key ring from his pants pocket, heavy with keys to six steel doors.

"Then you can come with me, pal," said Annie. "I want an escort. It could be sabotage."

Mohan understood the meaning of that word very well. He opened the small round view port in the door and peered through. He could see the length of the A-deck promenade. It was lit quite well; there were two or three second-class passengers, all Asiatics, outside the door to their dining saloon at the far end, fifty feet away. But the opening of the door was an exercise in caution all the same. The other guard covered his colleague from behind as Mohan followed Annie out.

Annie clattered up the steps to the boat deck, followed by his escort, and thence by a ladder with a Crew Only sign to the deckhouse roof, cluttered with ventilators and fan housings. They walked aft to the funnel. It looked big, its pale blue paler in the starlight, smoke coiling sternwards in the breeze of the passage.

Annie unhitched the rope that ran up the funnel to the antenna, and rapidly lowered it. It was like letting down a clothesline. He heard the sound of the Victrola in the first-class lounge which opened onto the promenade deck just below, and Al Jolson's awful voice singing some ditty. There was laughter, too. There were about fifty first-class passengers aboard, whitees mostly, British and American and German, and a few Filipino businessmen, as always very scrupulously dressed, some with wives. And a half-dozen Chinese of the same type, but without wives. Even well-off Chinese usually traveled second-class; why waste money? (But they used to tell each other it was to avoid having to mix with white people.)

Of course, there was nothing wrong with the antenna's glass insulator, doughnut-sized and strictly speaking unnecessary. But Annie tinkered with it and the antenna wire, cussing softly under his breath to impress Mohan. "Shorted out," he kept repeating. "See this?" He held up a bit of wire previously secreted in his pocket. "Sabotage!" he said, through his teeth.

After making those phantom repairs and hoisting the antenna again, Annie led the way back down to the A-deck doors in a hurried and furtive fashion. He kept grunting one-liners at Mohan about the antenna being deliberately fucked, and the Sikh flicked off the safety of his shotgun and covered their joint retreat with darting eyes. It should be mentioned that these Greener guns, twelve-gauge pump-action repeaters loaded with seven 00 buckshot shells, were a very good choice of weapon for a close-order ruckus with Chinese hoodlums. The Greeners were similar to the Winchester "trench guns" with which General Pershing had equipped thirty thousand of his men in France in 1917.

Annie rapped on the steel door. Mohan was behind with his back to him, covering the A-deck promenade. The view port in the door swung open and Peter Storch's eye looked out, into Annie's. "Sabotage," said Annie softly.

"Good lord," came Storch's voice. "The swine!"

The clank of the lock. The steel door opened. Annie was going through when there came two shots, almost in his ear, and Mohan toppled to the deck without a word, two holes in his head.

Annie rotated on his axis, an exquisite pirouette, drawing his revolver with great swiftness. There was a Chinese fellow hanging upside down from the boat-deck railing immediately above with a big automatic held in both hands, which he discharged at Annie. But he missed — on purpose, of course. Annie fired at the upside-down face six feet away. *Click* went the firearm with its bent firing pin, and *click* and *click* again as he fired at two more men swinging in over the rail like monkeys from the boat deck above. They had pistols; they ran for the door firing as they came, bullets splattering on the steel but taking care to miss Annie, who nevertheless hollered "Shit!" and fell like the tower of Babel, taking care to trip over Mohan's body and thus to collapse full-length right in the doorway as the other Sikh fired his Greener through it, though most anxious to slam it shut.

It was beautifully timed. It was a circus fall, in honor of Annie's mother's favorite lover, an acrobat of Italian extraction.

As Annie went down with such perfection, Peter Storch was letting off his .44 through the viewing port into the vanguard of the attackers. He got one, and the guard got one — how could they miss at that range? But the next two reached the door, Annie trying to squirm through it and the big Sikh trying to jam it closed on his leg. Annie was cursing, his revolver going click instead of bang. A short pirate who looked like a traveling Chinese salesman ran across his back and died in that doorway as the Sikh blew him apart. The man fell on top of Annie, screaming deafeningly. Reacting with great presence of mind, Annie grabbed the man's writhing body and used it as an additional doorstop. The Sikh was thus obliged to try and haul both of them, Annie and the destroyed pirate he was pretending to wrestle with, through that door so that he could close it. It was an impossible task, and the Sikh got shot attempting it. The ear-numbing sound of gunfire in closed quarters seemed to be coming from all over the ship, but Annie could hear McIntosh's voice roaring through it, "Shut that damn door!"

Also lying on his stomach but fifty feet down the A-deck promenade, Ying K'ou, the leader of Madame Lai's men, took very careful aim with a Mauser automatic pistol, bracing his wrist against the stanchion of the ship's rail. He put one slug straight through the view port, no more than four by four inches was his target, and mostly blocked by the muzzle of Third Officer Storch's massive Colt, which had already got at least three hits to its credit. The avenging bullet, made in Germany, struck the .44's cylinder a glancing blow and ricocheted at seven hundred miles an hour into Peter Storch's mouth, open with the concentration of his marksmanship. Emerging sideways behind his ear, it spun off into the sea, the young man's ghost following closely.

In the doorway to the citadel of the *Chow Fa,* and on each side of this door, there was a heap of bodies, some dead, like Peter's; some wounded, like that of the Sikh, who had two bullets in him, and also that of the man who had shot him, though the shotgun had taken a lot of his arm off. There was one alive and well and safe at the bottom — namely, Annie Doultry.

Stoddy McIntosh, first officer, came charging out of his cabin on the upper deck in his undershorts with his Winchester, still shouting, "Shut that damn door!" He looked down the companionladder well and saw the thrashing carnage below. He went straight on down to join it without hesitation, blasting away with the repeating rifle. One of his shots screamed off the steel deck an inch from Annie's head, which still lay upon it, but that was the closest Stoddy got to hitting anything important. There were about six live pirates through the door by now, some of them with a gun in each hand, their brains swamped with adrenaline. Two were already in the wireless cabin. One of the others shot the first officer through his middle.

Stoddy sat down on a step of the companion ladder and shook his head self-critically.

Peter Justice was sitting half-asleep and stark naked in front of the radio, trying to make it function, when the attackers burst in. His hands rose high in the air, but it was a miracle they didn't shoot him too.

Lying on his back, Annie gazed at the stars through a mist of gunsmoke and the bitter perfume of cordite. Two dead men lay atop him. Annie made no attempt to move them.

Ying K'ou, who was dressed in a smart Shanghai suit, stood over Annie's face and grinned down at it. There was firing still going on, mostly down at the engine-room doors, where one of the guards was being a hero with a steam hose. The second engineer, who was on duty, had got himself shot in the hand; but he was keeping the doors closed despite some pretty horrible threats. Two of the pirates had been badly scalded by that steam hose. Where Annie lay, it was quiet now except for some moans and curses, some in Sikh talk, for the big guard was still alive, lying a few feet away just behind the steel door that he had tried so valiantly to close. Annie was covered in blood. Most of it was from the pirates' point man, who had had first taste of the shotgun. But Annie himself looked in a bad way; he looked wounded. His eyes looked like those of a man close to death. Maybe Ying K'ou's grin was supposed to be encouraging.

Annie could see Stoddy McIntosh sitting up there at the top of the companion ladder, his chin on his chest. Ying K'ou, who was no more than twenty-five, went up the steps to the bridge, which his pals had already taken over, pushing his way past McIntosh without a second glance, for anyone could see he was far gone.

Annie dragged his body out from underneath the corpses that encumbered it and pulled himself over to the ship's rail, leaning against it in a sitting position. Two more Chinese with guns came through the door, stepping over the bodies of their comrades. They glanced at Annie but ignored him, for they had strict orders to leave the *gwai lo* with the beard alone, whether he was alive or dead. One of them collected the scattered weapons, including the shotguns of Mohan and the other guard. The latter was unconscious now, or maybe dead. Annie hoped this was not the case, because it would give him a serious problem, a witness problem, since Peter Storch was already a goner. Annie reflected on this issue for a moment or two, as he listened to the occasional muffled shots from the engine room far below, and louder gunshots from the first-class saloon, where they were herding the passengers, frightening them by shooting up the mirrors and hunting scenes. He could also hear the sea, and McIntosh's labored breathing. But Annie had reached a decision; and having done so, he dug into his pants and, with sucked-in stomach, his undershorts, and hauled out his Walther. Next he ripped open his white uniform shirt and with a steady hand gripped a big chunk of his own flesh that in a lesser figure might have been called a "love handle." It was a chunk of solidity, including under its fatty tissue the massive oblique muscle that had given his physique when he was a young man that Hellenic silhouette. And so thinking, he aimed his pistol at this armful of flesh, the muzzle no closer than eight inches to avoid a flash burn, and pulled the trigger.

The slug propelled itself straight through that side of beef. With its exit came plenty more blood and pain enough for Annie to say "Aw, fuck" to the corpses around him as he slipped his gun between the rails and let it fall into the frothing sea far below.

The chief engineer, the cadaverously thin but chubby-natured David Ogden, a Londoner, slept through the worst of the action. He was a drinking man, with a locker full of gin in his cabin, and when he woke up with a gun in his neck he thought it was the DT's again. A contrasting-natured man, Harry Stokes, the Skroff, a peaceable occupation by tradition, was awake and going for his Winchester two seconds after the two shots that had killed Mohan.

Harry had the wisdom to go up to the bridge, instead of down like McIntosh, to get shot. In Peter Storch's enforced absence he found he was the only officer there, and he had slammed the bridge grilles at the top of both companion ladders. These were steel-barred gates, not solid like the ones below. From behind the starboard gate he could see down the well to A deck, and he kept up a steady fire on

343

the hostiles. He got one in the leg. But since neither of the helmsmen would help him (they kept their heads down), he couldn't cover the port side too and found himself sprayed with bullets by two men who were shooting blind through the grille on that side. Harry had no hope of surviving such a situation. He surrendered, still intact.

The six off-duty Sikh guards were surprised in the two cabins that they shared in the after part of the ship by a fusillade that shattered the locks on their doors at the same moment. One of them was shot dead in his bunk for no apparent reason save piratical exuberance. The other five were tied up with wire and locked in one of the cabins.

Captain Bristow had on a pair of extraordinary — for a merchant marine master — pajamas of green-and-white-striped silk. He had surrendered, wisely, after firing several symbolic shots from his pistol. The two Chinese quartermasters had done likewise. Third Officer Storch, Stoddy McIntosh, and Radio Officer Doultry were the only casualties among the ship's deck officers.

The defenders of the engine room held out defiantly until Ying K'ou dragged

Captain Bristow down to their staunch doors and said he would blow his head off. Captain Bristow was no coward and he said nothing, but the third engineer realized enough was enough and opened up.

Ying K'ou, like most of the twenty-eight men with him, had traveled second-class. They were all well dressed and respectable looking. Three had traveled first: a venerable "merchant" with his secretary and concubine, well-heeled and lavish with the tips for a Chinese. His luggage had been inspected, but with formality and not a hope of discovering the numerous handguns concealed in the double bottoms of his trunks.

They herded the officers into the chart room, which led off the wheelhouse aft. Peter Storch's body lay where it fell. Annie, a terrible gore-covered figure, his ripped shirt flapping open so that his wound was plainly visible, helped Harry Stokes carry McIntosh back to his cabin, where they laid him down. There were no doctors in the audience. In the first-class saloon, the wife of an American businessman was screaming at a pirate who was playing with her husband's glass eye, rolling it up and down the bar. The others were systematically going through the passengers' cabins, dumping all valuables in heaps on the dining-room floor under the stained-glass skylight. It was their democratic system: everything valuable went in that pile, and no sleight of hand. But clothes were different; a couple of Ying K'ou's men were sporting new straw boaters, and another had donned a tuxedo that was to his liking, though on the big side.

In the chart room, Captain Bristow said, "You better see to that wound, Doultry. Well tried, old boy, damn well tried."

Ying K'ou told the helmsman to keep exactly to his scheduled course for Hong Kong. The *Chow Fa* steamed on at her steady sixteen knots. The time was about 10:45 p.m. Then the young man went into the chart room and pointed a Greener at Annie's face and said, "Now you come down, make wireless okay to Hong Kong."

"Fuck you," said Annie.

Harry Stokes was bandaging Annie up. Captain Bristow said: "Doultry, do what he tells you. That's an order."

Annie went down to the wireless cabin, escorted by three men. There he produced from his pocket the component he had removed from the transmitter, replaced it, sat down, and sent the "negative" signal and received an acknowledgment from

Hong Kong, still five hundred miles distant. "I sent it correctly, fair and square," he said to Ying K'ou. "Because one of you bums is supposed to understand Morse code, okay? You tell this captain one of you understands this wireless shit, you had me covered all the way."

"I understand Morse code," said Ying K'ou. "You like I send for you? Tippee-tippee tap? In Chinese?" He was in a very good mood. He was a good-looking little bastard, too, with the face of a Mongol aristocrat and the body of a cheetah. When he wasn't grinning, his was a cruel face, smooth-cheeked, the muscles of the cheeks beautiful. Harry Stokes couldn't take his eyes off him once Ying K'ou had left Annie and returned to the chart room. But hasty conclusions should not be read into this. At a very well-timed moment, Harry produced his key ring from his pocket, dangled it in front of Ying K'ou's nose, and said: "See this one? And this big one? They're the keys to the strong room, you bugger." With that, he threw the whole bunch out of the chart-room window, far into the sea.

Ying K'ou just laughed at him and went back down to the wireless cabin, where Annie was closeted, ostensibly under guard. In fact, Annie was sending another signal: "Humpty Dumpty had a great fall," it went. He sent it twice, in fact, on the agreed wavelength, before getting a response: "Receiving you loud and clear," in Chinese. After that, in deference to the remote possibility that the dialogue would be picked up by somebody by chance, no more was said by Madame Lai's new radio operator, a boy of eighteen, on her brand-new Marconi outfit aboard the *Tiger of the Iron Sea*.

Madame Lai had taken the *Chow Fa* with twenty-nine picked men — and Annie Doultry, who picked himself. Of these, four had been killed and five wounded, two of whom died the next day. The ship's company had lost Third Officer Storch, two of the Sikh guards, and a Malay stoker who caught a stray bullet in the head in the engine-room fight. Of the wounded, both First Officer McIntosh and the big Sikh were in poor condition.

There was no morphine in the ship's medical kit. What an irony, in drug-swamped China. They had laid Stoddy on his own bunk, and Annie sat with him. He was in great pain, his legs paralyzed, for the Mauser slug had evidently traversed his gut and lodged in his spine. Captain Bristow was there too.

One of the pirates, a young fellow, came in with some opium and a pipe. Annie melted it with his new lighter in the proper way and made McIntosh smoke it, although he objected. But it made things easier for him.

Naturally, Annie's jammed revolver had been collected by the pirates along with all the ship's other weaponry. But he had arranged to get it back — unloaded, of course. Ying K'ou's second-in-command, a fat but not jolly desperado in a formal blue Chinese business suit, name of Li Yung Fen, returned it to him in McIntosh's cabin. "No good gun," said Blue Suit with a smirk.

Annie took it apart right there. The bent firing pin was painfully obvious, and Annie said, "Ah! Look at this! The pricks. The pricks!"

Captain Bristow looked at it and shook his head. "You left it lying around, I suppose?" he said. Annie stared at him and then at the floor. "Only in me cabin," he murmured. "In the locker." Bristow went on shaking his head.

"That chow boy, Fong," said Stoddy McIntosh. "I never trust them chow boys.

I never liked that Fong."

"The vandalizing of that aerial," said the captain, "was the baited hook that flummoxed us."

"Aye, that it was." McIntosh reached out and touched Annie's hand. "You're a lucky sod, Annie. A lucky sod." He was well away on the opium. "I never did like these here stinkpots, to tell you the truth."

Annie hated the sight of blood. In the ring, especially, a cut on a fighter's face made him wince with sympathy, and nauseous. So when they escorted him down to his wireless cabin again at three a.m., he took the opportunity to ask Ying K'ou to please hose down the deck by the door on A deck. His request was complied with.

He sent the "negative" signal again, under loud threat of deaths slow and grisly to impress the audience. In fact, the whole system was stupid, for no shipmaster would allow a radio operator to refuse and take the consequences from the ingenious knives of frustrated Chinese pirates, even if such a hero existed.

Stoddy McIntosh died around four in the morning. As it happened, he was alone with Annie, Harry Stokes having gone to fetch the blue-suited guy with the opium pipe, who had been most considerate.

Stoddy was gripping Annie's hand; so the latter felt the gradual sensation of the slackening grip, and watched the man's face closely as the soul departed the body.

As many have recorded, there was definitely the impression of an exhalation, of a giving up of something, of an exit made. Though it is a matter of record that Anatole Doultry was an atheist, that he did not give credence to religious or mystical notions, whether Christian or pagan, there is no way of knowing whether or not this unbelief was a fundamentally true and accurate reflection of his convictions. He was a deep thinker, after all. The layers of his deceptions were like the layers of an onion's skin. Still, Annie dreamed of a kernel of truth. But, as anyone knows who has tried to peel one, there is no onion within an onion, just the multitudinous layers of its substance, necessarily finite; and then there is nothing.

When three a.m. came around, Ying K'ou sent the "negative" signal himself, just to show that he wasn't kidding. He didn't even ask Annie how it went, what the code was. He had watched the wireless officer do it twice, and read the letters right off the clicking key like a pro. He was an intelligent young man.

The Sikh guard with two bullets in his thorax did not die. He had an exceptional constitution and survived for many years thereafter on one lung. They put him in Peter Justice's cabin, and people took turns to sit up with him. Ying K'ou allowed the officers normal freedom of movement, since they were sensible and reasonably cooperative. After his bleeding stopped, the Sikh was able to give Captain Bristow a coherent account of what happened at the doors to the *Chow Fa*'s conquered "citadel." He made a point of praising, in a manly way, Radio Officer Poultry's bravery in trying to shoot it out with a gang of pirates with a misfiring revolver (which the Sikh attributed secretly to insane white man's exhibitionism, but he was too much of a gentleman to say so). Nor did the guard labor the point that when Annie fell, shot in the side, he made the closing of the door impossible, thus sealing the fate of the ship.

After this conversation, Captain Bristow gruffly told Annie he would be recommending him for a medal from the governor of the Crown Colony of Hong Kong.

The *Chow Fa* kept her course the following morning and made signals in the bright sunshine to a merchant vessel and HMS *Athena*, a destroyer on regular patrol. The absurd signals — negative indeed they were — were routinely sent and acknowledged by the station on Cape d'Aguilar (though reception in daylight was not as good). The passengers were fed and kept amused by one of the pirates, who dressed up in the chief steward's outfit, complete with gold-braided cap (a cap that later was sold and eventually turned up on the head of one of Madame Lai's gunners).

Predictably enough, a number of passengers wanted to send wireless telegrams to say they would be delayed. This was not permitted, but Ying K'ou said it would be okay to send any normal messages, business or personal, and even messages that gave plausible reasons for changes of plan that effectively postponed people's appointments or subsequent travel arrangements. Annie was given the task of explaining this to the passengers, because he had suggested this concession, to keep up a normal flow of radio messages from the *Chow Fa* during the day's run. Dead silence would have seemed suspicious. Several passengers seized the opportunity, with gracious thanks to the handsome young Chinese devil standing with his Luger pointed at Annie's kidneys at the end of the saloon where they were gathered. Not one of them saw the trick for what it was; that is how little they understood the radio situation, in those days. Anyway, as Annie pointed out to Captain Bristow, the pirates could have invented all sorts of fake messages to send themselves — or even real ones, to their own anxious relatives.

At two p.m., Ying K'ou ordered the helmsman to head eight points northward. By seven o'clock, in the aurora of the lowering sun, Annie could make out from the bridge, where he was smoking with Captain Bristow, the glister of the Pratas reefs on the northwestern horizon.

As darkness fell, the *Chow Fa* anchored in the gentle swells a mile south of the Pratas in about twelve fathoms (or seventy-two feet) of water. Three junks were anchored in the lagoon, inside the reef, where only a junk would dream of going. Two of them had sailed up already and came out through a passage, their canvas stately in the twilight's afterglow. The *Iron Tiger* herself stayed in the lagoon, partly hidden by the low profile of Pratas Island itself. But those tall masts were instantly recognizable to Annie. He could even see, shining with its newness, the antenna strung between her main and mizzen.

Annie's wound was no joke. It was hurting like hell. Like everybody else, he had slept very little. Nobody talked much. Annie had talked hardly at all, save about the wireless operations, since McIntosh died.

The two junks came alongside, on the port side, and made fast to the *Chow Fa.* They were Madame Lai's two fastest boats, half the size of the *Iron Tiger,* but with those very smooth bottoms her hands had once described. There were shouts of exuberant greetings, and then Ying K'ou ordered the steamship's crew to let down ladders, and another forty of Madame Lai's men came aboard.

These boys were the real thing piratewise, in all their panoply, not disguised as second-class traveling salesmen. They wore their red head scarves and their bandoliers and knives, and let off a few hundred rounds for fun, into the funnels mostly. They put the fear of God into the passengers, for they had a consuming passion for one thing, and one thing only: silver! the metal of the moon!

chapter 8
The Wisdom of Pearls

The true pirates, the old-fashioned rogues with the red bandannas, came over the sides of the *Chow Fa* just as determined and bloodthirsty as red ants. From his position of half-collapse, Annie quickly recognized their dilemma — and felt a twinge of sympathy in the throb of his wound. For these were the lads who thought of themselves as pirates and who had probably all seen Doug Fairbanks or some other movie swashbuckler shimmy up a rope, clamber over the side of a ship, run up a pirate flag, and ravish a protesting wench. They knew what was expected of them. Indeed, they expected it themselves. And though Annie had acquired much respect for the discipline and the human insight of Madame Lai, he could feel an unexercised energy or desire in these wild young Chinamen that might just lead to trouble. He crossed his fingers as best he could that every one of them would remember that Annie

Doultry was on their side.

The men from the *Iron Tiger* were, in an odd way, superfluous. The job of taking the *Chow Fa* — tricky and dangerous — had been accomplished by just a few pirates masquerading as respectable passengers, by Annie's sly intervention, and thanks to the strict but predictable regimen of the *Chow Fa* itself. It was natural that the red-bandanna boys would feel at a loss, without a fight to fight. And as it happened, no less a figure than Tang Shihping, Madame Lai's chief gunner, was foremost in this sense of grievance. Not a single shot had had to be fired from the *Iron Tiger*'s guns. Where was the Tiger? What was the Iron? And so Tang had come onboard the captured ship with a shirtful of dynamite (a natural resource of his department of control) and an irresistible urge to set it off.

His target, of course, was the strong room, with its crates of silver. Yes, the doors could have been unscrewed with patient and prolonged endeavor, or taken out with a fraction of the charge employed by Tang. But the master gunner wanted a big bang, and everyone naturally assumed that his expertise was reliable in the matter of adjusting the size of the bang. Alas, he used far too much dynamite — four sticks when one would have sufficed. But those three extra were the mark of emotional need, and they were a match for the fervor of the pirates. Annie did note in passing that the sticks of dynamite were very nearly the same red as the bandannas the pirates sported — or the blood that raced through their giddy heads.

The roar of the explosion was so unexpected that Annie hadn't had time to duck or look away. Two of the pirates — desperate to be the first in the strong room (something to tell their grandchildren) — were picked up like rag dolls and flung aside; so much for grandchildren. From where he was, Annie could see not just their scorched remains, but the scattering of their parts, enough to eliminate the chance of reproduction, and of life itself. The noise of the explosion and the loss of two pirates in a snap of the fingers might have deterred the others; but it only made them bolder, or more crazed. In the smoke, there were hands willing to tear down the shreds of hot metal, never mind the fragments of lost comrades. And as the smoke slipped away in the sea breeze, there was the first sight of crates. It was then that Ying K'ou, still wearing the smart Shanghai suit of gray pinstripe that had disguised him as a passenger, strode forward with several of his Secret Wolves and began to haul the crates out into the light.

This was the climax of the whole operation. Madame Lai was now to be seen on the bridge, like an empress surveying the plunder from foreign wars. Ying K'ou looked up at her for the crucial order, and Annie saw the woman's pale hand flutter — it was a signal, but it was also like an involuntary grasping motion, as if a wanton lived within the empress and longed to tear the crates apart herself.

But it was Ying K'ou and a foot-long iron bar that accomplished the savage destruction of the first crate. He it was who tore away the thin wood and the delicate protection of so many folded newspapers.

And so it was Ying K'ou, so dapper in Shanghai gray, who got the first glimpse of pig iron — rough lumps of unshaped metal, not nearly as sophisticated as the iron bar with which he had opened the crate! He held up one lump of the stuff, as if it were a heart taken from a sacrificed animal, and the babble of noise ceased, like a wind at sea suddenly dropping. Indeed, there was a moment of crushed silence, so funereal, so aghast, Annie could hear the creak and flap of the ship at sea. It took that instant for the truth to sink in. Oh, to be sure, other crates were ripped apart in the frenzy that would very rapidly cry out for revenge — seven other crates in all, and pig iron in every one. At one moment, Annie looked up and saw the stricken face of Madame Lai; at the same instant, she turned to gaze down at him, and in her hard features he felt a first wondering — "Doultry, is this your trick?" — and he knew he'd never met another soul on earth (not even his wife's mother) of whom he'd have more dread if she was pursuing him.

Annie could see that the pirates were very close to mutiny or, worse, to a feeling that, every law of fate having been out-raged, there was no limit to what they might do. Very quickly, the surviving crew of the *Chow Fa* and most of the wealthy passengers were assembled. As if he were to blame, for first revealing the odious pig iron, Ying K'ou was shouting out his in-tent to slaughter every ship's officer left alive. His furious glance clearly included Annie Doultry in this plan. Best of all, he would disembowel Captain Bristow and offer said inner organs to Madame Lai. For a moment, however, that commanding lady was nowhere to be seen. Had she determined that discretion was better than presence in so awkward a situation for an omniscient authority?

There might have been an orgy of murder but for Tang Shih-ping, the chastened chief gunner. He was a dutiful man, a man trained in exactness, as gunners need to be. He was horrified at his own earlier excess of zeal; he, if no one else, was pained by the loss of those two pirates in what was Tang's big bang. And, like a navy man, Tang now strode forward. He actually stood on one of the unopened crates and held a sword aloft, a sword he had picked up from the deck.

"Are you mad?" he cried out to his own men. "Have you forgotten the rest of the strong room? Are you helpless? Have you not thought that the silver might be hidden? Might need artful searching?"

So it was greed that stilled the blood lust in the pirates, and shame that sent them scurrying this way and that, like rats looking for cheese. Tang had made a lucky guess. For in the strong room, behind the crates, there was discovered ten thousand dollars' worth of gold, being shipped to Shanghai to bribe a warlord. It was something — a tip, if you like! But it drove the pirates to a far more diligent search of the passengers, and that produced some good jewelry, some pocket money, and a fine selection of cigarette cases from Tiffany (as well as several bleeding passengers).

It was now that Madame Lai appeared on deck, as much to congratulate her men on every devious picking as to keep a close account of it in her mind. She made no effort for the moment to speak to Annie Doultry. Not that he was good company. He had a small but significant gunshot wound (one the idiot had inflicted on himself). He had put himself in the way of hanging for a quarter-interest in some pig iron plus maybe $2,500 and some odds and ends of jewelry. He had also helped preside over the death of Stoddy McIntosh, not really an old friend so much as a new friend, but one who had reminded him of what might have been. In Stoddy's cabin, it was Annie who gathered together the few things left from a life at sea, and notable in that roundup was an old, cracked photograph, sepia and faded, of the *Thermopylae*, the ship he and Stoddy had sailed on as kids, the lovely *Thermopylae*, the closest rival to the great *Cutty Sark* at sailing the Indian Ocean. Annie began to feel some horror — it was more than remorse — that his gamble had ended so badly for others.

But then he was roughly hauled on deck, where Ying K'ou (who had at last abandoned his gray jacket) was picking hostages: he had selected three wealthy Chinese and was calculating a ransom of maybe another $100,000 from their business partners. And while he was about it, he determined to take two officers — Purser Harry Stokes (had Ying K'ou noticed the guy's avid, sidelong staring?) and . . . "You, *gwai lo*," hissed Ying K'ou. He was pointing at Annie Doultry and leaving no degree of malice in doubt.

So it was that Doultry and Stokes and the three Chinese were taken back to one of the pirate junks. Night was not far away now. So the Secret Wolves methodically smashed the radio and disabled the engine on the *Chow Fa* and left it and the majority of its passengers to drift. The crew could manage repairs and the ship would make harbor safely enough, with the passengers competing to tell and sell their stories of how the fiends had taken every last dollar and nearly cut every throat. The legend of piracy never ends.

Meanwhile, as night fell on calm seas, the junks went back to their mother ship, and in the early hours of the morning pulled alongside the *Iron Tiger* at anchor in the lagoon off Pratas Island. It was a sweet place, at the most pleasant time of year; yet Annie Doultry could not help feeling it was a threshold of doom.

"So what do you think, Annie?" It was the tenth time at least that Harry Stokes had asked him. There they were, confined in a small cabin, and Stokes hadn't had one thought of laying a hand on Annie. Instead, he was pestering him with the interminable and unanswerable question with which a man may try to convince himself that he is not sitting in his own death cell.

Annie was about to give a brutal answer when the door of their cabin was unlocked and two pirates pointed at Annie in a way that left no doubt that he was to go with them.

"God help you, Annie," muttered Harry.

"And you, fruit," grunted Annie.

Annie was taken to the cabin of Madame Lai Choi San herself, where the woman stood waiting in the light of one subdued lamp. Nothing about her stance now was seductive.

"Captain," she sighed. "We not so lucky. Did you betray me?"

"Me?"

"Everyone asking."

"Because I'm the *gwai lo,* the one whitee in the plan? You think I shot myself?"

"I think you might. You talk to Company? You warn them?"

"If I talk to the company, what do I get? A medal, a reward? How much? $5,000? And for that I risk having your fellows lift my head from my neck? Instead of a quarter of $400,000? That and more. How does anyone as smart as you see it that way?"

Madame Lai stared at him, and then at the distance, as if to measure this strange man against all she knew. "Maybe. I thought you like me, Cap?"

"Like?"

"Like Chinese woman?"

Annie reflected. "I don't think 'like' was ever the word."

This conversation might have become warmer and more interesting. There was wine waiting on a table, Annie noted. But at that moment, Mr. Chung slipped into the cabin carrying a small leather attaché case. His face was fixed and frozen, not just because he preferred to offer no reaction to seeing Annie and his mistress alone together, but because of some news he had.

"So, Chung," said Madame Lai with barely masked impatience. "No silver?"

"The silver, I tink, was a flont."

"A front?" asked Madame Lai. "For what?"

"For this," whispered Mr. Chung.

And he put the small attaché case down on a table. "I find this, under the bunk of a second-class passenger. I notice the leather is velly new. Velly good English leather. I wonder why."

So saying, Mr. Chung lifted the lid of the case and brought the lamp closer so that it was like moonlight. It revealed a bed of white cotton wool, and resting in it, like eyeballs, all in tidy rows, were pearls. A great sigh slipped from Madame Lai's tense being. These were no ordinary pearls. There were white pearls, smoke pearls, creamy pearls, pearls the size of fingernails, of knuckles, of roulette balls; and best of all, there were a dozen large green-black pearls, the very richest the sea has to offer.

"How many?" asked Madame Lai. For she knew Chung would have the tally already, and might even have one or two pearls in his own pocket as a keepsake.

"Thlee hunnerd and eight," said Chung. "I count 'em twice."

"The value?" demanded Annie, a part-

366

ner again in the enterprise.

"Conservaly," said Chung, and it was plain that he was a cautious man, "four hunnerd thousand dollar." A pause. "Amelican," he added.

Madame Lai and Mr. Chung were busy with plans and calculations, not to mention the sheer physical gratification of handling every pearl, guessing its weight, and cooing over it. Annie had mixed feelings. He went up on the deck of the *Iron Tiger* and stepped as gently as he could among the bodies of the wounded and the dead. He did not count. He did not have Mr. Chung's clerical turn of mind. He preferred not to know exactly how many of the pirates, the crew, and the Sikh guards had died for the "mistake" of three hundred and eight pearls.

He found himself at the taffrail by the rope locker: it was the place where Madame Lai liked to sit in command. Annie did not bother to make a decision. He simply took off the uniform he had worn on the *Chow Fa* and tossed it into the sea. He had some old clothes, pirate clothes, and they did not really fit him well. He was a bigger man by far than most of the pirates. But he felt more at ease, like a ship that had sailed too long under false colors. So he leaned against the taffrail and smoked one of his last Woodbines.

Sooner or later he was going to need a fresh supply — or give up smoking — or draw a last breath.

"You are melancholy, Captain?" asked Madame Lai. Even at dead of night, in a position of such advantage, he had not heard her creep up on him. It was as if she might have been a ghost. Though, under a dark red dressing gown, very loosely tied, there were enough hints of her bodily substance, there in the real moonlight, not the one preserved for the unveiling of pearls.

"I regret the death of McIntosh," he told her.

"Three months ago, you not even know McIntosh alive."

"Three months ago, darlin', I didn't know you existed."

"You mean, you be sad if I caught bullet?"

Annie looked at her carefully. It was always the same: she was beautiful, or handsome, but lethal, too — the way a snake looks if you catch its eye. "Well, as fer that," he said, and he was home in Edinburgh again, "I'd have to see it to b'lieve it."

"So now you think you solly for this McIntosh." She made him sound like a used raincoat. "You solly for yourself, Captain."

She was right, he knew it, without anger or resentment. He knew he was some way short of that abrupt Chinese knack of hers, to be crazy about a thing and then to crush it. But with all her hidden nature, why was she drawn to him?

"Hunnerd tousand dollar, Cap'n Dowlty," she said, and he knew she was working to sound as Chinese as possible to torment him.

"What's a hundred thousand dollars?" he said to himself. "Seen one, you've seen them all."

"You wanna come to cabin?" she asked. "Hold the pearls?"

"No thanks, darlin'. I'll smoke a while and think."

"Mebbe no one ask you no more."

At dawn, as the crew of the *Iron Tiger* were taking their breakfast (not a pretty feast by modern standards or etiquette), Madame Lai Choi San came on deck and called for quiet. She was wearing a scarlet robe, on which the rampant figure of a tiger was embroidered in gold, and she had taken pains to place herself directly in the way of the rising sun. It was hard to escape the impression that she was the new dawn, or was a force fit to compete with the sun. Annie thought, What a trick this babe would have been on Broadway, or in Hollywood!

"My children," she began, and a kind of moan of appreciation went through the collective body of these coarse pirates. It was as if healing was coming to them. It was as if in profound senses, deeper than they had ever known in life, she was their Mother.

"My children," she said, "you have endured much."

There was a murmur of assent.

"You gave your courage and your skill for a great venture. And you were horribly disappointed. I wept for you. I could not speak to you for sadness. But this morning I am here before you, my children, without a trace of sadness."

Now, this was unexpected. This was the Mother who truly knows more than her children have ever dreamed of. The pirates began to smile. The scars on their faces were lifted away. It was as if their Mother was there to tell them it was their birthday. They felt something grand was coming.

"How would the sadness have room," said Madame Lai, "when there is such *triumph!*" That last word was shouted out. And Annie could see kid pirates turning to each other with a "What did she say?" The word was so daring, so out of the blue.

"The gods are with you, and I am with you. During the night — I could not sleep" — and at that point Madame Lai slipped a pretty little wink to Annie — "I was searching the luggage of the passengers. And we were rescued, my children. For in one humble case I found pearls, amazing pearls."

At that, she plunged her hands into a bowl that had just been put before her by the number-one amah, and the hands, those supple hands, came up dripping with pearls so large, there were retired pirates years later who said they were like golf balls. The crowd was going mad with joy, wonder, and vindication. They were as one again, a family, a force, and the children of their Mother. "I am told," she said, "that here is value — at least three hundred thousand American dollars!"

Pandemonium!

The sun rose higher, seemingly pumped up by the hysterical enthusiasm of the crew of the *Iron Tiger*. Every gong and drum on the ship (enough for a modest orchestra, Annie reasoned) was beaten. There was no design to this "music," of course, except that the tremendous delight of the ship's crew fell into an intense unison of its own until one pulse was beating. Annie was impressed as never before in his life by how a band of individuals could become a mob or a single force more potent than the sum of their numbers.

Firecrackers exploded. And then the effigy of Tin Hau, goddess of the pirates, was paraded around the decks, with everyone falling prostrate as it passed. The Spartan "breakfast" passed directly into feasting and revelry. There were patient lines of unruly pirates waiting to shuffle past the bowl of pearls itself, with every face riveted on the opalescent glories, and so many hands reaching out for just one touch. And there was Mr. Chung, in polished spectacles, waiting to see that no touch stuck.

It was amid this riot of spontaneous ceremony that Madame Lai found Annie on the deck.

"You are not drinking, Captain?"

"The day is very young," he answered, with a wry smile.

"I unnerstan'," she said, and there it was

again, that rougher Chinese voice, as if to mock the way Annie's talk swung between Edinburgh and America's Pacific Coast. "Perhaps I may show you something of innerest?"

Annie followed Madame down to the chart room. There was far less space than before, for this blunt reason: on a table that took up half the room was the very best and most up-to-date Marconi radio money could buy.

"A plesent for you, Captain," said Madame Lai.

"For me?"

"If you are going to sail with us, I wanted you to have a radio to play with. The velly best. See how you like it."

Oh, Annie liked it, he was bound to admit. He sat himself down in the chair made available, and in a few moments he saw that this was the new model he had heard about. But how had Madame Lai got hold of it?

"Captain," she said, before he had time to ask, "I was anxious to get you velly fine gift. Nothin' too much for my fliends."

Annie smiled at the intricate machine as a flight of fresh cunning, a real joke on Madame, occurred to him. "May I?" he asked, indicating the apparatus.

"Surely," smiled Madame Lai. She lifted her hand, and a pale kid, no more than sixteen, appeared, bowing to Annie. "This is Mai Ying," she said, "from Hong Kong Wi'less Teleg'phy School. You know?"

"The best," agreed Annie.

"He number-two wireless man. You teach him, Cap."

So that was it: Annie was getting a gift, but at the same time he had this wand of a boy to watch what he was doing, to make sure he wasn't doing too much. Very well then, if a trick was to be played, strike fast, thought Annie.

He quickly turned on the transmitter and tuned it in on the wavelength kept for *The Sea Change* (not a detail this story is going to give away). Then, for all his recent excitements and injuries, he steadied his hand and tapped out:

They sailed away in a Sieve, they did,
In a Sieve they sailed so fast,
With only a beautiful pea-green veil
Tied with a riband by way of a sail . . .

"What is this?" demanded Madame Lai of her boy Mai Ying.

"Too fast for me," said that youth grimly.

"It's just a nonsense song of Mr. Edward

Lear," explained Annie. "Called 'The Jumblies.' "

"Nonsense?" said Madame Lai. This was a concept she could not quite focus. It made Annie smile and nod inside himself — there was no room in Madame's Chinese soul for sheer play, whereas for Annie it was life itself.

"Mr. Lear was a great player with words," he said. "Ideal for tests of transmission. He liked to make up poems with no meaning."

"How is that possible?" asked the suspicious Chinese woman. Play for her was a practice that required a cat and a mouse, and it was only its best cold fun if she was the cat.

"Well," said Annie expansively, "it's a British thing, I suppose: soundin' full of sense, but mad as a hatter, too. Here's some more." And his fingers turned to the Morse key in a blur of speed — it was the best bit of radio work he'd ever done.

They sailed away in a sieve, they did,
But that brought them to Chep Lap Kok,
In a Sieve to sail so fast
And be there Monday at last.

The virginal face of Mai Ying was

twisted in perplexity. "We no do this at school," he said.

"Why, sonny, I'll teach you," said Annie. "This sonny's a mate o' mine," and he embraced the boy. In truth, he was a little drunk on the sheer music of "nonsense" words. Annie could talk like that for days once the rhythm got into his head.

"Mai Ying," said Madame Lai sternly. "You have much work to do." And the stripling bowed and blushed, just as he marveled at the rapid hands of Annie Doultry. It was no pain at all for Annie to sit with the boy — he was a willing learner, and polite — for hours at a time, reciting yards of Mr. Lear's sublime silliness. And so the *Iron Tiger* and its supporting junks sailed on across the South China Sea, with unabated revelry aboard, and twinkling tales of Calico Pie and an Owl and a Pussycat filling the airwaves.

And so, in a matter of those few hours, the pirate fleet came in sight of the island of Lantau, off the Macao coast. It was a fine resting place, for that coast in that time of year possessed mists the way a drunken man has headaches. Shapes were blurred, shifting, here one minute and gone the next. Though Annie was certain, for a moment, that he had picked out the odd shape of Chep Lap Kok, a smaller island between Lantau and the coast.

The fleet dropped anchor, and even in the mist some word got out. Sampans began to appear from Lantau, bringing girls to join the party on board the *Iron Tiger.* This party of the pearls had never ceased or slowed, but soon the decks were crawling with bodies: bodies in the furious activities of love — if you like, just like a can of live bait. On his way to the cabin of Madame Lai, Annie Doultry had to step very carefully for fear of squashing tender parts. And, cool as he was in this ongoing crisis, he was not entirely unappreciative of the sight of so many girls flat on their backs, being fucked like crazy, but still grinning up at the *gwai lo* as if to say, "You wanna be next, whitee?"

In the cabin of the commander of this exceptional band of pirates, Annie told Madame Lai, "Your boys are going to sleep well tonight."

"They have earn it," she said. "We all earn it. You sleep too, Annie Dowtly?"

There can be no wonder if our readers and our rough hero sigh together at this point — for hadn't he and you all seen it coming that Anatole Doultry (named after a novelist) and Madame Lai Choi San (a great femme and very fatale) were destined for their own night of love? If love is the kindest word for it . . . Annie had never quite made up his mind, so maybe the matter is best left in your judgment. But, a warning, if you're a little squeamish about the things a grown man and a mature woman might get up to in a cabin at anchor on the South China Sea, why then you might care to skip forward a few pages. If not . . .

She was quite naked in the lamplight, and Annie — frankly — was surprised, or was it just that the truth struck home at last? For while the naked Madame Lai was ineffably splendid and promising, the world traveler in Annie Doultry saw this delicious contrast: for whereas in her breasts, her shoulders, her bum (oh God, her dumpling of a bum!) Madame was clearly Chinese, still in her legs, in the long flat of her stomach and in the curve of her throat she might be . . . European? And so, the possibility came home to Annie at last: this authentic Chinese warrior could be a mixture (just like himself), some sort of Eurasian, a compote of all the world's skills and sins, and brimming over in her great wish to be fucked by the *gwai lo* — her *gwai lo.* It heartened Annie, for he loved the recipe of dirty mixture in life.

Looking through the keyhole to the cabin, the inexperienced eye of Mai Ying (so much to learn) saw the rough clothes fall away from Annie's physique, as if a great statue were being unveiled. And the boy gasped — he may never have been the same afterwards — to see that other statue, the leaning tower of piss, the very manhood and cock-a-doodle-doo of Captain Annie. But Madame Lai could not take her eyes off it. Sitting up in bed like a little girl saying her prayers, her face dipped over the great phallus, and — the boy at the keyhole could not believe what he saw — her small plum of a mouth seemed to open like a valve to take in several inches of the Scottish caber.

In a moment Annie was on his side, Madame Lai was like a plant growing over him, and her little fist (holding the biggest black pearl) was up his asshole planting the pearl in the most appreciated place.

"Oh, Lord," he cried out. "I'm a-comin'!"

She could not answer. It is the one drawback of fellatio as conscientious as hers that it eliminates the chance for small talk and poetry alike. But nothing is exactly perfect in this life, and for Annie Doultry the delicate but firm pressure on his rear parts was in perfect harmony with the eruption of his cock. He came and he came — we are dealing with a hero here. At one point his lover backed away to inspect the unaltered gush of it, like a plumber saying to a customer, "Don't blame me. This water supply will stop when the dams empty."

Eventually, Annie Doultry was done, and Madame gazed down at his dwindling cock with satisfaction — though not of the fullest kind, not yet — just as her chin was aglow with the scales of his semen.

"Cap'n Annie," she said. "You got water for a desert."

"And you, my beauty," he said.

"You love me?" she asked.

"Me?" said Annie, acting out surprise. "Love you?"

"Yeah," she sighed.

"So tell me, lady — your mama?"

"Yeah?"

"Was she from Liverpool, Marseilles, or was it Galveston, Texas?"

She looked at him in awe and then anger. For this was a worry that she had never been able to forget — and it was possible that her position as commander of pirates would be endangered if any hint ever got out.

"I saw it in your cunt," he said.

"An' I put pearl in your asshole," she told him with a cheeky grin.

Mai Ying's rapidly corrupted eye then saw Annie get up and advance to the table where the bowl of pearls stood. He took up a scoop of that giant caviar and returned to the couch, his clenched fist dribbling a few pearls.

"Now, darlin'," he said, and he — Mai Ying could not believe this — he appeared to push his hand between Madame's legs and fill her precious vaginal cavity with the stolen jewels. She yelped — there was real pain as well as surprise — but in a second or two she was moaning and seething, for he had flipped her over like a pancake and with his other hand he was in her back passage and able to massage the collection of pearls. Madame Lai could hear them squeaking together and she did not know if she could live with the insane pleasure of it. But Annie knew just what he was doing, and thus the grinding of the pearls at last found the inner lining of her clitoris and reduced that commanding woman to a state of rapture and surrender that was heaven and hell: heaven because she'd never known such soaring ease or abandon, but hell because no man had ever seen her so out of control. And Madame Lai Choi San would sooner kill a man, any man, than cede him control.

How many hours later? Who cares? Who was counting? It was still dark. Annie Doultry woke and could feel the gentle sway of a ship at anchor. He was surely in Madame's cabin still. Yes, to be sure, for there off to the left was the subdued lamplight in which they had made love. There was no doubt about that. Annie could feel the empty hot places in his cock still, and there was that gorgeous boil in his ass. But what the hell else was it? What was it he was smelling? Somewhere very close at hand there was something as sweet as roses yet as rotten as death, at the same time.

He needed a moment for his eyes to adjust to the half-light. And so it was, looking directly down the length of his own chest, he saw, just north of his belly button, a most artistic pile of . . . was it a firm chocolate custard?! What the hell? Then he heard a sweet little snoring noise. He looked off in that direction and there was Madame Lai, curled up in ecstatic sleep. Good Lord! Annie realized, the sweet little bitch had left a loving portion of herself on him.

Annie didn't know whether to laugh or be outraged. But suffice it to say that he was inspired. He felt around him for something, anything, that could manipulate her pretty whirl of shit — it was a ladylike spiral, to be sure. All he could find was a knife. Nothing better suited for the task — for it had a broad blade — except that he could not lift off the pile without taking several tendrils of his own bodily hair, and having to stifle any protest at the pain of that operation. But working with dainty care, Annie was on his feet, with a flat knife and a firm cluster of milady's waste. More carefully than any chef, and without losing any of its shape, he slipped this dessert onto a plate. He looked at it for a moment, and then he knew. A hand crept up his own asshole and there, there it was, like a cherry on the chocolate pudding — the finest black pearl. Yes, he liked the effect very much — it had elegance as well as insult.

All he had to do then, using one of his large Army & Navy store woolen socks, was gather together anything else in that cabin that he might need.

Annie came up on the deck as silent as a ghost — a ghost wearing just one sock. Not that he would have attracted special attention in that scene of naked slumbering after the orgy. And so it was that his pale form slipped over the side of the *Iron Tiger,* and used a rope — taking care that it not burn his balls — to lower himself into the warm waters of the South China Sea. And from there he had nothing but his slow, ungainly breast stroke to help him, a stroke that strangely enough kept veering to one side and thus required correction.

In the first light of dawn, Annie came out of the ocean on a stony shore of Chep Lap Kok. He paused, as if aware that he was alone, naked, and without food or arms on a desolate shore. But then he saw the sails of *The Sea Change* coming through the mist. He grinned, and began his painful walk along the stony beach.

Aboard *The Sea Change,* Barney was himself at the wheel, keeping as close to the shore as was reasonable. A few sea birds hovered over the ship. Then, as a fresh cove came into view, Barney saw a familiar figure squatting at the water's edge. The two men waved silently and Annie made the last slow swim out to his boat. As he came up over the side, his wound began to weep again. It was enough to convince Barney that Annie had surely had the worst of any adventures.

"Goddamnit, Annie!" he groaned. "You a loser agin?"

"Just me and me socks, Barney," said Annie.

"I thought you los' your min' wid all dat Edward Lear stuff!"

"You liked that, did you?"

"Crazy man!"

"Thank God for craziness then," said Annie. And at that point he held up his second sock, bunched and baggy and so heavy it had kept taking his swim from its straight course. He pulled back the wool and revealed a great mass of pearls. The wisdom of pearls.

"Jesus, Annie. How many?"

"About three hundred and seven, at a rough guess."

Barney's inquisitive nose was dipped down toward the jewels themselves. "I still smell de oyster, Annie!"

"Ah, well," sighed his captain, "freshness is everything, Barney."

At last, Barney looked up at him with a harsh grin. "Annie, you dun good, man."

"Well, thankee, Barney. And you were here when I asked. Now, I could use some clothes, a fast course out of here, and even my breakfast."

"We got folks ater us?" asked Barney.

"Sooner or later!"

At that very moment, a deeply contented beauty, a woman of uncertain origins, awoke from the sleep of sexual content hardly knowing how close to ruin and wrath she was. Sometimes, perhaps, it is better to stay sleeping.

Madame Lai Choi San opened one eye and then the other. She uncrossed her legs and felt the slow ooze of her own bodily fluids. She felt at peace . . . until she perched up on one elbow to find her somnolent lover. She knew that white type. They slept for days after sex. But Annie Doultry was gone. And in a matter of moments, the woman found the recommended breakfast for a pirate commander. Was it his rough jest or a harbinger of subtler cruelty? She saw the empty bowl on the side table and then she knew without feeling that every pearl had been picked out of her own body.

She considered.

She screamed.

She roared.

She howled.

Her own officers were gathered outside the door of her cabin, but too fearful to enter or to knock. There are depths of pain and wrath in the human cry that are not to be intruded on.

But Ying K'ou got the radio boy to look through the keyhole, and so it was that lad's terrified whisper that described the scene to the others.

"Madame — she naked. She kneel before goddess Tin Hau. She has knife and oh! she has cut herself! She is swearing eternal vengeance."

Whereupon Ying K'ou, surely on the point of command, went back on deck and gave the order to raise all speed.

It was a fine day, with a strong wind driving *The Sea Change* through the Hainan Straits. Destination? Haiphong perhaps. Or Singapore. For the moment, Annie was enjoying the speed of his own ship and the great cache of pearls tucked inside his shirt. The piano was up on deck and Barney was giving voice:

"Oh, you beautiful doll,
You great big beautiful doll!"

But a call from below interrupted them.

It was a young seaman. The radio was making noises. Annie stood up, grinning. He looked back the way they had come. Nothing. He used his binoculars. Nothing. Then he went down below, as he knew he must, to take his medicine. His Morse was so good he could tell the raw touch of Mai Ying, a Mai Ying with Madame Lai standing over his shoulder. The boy would improve quickly. But for now the message was halting, with mistakes here and there. Still, Annie was in no doubt of what it said:

"Annie Doultry, I am coming. I will never let you go."

"We bein' chased, Annie?" asked Barney.

"Chased?" asked that phlegmatic gambler with life and the wind.

"Don' worry, Cap," said Barney. "We git way!"

"Barney," said Annie Doultry, "this is the rest of our lives. We are dead men."

"Dead men? Whaddya mean?"

"That's how the game always ends. Never been any different. So let's have fun while we can!"

That said, he tapped back a reply message: "Morning, Pearly. I'm headed west."

On the *Iron Tiger*, there was confusion when Mai Ying reported Annie's message.

"An obvious lie!" hissed Ying K'ou, waiting for his commander.

Madame Lai Choi San smiled. An obvious lie? An insolent admission? It hardly mattered. If she set off in the very worst direction, why, the roundness of the globe would settle that. Sooner or later, she would find him. And she would sail for the rest of her life to cut off his head — but only after other parts. But if Annie was the man she knew?

"We sail west!" she shouted at the wind.

afterword
The Mystery of Collaboration

David Thomson

More than twenty years after it was written, a novel appears, *Fan-Tan*, as vivid as it is unexpected. It would be hard to say which of its two authors was more charismatic or daring, or which had the more complex life. But they had things in common, including a tendency toward stylish self-destruction and a taste for creative experiment, and they enjoyed each other's company, albeit in a competitive spirit. The ordinary reader coming upon this book may think he knows who Marlon Brando was, so "Tell me about Donald Cammell," he asks. As if Cammell might present the easier task. I'll do my best, but don't be too surprised if his strange story only leads back to the enigma of Brando.

390

Donald Seton Cammell was born in Edinburgh in 1934, the son of Charles Richard Cammell (1890–1969), who had inherited the Cammell Laird shipbuilding fortune. Charles had taken a first wife to live in France and Switzerland in splendid châteaux where he collected a great library and had three children. But then after economic crash and divorce he returned to Edinburgh in 1932 and married Iona Macdonald, a beautiful young woman, a doctor's daughter from the Highlands. Donald (one of three sons from that second marriage) was brilliant, handsome — and anxious (he had a serious depressive episode as a child). But his upbringing was richly colored by the literary and artistic circles his father cultivated.

Driven to work by his heavy losses, Charles became an author and a journalist, and eventually he was literary editor on *The Connoisseur.* He was Scottish fencing champion in 1937, as well as a regular contributor to *The Scotsman* newspaper before moving on to books — *Faeryland; Verses for the Centenary of Lord Byron*; two books of memoirs, *Castles in the Air* and *Heart of Scotland*; and *Aleister Crowley: The Man; the Mage; the Poet.*

Crowley (1875–1947) was a self-pro-claimed "beast" or the "worst man in the world." As such, he professed to practice black magic, ordinary magic, debauchery, and poetry, though not necessarily in that order. Crowley and Charles Cammell were friends, and the influence on Donald was enormous. Some said Crowley was a cheerful charlatan; others reckoned he believed his own talk. What's certain is that he was an early source for Donald's fascination with beauty, sex, madness, death, and the occult — though not always in *that* order. He was also just one of the links between flamboyant Victorian decadence and the druggy aestheticism of London in the swinging 1960s, the Faeryland where Cammell would come alive directing the extraordinary film *Performance.* Crowley and Donald Cammell shared many tastes, including that of working at night.

Donald's childhood seems to have been secure and happy, with a fond, eccentric father, a mother he adored and who adored him, as well as a younger brother, David, who would become something of a disciple and the business assistant to Donald's wild schemes. (There was a third son, Diarmid, younger, but very distinguished too — he would become a chess champion.) He was educated in Devon (a wartime evacuation), in the Highlands, taught by priests, at a prep school in Fort Augustus (from which he ran away), and then at Shrewsbury House, near Thames Ditton, and Westminster. He drew and painted for most of his childhood, and was encouraged by his parents. That sent him to the Royal Academy at the age of sixteen, but was it all too easy? When his father wrote another book, on Piero Annigoni, a photorealist portraitist who could "do" Renaissance light and who was renowned for his flattering picture of the young Queen Elizabeth, Donald went to study with Annigoni in Florence. This was apparently a devoutly bohemian household, a setting that encouraged the young man in his sexual explorations.

By the age of twenty (in 1954), Donald Cammell was a hit in London, a sought-after society portrait painter, a womanizer, and a man-about-town, but subject to fits of gloom — of course, 1954 was also the year of *On the Waterfront* and movies were beginning to interest Donald. He married a Greek actress, Maria Andipa, and they had a son, named Amadis. But the marriage didn't last, and Donald made the decision not to see, or know, his own son. He had been diagnosed as a manic-depressive, and he would seek many different forms of treatment. Still, he was determined not to have children. (It would be decades before Donald sat down for lunch with Amadis in London — a pleasant meeting, but nothing that stuck.)

Donald was restless in the London of the 1950s, a world as yet unacquainted with the sexual revolution, the New Wave, or the range of literary ideas that would soon fill Cammell's head. He had money as a painter. He moved to New York for a time, and often visited Paris. It was there in 1957 that a friend, the actor Christian Marquand, introduced Cammell to Marlon Brando (Brando would name his first son Christian after the French actor). Marlon was in France playing a blond Nazi officer in *The Young Lions.* Donald was hugely impressed by Marlon's beauty and comic spirit as much as by his talent as an actor. A bond was formed in Donald's mind, even if Brando had so many admirers that he had learned to be casual or cynical with them.

At about the same time, Donald began a long affair with the Texan model Deborah Dixon. They lived in Paris, but as the ferment of novelty built in London in the 1960s, so they visited more and more often and found company with art dealers and writers, with Brian Jones and Mick Jagger of the Rolling Stones, and with the burgeoning world of London filmmaking. Paris and New York had given him an air of extra sophistication — the actor James Fox would call him "the most attractive bohemian in Paris." Donald had fallen for the writings of Genet and Borges and was drawn to the idea of the societal outlaw (while residing in Chelsea). He was also something of a libertine — Marianne Faithfull, then a pale flower-child, and Jagger's consort, would note Cammell's taste for threesomes.

It was at about this time that he abandoned painting and became obsessed with moviemaking. Some observed that he seemed relieved to be free of that parental obligation to do glamorous portraits of rich people. In New York, he had tried abstract expressionism, but the urge to paint was leaving him. He was beginning to favor rock stars, criminals, and people living on the fringe. He had an East End friend, David Litvinoff, who introduced him to real gangsters.

A woman who knew Donald at the time, Caroline Upcher, remarks on "his great charm. He was both gentle and a gentleman, very kind and with impeccable manners. But he was quite louche, hugely attractive, and attracted to women, but interested in homosexuality. He was a stirrer and there was a slightly voyeuristic part of him. I suspect it could be cruel sometimes. But his voice was so important — upper class, with a mid-Atlantic drawl."

In becoming friends with the Stones, Donald enjoyed their insolent attitude to society and their own admirers. The Stones were several steps closer to anarchy, the surreal, and art-school outrageous than most rock groups. When Mick Jagger pouted about getting no "Satisfaction" (a summer '65 hit), he was boasting of a compulsive sexual hunt, while warning admirers not to like or trust him. Jagger was deliberately exploring an air of depravity, a kind of public orgasm, and this was telling on the less stable Brian Jones (the most restrained Stone in performance, but giddy with desire in person). When Jones's girlfriend, Anita Pallenberg, left him (and started an affair with Keith Richards), Jones sought refuge in Cammell's Paris flat. In that respect, he was a model for the rock singer, Turner, who has gone into hiding in *Performance*. And Pallenberg — who had also slept with Cammell — would become not just the obvious female lead for the film but also its most threatening sensibility. It was in Pallenberg's being and her own devouring glances that *Performance* felt like the cast were acting out their own psychodramas. At the time, some assumed that Donald was bisexual — he was certainly interested in those who were.

In 1968, two films emerged that bore his name: *The Touchables* and *Duffy.* In the first, from a story by David Cammell, written first by Donald and Anita Pallenberg but credited to Ian La Frenais, a rock star is kidnapped by some female fans and mildly tortured. In the second, two brothers reckon to swindle a wealthy father of his money. They are helped by an American, Duffy, played by James Coburn. The brothers are played by James Fox and John Alderton.

Neither film was good, but Donald found favor with a young American in London, Sandy Lieberson, once Donald's agent and now a producer. It was Lieberson who encouraged Cammell to think of his next project as something he should write and direct. In its first life, it was a long story called "The Liars," in which an American gangster on the run comes to

London and hides out in a house owned by a retired rock star. At that point, Cammell wanted Mick Jagger as the rock star and Marlon Brando as the gangster. He and Marlon talked about the project, but Brando passed on it. The role of the gangster was then made English and it ended up with James Fox (the young gent from *The Servant*), and an actor Donald longed to transform from gentleman to gangster.

Fox would be so caught up in doing *Performance* that he was derailed for a time. After the film, he gave up acting and joined a religious mission. He did not act for ten years. Without any malice or grievance now, he looks back and says, "Donald could be dangerous. Both creatively and in what he'd do to get what he wanted out of you. He wasn't a typical film man. But that's why so many of us in film were so drawn to him. He had new ideas, and though there was a dilettante side and some of his stuff doesn't work at all, still there was a bisexual thing in *Performance* that was new."

Cammell asked Nicolas Roeg to be his lighting cameraman on *Performance*, but Roeg was anxious to be promoted. And so Cammell generously agreed to codirect with Roeg, who was still in charge of the photography. But it was clear to everyone from the outset that the script and the ideas belonged to Donald Cammell. By ideas, I mean not just the poetics of interchangeable identity between Chas and Turner (Fox and Jagger), but the background story of London crime (derived from the unpredictable and very violent Kray brothers) and the house in Powis Square that is a hotbed of sex and drugs, cut off from any outside world. All the cast were Donald's, a mark of what Lieberson called his being "a great orchestrator of people."

Performance is a cult movie that has lasted beyond its immediate notoriety. It is violent and sexual not just in outward ways but even more so in inner suggestion, and it ends with the camera serving as the bullet with which Chas has shot Turner, a bullet that passes through his head to confront the face of Jorge Luis Borges. Not one in a hundred of the general audience knew it was Borges, or what that might mean — but there was the glory and risk of *Performance*: it was a studio entertainment and a very private spell at the same time.

The film has always provoked sharply varying reactions, not least at Warner

Brothers, the company that had paid for it. They stopped shooting briefly and then took the 1969 cut (made by Donald) back to Los Angeles for clarification. Cammell and Mick Jagger protested: "This film is about the perverted love affair between Homo sapiens and Lady Violence." In 1969 you might have put that on a movie poster. But the film's new editor, Frank Mazzola, was unexpectedly sympathetic to Cammell, and the cut remained under Cammell's control (though he did agree to bring Jagger on earlier to appease Warners). It was released in America in 1970 to no business and damning reviews. Richard Schickel, in *Time*, called it "the most disgusting, the most completely worthless film I have seen since I began reviewing." But when it opened in London, in 1971, it was hailed as the epitome of modernism and celebrated by the new magazine *Time Out* as a measure of Britain having come of age.

Marlon Brando thought it exactly the kind of avant-garde picture with which he had dreamed of being involved but that never seemed to materialize in America. For so many reasons by the late 1960s — Vietnam, civil rights, the fate of Native Americans, plus the state of Hollywood —

Marlon Brando was out of love with his own country and his own genius as an actor. Not only was *Performance* filled with great artistic daring and earnest pretension (just the mix in Brando's creative personality), it also had an air of taking acting beyond the prim boundaries of show business and into the actor's own persona. A few years later, in *Last Tango in Paris*, Brando would find ways of channeling his own life and feelings through the character he played, and I suspect that resolve was given new hope by seeing *Performance*.

But the whole experience had propelled Cammell back to America, where he hoped to be "discovered" as the director of a brilliant cause célèbre, but also a picture that may be the best portrait of the high-toned romantic decadence that enchanted London in the late 1960s and that had struck Cammell as a more beguiling art than painting.

With Frank Mazzola as his editor, and with cameraman Vilmos Zsigmond, in 1971 Cammell went to the Utah desert to shoot a mind-trip short picture called *The Argument*. It starred his new girlfriend, Myriam Gibril, but it was only meant as a photographic test — it was not finished until 1999, three years after Cammell's death. But in 1977, for MGM, he did get another directing assignment, on *Demon Seed*, scripted by Robert Jaffe and Robert O. Hirson from a novel by Dean Koontz. It involved Julie Christie as a woman who is raped and impregnated by a rogue computer. It was a failure wherever it played, though it attracted a few good reviews. Donald had been horrified at the committee-like structure of the studio, and he thought of taking his name off the picture. Granted that as a painter Cammell had had a bored facility, as a filmmaker it was possible that he was full of innovative ideas yet devoid of narrative fluency or the willingness to compromise with studio needs.

In Los Angeles in the 1970s, the friendship between Cammell and Brando had deepened. These were the years of Brando's revival — with *The Godfather* and *Last Tango in Paris* — and then of an even greater turn toward despair and cynicism, culminating in his virtual sabotage of *Apocalypse Now*. But in 1974, Brando had a serious falling out with Cammell when the Scot began romancing the underage China Kong, the exquisite child of Anita Loo. That affair was unusual enough; in addition, Anita had been Marlon's lover, on and off, over a long period. So the actor was fond of China. It was a joke in the Kong family that he was her "godfather." He had often invited her out and played with her, and he was conventionally but startlingly angry when Cammell (aged forty) began taking China out of school to the desert on romantic idylls. It should be said that, all his grown life, Brando had been fascinated by Asian women or women of mixed blood. That was one of the reasons why, after *Mutiny on the Bounty* (1962), shot in Tahiti, he purchased his own Pacific island retreat, the atoll of Teti'aroa.

Cammell married China in 1978 and not long afterwards Brando offered his apology for being so disapproving, along with his congratulations. It was then, in 1979, that Brando himself made a proposal of collaboration to Donald Cammell. It was *Fan-Tan*, and both the initiative and the idea for the China Seas story came from Brando. He had a notion to make a film about a Scots-American sea captain in his fifties (Brando was fifty-five in 1979) who signs on with a band of pirates led by a fierce Chinese woman. Brando wanted someone he felt he could trust to turn this idea into a script and who would then direct the film. But in his mind it was always intended as an independent production, not the kind of Hollywood compromise he hated.

He hardly seemed to notice that *Fan-Tan* was also an old-fashioned adventure — a rattling good yarn, perhaps, but the kind of picture that might have been made long ago. With one exception: it did have a special openness to the attraction — sexual and intellectual — between the West and the East. Cammell said that he was interested.

Their 1979 work produced a 165-page treatment, dated May 1979, that was meant to make use of Teti'aroa and was filled with a naïve love of the South Seas. The action of this novel was covered in the first third of the treatment. The rest involved a trip to Tahiti and an account of the development of those islands. Annie Doultry and Madame Lai were sharing the action with many other characters. Much of it came from Marlon's own improvs as they worked, and it is palpable in the novel that Annie Doultry is a version of Marlon: playful, naughty, ruminative, and with very mixed feelings about loyalty. If you look at *The Missouri Breaks* (1976), you will find a Doultry-like Brando who experiments with accents and costumes, and who sometimes pretends to be female. Marlon's grasp of Annie was always the drive behind the project.

Here's an extract from the tapes of Brando and Cammell talking, in which Marlon becomes Annie Doultry — it's a scene from the latter part of the treatment, nothing that figures in the novel. This is Marlon talking:

"Well, okay, Doultry says, I'm going to get drunk tonight. I'm going to have some fun. Who knows what tomorrow brings? Here's to the seagulls. Goodbye, darling, have a nice night. She goes. So that she herself is sort of being devil-may-care with life and thinking, oh what the fuck. . . . And here I am, I might as well enjoy myself. So she goes in and I think that Doultry sees her sitting down and he comes over and he says, with a couple of drinks . . . I may not look like it, but I'm a patient and you're just what the doctor ordered. . . . He opens up with that and she says, I don't think we've been introduced. And he says. . . . She's sort of being a little stiff and proper. He says, this is the South Pacific . . . my name is Doultry. She says, how many times have you said that? I don't know — 328. Why? She says, anybody ever call you dolt? My mother used to call me dolt all the time. And that kind of dialogue goes on."

There's no better way of describing Teti'aroa than in the words of China Kong. She traveled to the island with her husband for conferences on *Fan-Tan* and stayed for six months — where could they be better staged than within sight and sound of the sea?

"Teti'aroa was an island paradise, but paradise done Marlon's way: sprinkled with thatched-roof huts, each roof formed in perfect clusters of bound reeds. The posts and beams joined without a single nail, gigantic conch shells as sinks, linen so crisp you never wanted to get out of bed, and to top it all off, a French chef prepared all our meals. They wrote daily: talking, acting, recording, bringing characters alive. The sight of the two of them running up and down the island's private landing strip was truly amusing: the slight and the slightly larger silhouettes, Marlon with his ripped white T-shirt, a la *Streetcar*, and Donald with his trademark Panama straw hat. Only a few other times had I seen Marlon so delighted."

Brando was a generous host to the couple; there was a contract between Donald and

Brando's company, Penny Poke Farms, and money passing from Marlon to Donald. But Marlon was strangely reluctant now to push the treatment on any studios. He hated the idea of a big company taking over because he said it would mean the loss of independence. But how could this epic be filmed without someone's money? Had the whole thing been his idle dream, a way to make Teti'aroa fun for a few seasons?

At any event, Donald telephoned his brother, David, in London and told him, "It's not going to go ahead. Marlon likes torturing people," whereupon David and Donald thought of doing the story as a book first. Surely the book would help the film get made? Marlon agreed: if they had a best-seller, that income might finance the picture!

David called on Caroline Upcher, the fiction editor at Pan, and then Sonny Mehta, the publisher. Caroline remembers that Donald was a bit jokey about the whole thing — he called it "a good yarn." Sonny was interested. David enlisted the agent Ed Victor, an American based in London, and terms were agreed. It turned into a special joint contract, dated July 7, 1982: "A book will be immediately written by us, to be based upon the prior work written by you. . . ." This was in the form of a letter from Marlon to Donald, and it called for a few editorial meetings, "after which time you [Donald Cammell] will do the actual day-to-day writing. You and I will review the proposed manuscript together, with final editorial/creative control remaining with me [Marlon Brando]."

There was at the same time a contract with Pan that called for an advance of $100,000. (The U.S. rights were never dealt.) Although Marlon had an equal claim on that money, it seems that the entire sum due on signature ($50,000) was paid to Donald.

And so, at some time in 1982–83, Donald Cammell wrote the novel *Fan-Tan*, or an incomplete version of it, according to their earlier conversations and in keeping with that first treatment proposed by Brando. Marlon had acted out scenes. And he annotated Donald's drafts. Cammell did research in the library at UCLA, and found a real woman pirate as a basis for Madame Lai Choi San — Marlon had heard of that woman first and had been intrigued by her. Donald and China went to Hong Kong to study the construction of boats, and Donald's lifelong interest in

408

shipping prompted him to include architectural drawings of the supposed sister ship to Annie Doultry's treasured boat, *The Sea Change*. China remembers telephone calls to Marlon from Hong Kong where the two men were revising pages of the novel.

The novel is based on the first fifty or so pages of the 1979 treatment, but the novel develops certain scenes not included or barely mentioned in that treatment — the playing of fan-tan; the rite of initiation; the typhoon (perhaps the most striking piece of writing); the capture of the ship; and of course what has become Chapter 8 in this volume.

Cammell did this writing on his own (in longhand), although he submitted the typed novel (minus an ending) to Brando. There were phone conversations over it. In time, Cammell came to wonder whether Brando had ever bothered to read the whole thing. There is no record of any detailed response. In due course, Brando simply let Cammell know that he did not wish to proceed with *Fan-Tan* as either novel or movie. By their original agreement Brando retained the creative rights. It was his property.

Donald Cammell was furious. He felt

betrayed. He believed that the book had considerable merits, and having worked to write a novel, he found he loved the process. He still dreamed of doing the movie. He sometimes reckoned that Marlon had been capricious and manipulative, never intending to go ahead. I will return to this, but for the moment it is important to trace the history of *Fan-Tan.*

What emerged in the summer of 2004 (after the death of Marlon Brando) was a typescript supplied by China Kong to Ed Victor with the hope that perhaps now the book could be reactivated. It consisted of 283 pages of typed narrative, with another twelve pages that are "an OUTLINE of the last thirty pages of BOOK ONE" (this description is in Donald Cammell's own hand).

In other words, Donald had written all but the last chapter or episode of the book — the climax of the action. At the same time, the reference to "BOOK ONE" shows his awareness of the rest of the treatment. That he didn't write that up, too, I think, is a measure of sound judgment: the outline limps along without the battle between Annie and Madame.

The twelve pages of synopsis make up what is Chapter 8 in this presentation of *Fan-Tan*, and I have happily followed them in nearly every detail in my assigned task of completing the story and editing the text as a whole. I was engaged by the two estates (of Marlon Brando and Donald Cammell) and at the request of Sonny Mehta (by now in New York at Knopf), who once again found himself the publisher of *Fan-Tan*. My job was to finish the story according to the outline, and to edit or organize the existing text. There were repetitions that Cammell would have tidied up. There were also a few blanks where material was still to come — and it is clear that Donald still believed that Marlon might do some of that himself.

I hope that clarifies the provenance of this text, and I believe the result is close to the book Donald Cammell would have wanted to see in print. Can I say the same for Marlon Brando? That's more complicated. For instance, it's hard to explain another finding in the Brando files: a 1993 script version of *Fan-Tan*, based on the whole outline but credited to Brando alone and registered with the Writers Guild. I wonder whether Cammell knew of its existence.

You might think that Brando and Cammell never spoke to each other again. It is not that simple. In fact, in January

1986, the advance of $50,000 was repaid to Pan — by Brando. That is the clearest sign of his taking responsibility for the sorry mess, and it may have gone some way to reconciling the two men.

Donald Cammell's career did not prosper. In 1987 he directed another film, written with China, *White of the Eye*, in which David Keith plays a serial killer and Cathy Moriarty is his wife. It is a very striking movie, much enriched by being shot in the copperworks outside Globe, Arizona. But despite several good reviews, it was another box-office failure — a bankruptcy in the company making it had meant that there was very little promotion.

Marlon Brando saw *White of the Eye* and was impressed with its "originality, artistry and power." That is from a letter from Brando to Richard Hefner, chairman of the ratings board, in a successful plea to have the X rating changed to an R. Donald Cammell really did possess a talent and an originality that Marlon had longed for.

At that time, Marlon was nursing a project to be called *Jericho*. It was about a former CIA assassin named Harrington (also the name of Brando's most treasured psychiatrist), a man who knows the agency's darkest secrets and who is lured back into business. The story is one of mounting slaughter, as Harrington executes nearly every other character. As Cammell described it, "The overall image of the film is a man living with his own guilt over all the horror he's perpetrated. I felt I knew [him] as a performer and I could help orchestrate that performance, to see him bare his soul for once."

This time around, Brando began by claiming that it was a script he had to write himself. In the past, all too many ventures had failed — he surely allowed that *Fan-Tan* was one of them — because Marlon had left the writing to others. It is not an uncommon fantasy among Hollywood's great to think they could be writers if only they had the time, the patience, a pen, or the spelling. Then he wavered. In early 1988, *Variety* carried an announcement that Donald Cammell would write and direct *Jericho*.

The question of what Marlon Brando meant to write, or wanted to write, is unclear. Once before, on *One-Eyed Jacks* (1961), there had been every sign of his wish to be an independent writer-director. Indeed, Stanley Kubrick had walked away from that project when he concluded that Marlon was not prepared to have it made any way but his own. The shooting dragged on, as ruinous indecision overtook Brando. That was nothing compared with his dismay over the editing. Was it a lack of stamina or concentration? Or something to do with limits on his decisive creative intelligence in any area except that of acting? Finally, Brando quit *One-Eyed Jacks* and let others finish it.

Throughout his life, there was that failure to stay lastingly committed. But in the matter of writing there may have been another problem. From his school days onward, Brando suffered from a kind of dyslexia, never identified or treated, but the concomitant of and perhaps the spur to his astonishing mimicry or absorption of other people. Time and again, friends report how being with Brando was to be studied to the depth of your being, until he could do you, be you, imitate you. I don't claim to understand this condition, but I think it left Brando with rare, mixed feelings about writing. And I hear a confirming echo of that in what Cammell said when Brando dismissed the book of *Fan-Tan*: "He couldn't read it if he hadn't written it himself."

Was the tragedy ordained? If so, it is all the more wonder that Cammell had made

Annie Doultry so fond a portrait of Brando — a loner, a thinker, and a dreamer, whimsical and sensual, a joker and a mimic, a king of accents, a man given over to fate and gambling despite every protestation to the contrary, a man crazy about Asian women, and someone fatally born to betray his own pacts. Annie is also a man who loves sailing around the South Seas and who shares Marlon's passion for amateur radio.

Jericho never happened. You may say you guessed as much. According to Cammell, Brando took a script Donald had rewritten and ruined it, throwing out all the good, adding to the bad. In which case, you'd want to ask, why did Donald put himself in position to be betrayed again?

There are many likely answers; the first being that in the Hollywood scheme of things Marlon had power and Donald was the endless supplicant. Despite his hulking size and a chronic record of starting and abandoning projects, Marlon Brando was still a name that might draw backers. But more than ever, he was a bitter, teasing recluse who loathed and despised the picture business that pricked up its ears at the mention of his name. As China saw it, "Donald was a manic-depressive. Marlon wasn't, but he could get warm and get cold and he could be cruel. The two of them had a weird marriage. It was why they were attracted to each other."

This is not easy or comfortable stuff to find in our heroes, but there were profound streaks of fatalism and self-destruction in both Brando and Cammell that were played out to the sinister music of Southern California and the business. Nor should we omit the matter of beauty and what happens to it. The Marlon Brando of *Streetcar*, and of the ten years after that, was remarked on for his romantic looks. He was perpetually driven to turn that attraction into sexual conquest. Donald Cammell was not as famous or as much gazed upon by the world, but he was a handsome charmer, a lifelong pursuer of sex, and not confined by any rigid definitions of what was and was not heterosexual.

There is no evidence of a homosexual bond between Brando and Cammell — which is not the same as saying that both men did not think about it. Then notice this: Cammell kept his looks into his sixties and until his death, whereas Brando — notoriously — by the mid 1970s was someone who had squandered his own God-given looks. There is also the matter of China Kong, a lovely child and one that Marlon had happily played with, the daughter of one of his mistresses. But then Donald had appeared to steal that nymph when she was still underage. Did that bold act not deserve some rebuke? Was *Fan-Tan* itself not the story of a great betrayal, in which Marlon's character leaves a Chinese woman in rage (after he has taken her sexually)?

Jericho collapsed. So many other Cammell hopes had turned to dust over the years. He had had a notion of adapting Nabokov's *Pale Fire* for the screen — could there be a better proof of artistic ambition allied to impossibility? — and Nabokov had written back, thanking Donald for his "fascinating, beautifully presented" notes. There was a Jack the Ripper story he was working on with Kenneth Tynan. With David Cammell, he wanted to do a movie on the life of Emma Hamilton — Andrew Braunsberg was the producer on that project. Then there was *Machine Gun Kelly*, on which China was co-writer. (*Machine Gun Kelly* and *Pale Fire* — it is a twentieth-century collision.) He was asked to consult on a plot idea that grew into *Pretty Woman*, but only after Donald had

417

lost all contact with it.

The *Pretty Woman* episode is a good example of Cammell's dire luck. The project was then called *$3000*, and it was a down-and-dirty version of the film we know. Cammell advised on the script. At the same time, auditioning actresses for *Jericho*, he met Julia Roberts and recommended her to the producers of *$3000*. That insight worked, but only after Donald had been dropped and *$3000* became a more conventional romance.

We know, more or less, how Marlon Brando died — we all recall the sense of loss that came with the news, and many felt a great regret that there had not been more good films or more nights on stage. Instead, there is the woeful list of projects given up on, like *Fan-Tan*, out of some need for vengeance on a business that had disappointed the idealist in Brando.

Donald Cammell did make a last film, *Wild Side*, released in 1996. It starred Christopher Walken, Anne Heche, and Joan Chen and it is not without interest — nothing he touched was ever without interest, or free from undigested hopes. It is about sex, intrigue, betrayal, and too much cleverness, and it has rapturous lesbian scenes. But *Wild Side* was taken over by the company that made it, Nu Image, recut, ruined, spoiled. Cammell had his name removed, and it was a commercial disaster.

On April 24, 1996, aged sixty-two, in his home in Los Angeles, and in front of his wife, China, Donald Cammell shot himself in the head. He lived for forty minutes or so but he was dead by the time the ambulance reached the house at the top of Laurel Canyon. China describes what happened:

"The manic-depression was getting worse. And I became frightened because I knew he wanted to die by his own hand, with me there to experience it with him.

"For twenty years, I had accepted this eventuality, but now that the end seemed near, I was terrified. I tried to stop it from happening, which hurt him terribly, because I had always supported what he wanted to do, without passing judgment, and because, many years earlier, I had made a solemn promise to be there when the time came.

"Donald was afraid of going completely insane. And even though things in his life were going well — he had interest in his *Wild Side* Director's Cut, as well as financing for a project called *'33* — for the

419

last seven years, his personality was disintegrating.

"It started out that, at night, he would change from the Donald I had known into a person I called 'Uncensored Don,' a personality who said whatever was on his mind — Donald Cammell without reservations. This person was energetic, talented, and loved to perform. I believe Uncensored Don came out of Donald's frustration at not being able to express himself professionally.

"I would recount the antics of Uncensored Don to Donald, since he had no memory of those events. Eventually, it got to the point where Donald even became Uncensored Don during the daytime. For years Donald was entertained to hear of what he had said or done while in this state, but the additive effect of those experiences was for Donald a sign that it was time to shed his mortal coil.

"He had never done anything in his life just because that's how everyone else did it, nor did he die that way. He picked his moment.

"It has been suggested that Donald could not have lived for long after he had shot himself, but let me put that rumor to rest. Donald had studied the brain and all its functions for most of his adult life, and he knew where to put that bullet so that he would have the maximum clarity at the time of his death. He was an expert marksman and placed the bullet where he wanted it.

"He lived for forty-five minutes in a state of clarity and ecstasy that was, for me, unimaginable. He spoke nearly continuously, recounting people, places, and plans.

"Finally, the room seemed to fill with light, and he died.

"The death of Donald Cammell was not a sad event. It was exactly what he wanted, fireworks.

"The sadness came afterward, for all those who knew him and loved him."

James Fox, still a friend, remembers, "Everyone was surprised — not that it was done, but the violence of it. The more you heard, the spookier it became. But then I thought about the ending of *Performance* — shot in the head."

Later on, Brando was contrite. He said there was a bond between him and China — she had lost Donald, and by then Brando had lived through the trial of his son Christian for killing Dag Drollet, boyfriend to his half-sister, Cheyenne. Then Cheyenne had killed herself. There had been a time when Marlon and Donald had even thought of Christian playing a part in their movie of *Fan-Tan*. But in 1994, Brando had published his strange memoir — *Songs My Mother Taught Me* — and Donald was not mentioned in it. (It is a further irony that Chapter 40 of that memoir contains a description of Marlon sailing in the South Seas, and foundering on a reef, that is nearly as gripping as the typhoon in *Fan-Tan*.)

Hollywood is the history of all the films it has ever made. And that is enough for a crowded, crazy story. But it is more: it is also the darker, madder account of all the great dreams and projects that never got made. And finally perhaps the dreams unmade — like *Fan-Tan* — are more romantic or more dreamlike than the ones that came safely home.

note

In researching and writing this Afterword, I was helped by many people. I want to thank China Kong, David Cammell, Mike Medavoy (who also searched the Brando files for material), Ed Victor, Sonny Mehta, Sandy Lieberson, Caroline Upcher, James

Fox, Chris Rodley and Kevin MacDonald (for their excellent documentary on Cammell), Colin MacCabe (for talk and for his book on *Performance*), Chris Chang, Sean Arnold (for research in London), and Sam Umland, coauthor with Rebecca Umland of *Donald Cammell: A Life on the Wild Side*, to be published by Fab Press. I am also grateful to the work of Peter Manso, and to conversation with him.

A Note About the Authors

Marlon Brando made over forty films, including *The Wild One, A Streetcar Named Desire*, and *Apocalypse Now*, and won Academy Awards for his roles in *On the Waterfront* and *The Godfather*. His autobiography, *Songs My Mother Taught Me*, was published in 1994.

Donald Cammell was a celebrated painter, writer, film director, producer, and actor. Best known for his films *Performance, Demon Seed*, and *Wild Side*, he frequently collaborated with Marlon Brando.